STORM

PATRICIA BERWICK

This novel is a work of fiction. The names, characters
and incidents portrayed in it are the work of the author's
imagination. Any resemblances to actual persons, living
or dead, events or localities are entirely coincidental.

Published by Milton Books 2025
Copyright © Patricia Berwick 2025
The moral right of the author has been asserted

Milton Books 978-1-991184-8
A CIP catalogue record for this book is available from the New
Zealand National Library

ISBN 978-1-99-118487-0

All rights reserved. No part of this publication may be
reproduced, stored in a retrieval system, or transmitted,
in any form or by any means, electronic, mechanical,
photocopying, recording or otherwise, without the prior
permission of the publisher.

Cover image: Staffan Kjellvestad

Novels

2022
Island of Secrets. Milton Books, New Zealand.

2017
Fragile Strength (2nd edition). Milton Books, New Zealand. 309 pages.
Tablets of Ur. Global Publishing Group LLC. USA.

2015
The Shattered. Milton Books, New Zealand.

2014
Peril and Paradise. Berwick's Publications, New Zealand.

2012
A Fragile Strength. Read Pacific Ltd. New Zealand.

Children's Books
2024
Slinky Skink, Milton Books.

2023
 The Little Brown Frog, Milton Books.

2022
The Kiwi Who Could Only Say Keee, Keee, Keee. Milton Books.
Willow Wētā. Milton Books.

Prologue

I am so excited, that is, me, Amber Jenson. I haven't been home to the Marlborough Sounds in years. No idea why, study and work intruding on every thought, I suppose. When I was a child, my parents and I went to the Sounds every holiday and even some long weekends. They decided to live there when they retired. You see, they own a bach[1] there high on a hill overlooking the magnificent blue water that laps in from the Cook Strait. The bach is not small. It has four bedrooms, two bathrooms and a large open-plan living and kitchen area. There is a large deck surrounding the house. The decks allow us to take advantage of the weather and the views for meals outside or just sitting.

My memories are full of light and play. When we first went there, I met a boy who lived on the farm next door, Danny, and we soon became fast friends. We went everywhere together, whether walking, climbing, swimming, or kayaking; you name it, we did it with vigour.

When we were exhausted from all that work playing, we would end up at either of our houses and flop on a couch, holding hands

---

[1] Bach – a name for a holiday home in the South Island of New Zealand.

and gazing at whatever was playing on television. We became so used to each other that we knew what the other was thinking, like twins. Both families enjoyed our delight in life and our friendship.

All that changed when we went to 'varsity. Danny went up north, and I down south. We needed to go to the colleges with the best courses for our specialties, he for farming and me for anthropology. I thought we would see each other at Christmas, but that didn't happen. I had to work to ensure my student loan didn't balloon to unbelievable proportions, and I don't know about Danny.

I planned to return during the summer after I completed my BA, but I won a scholarship to go to the USA to study in graduate school. It was an opportunity I could not miss, and that move changed my life.

My parents still lived in Christchurch then, so I spent a week with them before leaving for the States. It was a busy week, saying goodbye to all my friends, attending farewell parties, and shopping for whatever I thought I might need. I had no time to think of the Sounds or Danny. I frequently wondered what he was up to and whether he had returned to the farm. According to Mum, he took his time about it because he returned just two years ago after being goodness knows where. His parents wanted to retire, and they hoped he would work the farm, hence his return. He is probably married by now, given we are both nearly thirty. I am not, but I live with Malcolm, the love of my life.

How did I meet Malcolm? Well, I studied hard at the University of Minnesota. My system was in shock because there were so many students on campus, nearly fifty-five thousand. That is the size of many of our not-so-small towns. It took ages to find my way around, but it had a big advantage. Because of student numbers, the variety of courses was huge, and I was like a child in a candy store wanting to learn this and that.

After a couple of years, it became old hat, and I took the time to attend conferences. Conferences are an excellent way to learn about the opportunities in the field, as well as to meet other anthropologists. Well, at one such conference, an amazingly handsome man took an interest in me. We were sitting at a bar, my friends and I, when this man came up. He was a speaker in one of the streams for the next event. He was a lawyer of some note, so my friends said. I wanted to go to a lecture on the implications of American law on non-Western Societies, so didn't bother asking what he was lecturing on. It was a topic that sounded right up my alley, and I was determined to attend. Imagine my surprise when this Adonis from the bar meeting, turned out to be that very speaker. He joined us for a drink after his talk. He was charming and made me laugh. My attention went from my companions to this new person. I learned he was taking up a job in Christchurch, New Zealand, I almost fell off my chair. Just that day, I had received a job offer from a firm in Christchurch. It was a research job and one I thought would be interesting. It seemed better than aiming for academia with its interminable politics and publish-or-perish syndrome. It seemed more like me. My friends and I were considering its relative merits when he, Malcolm, arrived. We quickly became inseparable, although I wondered what he saw in me. His comments about how beautiful and energetic I was satisfied me for a time.

It seemed natural for us to travel to New Zealand and then set up house together. I had a flat I bought some years ago, which I readily agreed to sell so we could buy a newer, flashier model that Malcolm and I could live in together. He liked the glitz and glamour more than I did, but I didn't mind. And so, life bopped along for me with a new apartment, a new man, a new job and many old friends.

Sometimes, I was frustrated with Malcolm because we always seemed to do what he wanted and go where his friends went. Without thinking, I relegated my friends to quick lunches during work breaks or meetings at the gym. My friends and I didn't seem to do anything together anymore. We did only what Malcolm wanted. Malcolm crept into every aspect of my life. There seemed little left for anything or anyone else.

But, the thought of this long weekend has created a change. I am thinking more of Danny than Malcolm. I can't imagine why Danny ever left my consciousness. We were so important to each other, but I have to admit, he could have visited me. I wonder why he didn't. I suppose 'varsity changed him too. I am curious about what he did when he left. He certainly didn't return home straight away. I guess that is his affair. However, it will be great to see him. I almost bounce in excitement as Malcolm drives us to Picton in my car.

Chapter 1

Twirling around in the sand on the beach below our bach[2], I am once more thrilled to be in this idyllic spot. Me, Amber Jenson, former holiday resident of the Marlborough Sounds and lover of all things the Sounds have to offer. I love the breeze riffling through my hair, the sun on my face, and the squeegee feel of the sand between my toes. So many memories, so much time spent here, careless hours of pure joy, and the many stress-filled hours spent away doing what? Important things, but were they? What is more important than time spent with the family, my friends of many years, enjoying each other's company?

No answers come to my questions, but I wonder why I am so intensely worried about this long weekend. True, Malcolm is unenthusiastic about this spot with its high cliffs and bush that rushes down to the pure water lapping against ancient rocks. He has no desire to swim, kayak or walk around to discover this place for himself. Such things are for the birds; besides, it is nearly mid-winter. What am I thinking? He is only used to cities and not just any city. He was born and bred in London. He finds the water

---

[2] Bach – a name for a holiday home in the South Island of New Zealand.

bracingly cold and uninviting to the timid, but kayaking is on top of the water, and walking heats the system with little effort.

Malcolm is out of his element, no place for a city dweller. He grew up in a big city, for heaven's sake. Even Christchurch is too small for him despite its new buildings, fabulous cafés and shops, magic art gallery, and library. My mother doesn't like the new city Christchurch has become because she remembers the old, elegant town with its English influence. That is the city that existed before the terrible earthquakes of 2010 onwards. It is all changed, but we young ones love it. I guess I'm not so young anymore, nearly thirty and unmarried. What a disgrace! Fortunately, my parents aren't sticks in the mud. They don't mind me sharing my bed with Malcolm, but perhaps Dad isn't keen on him. Maybe they hope I will get him out of my system.

My father exploded, "What is the matter with the man preferring wine to beer, and he doesn't watch rugby? He wants to watch football. Well, I might for a while, but I must watch the All Blacks, nothing better."

That statement didn't win friends or influence anyone, especially when Malcolm was in earshot. He is a public-school boy, and in England, that means soccer, not rugby.

So, we haven't got off to the best start this holiday, but it isn't helped by my desire to go and visit Daniel and his family. Malcolm is in a mood. I only asked Mother if Daniel was married. Given I have known him all his life, it seems a reasonable question. Apparently not. I don't have a past, an excuse for a *faux pas*. Malcolm is allowed one. Why not me?

So, here I am down on the beach by myself, kicking the sand, talking to myself, not even to the cheeky fantails that flitter around my head who have something urgent to say. I know the insects are disturbed by us, and the fantails enjoy eating them, but deep in my heart, I believe the legend that fantails are bringers of news. Bad news follows if they fly into your house, or so I am told. But that is in the South Island. In the North, it can be good news. I wonder whether the North or South Island mythology works in Marlborough Sounds, especially as North Island fantails exist here too. After all, it is just a short three-hour boat journey to Wellington from Picton and half an hour by plane. Of course, it was longer by canoes in ancient times, but that didn't deter the Māori. They seemed to whizz across the Straits constantly on quests for greenstone and domination of local tribes, which didn't make the locals here love the North so much. Still, I wonder what the fantails are telling me. Being trapped in this modern world makes it impossible for me to tell. The fantail cocks its head to one side as if listening to me.

What would Malcolm think of me considering what a fantail says? I answer my own question because I know he would think it was all piffle. Well, I don't.

Chapter 2

On the cliff, Daniel looks down at the prettiest scene he has viewed in years. He is considering all he can see, the bush, the sea, the beach and the house next door. But these are not what he is seeing. The prettiest sight is a girl dancing around on the sand as she did as a child.

When did she arrive back, and why hasn't she visited? She hasn't changed a bit in all these years, still the same lithe figure, the flowing black hair, shining skin, and joy of life. Still dancing around on the sand as though she has all the time in the world. I miss her daily. What happened to us? Life was all mapped out, or so I thought, and then we went to uni. We couldn't even choose the same one. She had to go way down south to Dunedin because she wanted the best archaeology school in the country, but I had no choice. I needed to take agriculture. Archaeology could not improve the farm, and Dad wanted to quit it to take Mum into town so she could socialise. She made the best of the distance from friends, but he knew she needed them all the same. They loved the isolation when they were young, but George and I came along, followed by Michael and Ian. George and Ian married, and that meant children. My parents missed being close to their *mokopuna*[3], their grandchildren. We children all grew up here on the farm, but George and Ian have chosen professions away from here, thus, the *mokopuna* are away from their grandparents. They are in a town not more than thirty kilometres from Picton, the nearest town to me here on the farm, but that is too far. It takes a half-an-hour trip by boat to reach Picton, then a drive of another half-an-hour to reach them. They love the farm but love the *mokopuna* more. The solution, I must be a farmer, well, I wanted to be a farmer anyway. It is not as if anyone forced me.

I needed an agricultural school. I could have chosen Lincoln – closer to Dunedin – but no, I had to go to Massey across the water, north of Wellington. Not even in sight of the South Island. It was the best choice for me because they were well into the environment and sustainable farming, not that Lincoln wasn't good. I guess it was my prejudice. I believed the courses to be better. I learned what I needed, and by then, she was off to some fancy college in the States. Too bright for her own good. I heard she received a scholarship.

She is here now, so perhaps we can get together. She looks happy to be back.

Out of the corner of my eye, I spot a tall blonde man walking down the stairs leading to the beach. He dashes across to her and grabs her violently. He doesn't seem happy with her. Oh! No, what

---

[3] Mokopuna - grandchildren

is wrong? They must be a couple. That kiss isn't something a friend would give, and she isn't pleased. She pushes him away. What is going on? Perhaps I should intervene, but then she always liked to fight her own battles. She wouldn't be pleased with me. 'Acting all macho,' that's what she would say. But I can't stand here and watch her hurt by some brute.

I sit on a rock where all is clear and from where I can get to her quickly if needed. I don't want her hurt even if I haven't seen her for years. Wait, perhaps help is at hand. Her father is dashing down. He must have seen what I saw.

My body relaxes. My muscles are aching from the stress I put them through. Amber's father is calling them for tea. What a *Matariki*[4] this is turning out to be; so much for family and togetherness, but my Mum and Dad will make up for that. Mum is in the kitchen cooking up a storm. We expect some relatives to arrive today or tomorrow, so we can watch the stars at sunrise together. It doesn't look like much of that will happen next door.

Perhaps I should have chosen another path, a path that took me away from here and all this. But I couldn't go anywhere else. The mountains, the Sounds, the birds, the bush; they are all home for me, and farming is a big plus. Such a way of life is hard but very rewarding. Amber used to love it. I wonder what she thinks now.

---

[4] Matariki – the Māori New Year. Many New Zealanders have celebrated it for years but 2024 was the first official year. A holiday was given for all.

Cities change people. I like them, but I could never live in one. Too busy, too many people, too much noise.

Right then, a *tui* shouts from somewhere in the bush.

A smile spreads across my face because I understand noise happens here too, but it is the noise of nature, not machines, people, and clatter. It nurtures me and makes me feel alive and whole. Hard to explain. I don't have to be anyone, act in a particular way, or walk when I want to run. My body needs clear air and an open view of the sea and sky. It is part of me. I used to think it was part of her. Perhaps not.

Chapter 3

What a shock. Malcolm has never acted like this before. His eyes change from deep to pale blue, and is that a flash of danger? My stomach shows fear even if I don't feel it in my head. It is unsettling to say the least. I shake my head, not sure what I am seeing.

"What is the matter? You are not usually like this. If you don't like being here, you can say so; no problems."

"And, what would you do about it? Run to your lover next door?"

This idea is beyond frustrating. Daniel - my friend who lives on the farm across the way, and I were too innocent when we were young to have an affair. We might have fooled around a bit, but that was all. We were best friends, but that was childhood. This is now.

"Such jealousy is utter nonsense. I haven't seen Daniel for years. He is probably fat and ugly now, for all I know."

My statement did little to cool the situation. Malcolm looks like he wants to whack me, something impossible to accept, and I won't expect that from him. I continue to rattle on, hoping something sensible will pop out of my mouth.

"We can leave first thing tomorrow. It would be rude, to say nothing about how unkind it would be to take off from here now. Mum has spent most of the day cooking for the meal tonight. They will be disappointed we won't stay until the next day for the dawn celebration for the rise of the *Matariki* stars. But, never mind, they will get over it."

Malcolm's attitude becomes even more bizarre. He looks like he will explode.

"*Matariki*! What kind of a thing is that? Who in their right mind would get up at sunrise to sit on a hillside in the frost to watch some stars? What if a cloud prevents the whole thing? It is just ridiculous."

I shrug my shoulders and try to contain the anger churning inside me. I remind myself that Malcolm is English and doesn't understand how important this event is to Kiwis. I had explained this weekend ad nauseum on our way here and even prior, when I proposed the weekend holiday some months ago. Even though I am not Māori, to me, it is the Māori New Year, a time to wish upon a star for something special, a time to remember those who have gone before and a time to spend with our family. I suppose I learned this from Daniel's family. Their family arrived here many generations ago. It is where they belong. I want to stamp my foot as if I was a little girl because Malcolm knows all this, but he still doesn't get it. He doesn't want to get it. Yes, that is more like it.

My voice rises a little and my eyebrows with it. "I have already said we could leave tomorrow, so why don't we go inside and enjoy the remainder of the day? Dad is coming down the steps. He must have seen how you acted."

"How I acted? What do you mean? All I did was kiss you tenderly on this beach you love so much."

My temper monitor rises. I find my hand flying up to hit him in the face which I know is a stupid thing to do, but that didn't stop me. His reactions are quicker. He stops my hand before it can reach him. His face screws up in a cruel smile emanating from deep within him. For the first time, fear really hits me. In his look, I see what he can do. Now, I don't want to leave with him, especially in his present frame of mind. Where has that funny, erudite man gone; the man I fell for so hard?

Suddenly, Malcolm steps forward and twists my arm behind my back, pulling me towards him. I am so surprised I don't react. My father startles us both when he bellows, "Come, both of you. It is time for dinner. Your mother will be upset if we are late."

Malcolm releases my arm, and a smile spreads across his face, a look that could melt icebergs. This man is the one I fell for, the quick-witted, easy-to-agree-with kind of person; handsome, with his bronzed skin, blue eyes, blonde hair and a physique build like Hercules. That smile could make me weak in the knees without even trying, but not today. I don't understand how his mood has changed so quickly. A brief worry flashes across my father's face.

He saw the full force of Malcolm's mood and the speed of its change. He shakes his head at me to show his disapproval.

"Come on, the two of you. We haven't got all day." While he speaks, he looks up at the sky. "See the clouds amassing on the horizon. I think there will be a storm before this day is out."

My father tries to lighten the mood, which must have worked because Malcolm moves towards the steps. I walk behind like a puppy, following in the steps of my master. Is this what I want for my life? I hope not. I make up my mind in an instant. I must end this relationship. Malcolm has shown a side of him which could appear at any moment. An attitude which makes me think I need to tread carefully. At the same time, I don't want to make a scene that would upset my parents. This is not the *Matariki* I expected when I arrived home.

While I think about breaking up, I glance up at the cliff. I glimpse a shadow moving in the gathering darkness. Perhaps it's Daniel. Did he view the whole thing? Oh God, I hope not. My heart flutters even though I have no idea why. Daniel must be well-married by now. Although my mother sends me progress reports about changes to the farm, she does not talk about Daniel's private life. All I know is that he returned from university and worked on the farm once his parents retired. He wants to change the farm into a sustainable business, whatever that means. My parents think it is a good thing. I am sure of it because It sounds like Daniel. He always wanted to save the world. I thought I was more practical. I only wanted to find out where we came from and why we weren't doing a better job of living peacefully in this magnificent world of ours.

We climb back up the steep steps to our bach, and Malcolm takes my hand. Perhaps he is putting on a show just in case Daniel is watching. I let him take my hand, but it doesn't make me feel better. I want to rip it away but we continue to climb while Dad follows up the rear.

The bach has four bedrooms and two bathrooms; well, there is an *ensuite* in my parent's room plus a family bathroom for the other three rooms. The living room flows into the kitchen with large sliding glass doors on two sides. It is hardly a bach in the old use of the word. It is a home where we can entertain outside even when it rains. The *Totara* wood of the house gives it strength, and its oiled timbers glow in the setting sun. The fairy lights Mum put up for *Matariki,* add to this. I love our bach and could live here year-round if I could find work, but now, I understand Malcolm could not and would not under any circumstance. I understand why my parents have decided to retire here. I couldn't think of a better spot.

Chapter 4

Well, that's a turn-up for the books! The Amber I knew, would have fought much harder. Perhaps she sensed her father's presence; that would put a capper on it, but then she followed that strange man like a lamb. She would never have followed me.

Oh no! They are holding hands. She must love the man to take his hand after that display of temper. I hope he doesn't beat her. I thought my dislike of him on sight was jealousy, but perhaps it was insight. He is nothing but a brute.

What am I doing up here anyway, spying? To be fair, I only came out to watch the sunset at my favourite spot. Tomorrow will be a busy day with my brothers, their wives, and all the rellies[5] coming for *Matariki*. Mum and Dad arrived yesterday to help me with the preparations. I thought I would invite the Jenson's, Amber's parents – not that they need an invite. They can just come, but I'm glad I haven't had time. I would have invited that man too and I could not stand by to watch that man upset Amber.

My memories of Amber and me are special: scrambling up the cliffs, even when it was impossible to reach the top. I remember

---

[5] Rellies – shortened form of relatives

one day when Amber decided it was a quicker climb to the top right over there. Even I could tell it was impossible, but not her. She had to give it a try.

She had a grin not only on her mouth. It reached right up to her eyes. "Come on, let's go. It is only about ten minutes to the top. There are lots of handholds. See, they are sticking out all over."

I obliged. Who led whom? It wasn't me leading her, that's for sure. She was determined. I followed. True, I didn't want to appear weak. I had to show her my climbing ability, even if I thought it would all end horribly. Fortunately, when we were about halfway up, and I was wondering how we would navigate the overhang, her father arrived on the beach.

"Get down here immediately, the both of you," he shouted, his face looking like thunder.

I began to back down, but not Amber. It took two more shouts from her father before she decided he was serious.

"You are grounded, girl, for the rest of the holidays," he shouted.

He was scared for us, and his shouts were a reaction to his fear. He was pleased when we were on the beach, safe and sound, but he couldn't stop his anger.

Amber's face didn't register much other than defiance. "What will I do? There is nothing to do in the house." She hadn't quite got the message. She couldn't see the danger or the fear in her father's eyes. She was annoyed at being caught doing something she knew she shouldn't do.

"We could play Monopoly or cards," I said, hoping she wouldn't say anything more to incriminate herself. I knew her father, and once the fear and anger disappeared, he would relent with a few rules, with restrictions that were probably sensible under the circumstances.

Amber screwed up her nose. "You know I don't like playing cards. Monopoly isn't so bad. Perhaps we can start a band and learn a few songs. That would fill the stretch."

At the time, I was sure I was tone-deaf, so my jaw dropped in amazement.

'Listen to yourself, boy,' my father would say. 'Where are your vocal cords? You must listen to the note, not your boots.'

"I don't think singing would do it. You know my voice. It is too low."

"Well, it's better than the squeaks you used to make before your voice broke. It is just getting used to singing at a different level. You will have a fantastic voice when you grow up." And she smiled at me, swishing her way up the steps, she put her arm through mine. She ensured she was in front of her father to show who was in control, grinning mischievously. I just knew she wanted to do something reckless. I had no idea what.

And yet, here is that same girl, obeying a tyrant of a man in a way that says this is how she should act. What on earth has happened in the intervening years?

I have no answers.

Standing up, I slouch along the bush path to my home. I know I must forget her. She is not the one to be in my future. Pity, no, it is more than pity. It is a great sorrow. I had hoped to wish on one of the *Matariki* stars to bring us together. It is not an option any more. Tomorrow, Mum will have organised some unsuspecting woman for me to marry on the spot. It is a regular event. I have no idea where she finds them all. She thinks I need someone, especially being out here alone for much of the year. She forgets I can go into Picton whenever I want, either by car or boat. The boat is better because it is quicker and I don't have to negotiate the narrow road with its tight corners to pay a visit to friends. Of course, with the car, there is no need to walk once I arrive in Picton.

That is another thing. My friends visit regularly, especially when the weather is good for fishing. They come out with me, catch their limit, enjoy the day or the weekend, and then return happily to their wives and families. I don't envy their home life. I love the solitude of the bush, watching the birds, the wētā and other insects, and going out whale watching when they decide it is time to grab some stingrays. The stingrays, in turn, catch jellyfish. It is the cycle of life. I even have a seal living on the point. He has made it his home, except when he goes off hunting or looking for his mate. She usually stays on the rocks with him until the young are safe, and then she is off; no nice Kaikoura creek for them to go up.

Amber and I had a wonderful time with her parents when they took us to Kaikoura for a weekend. We stopped at the creek and walked up the path, over a bridge and ended in a water hole full of prancing baby seals, not an adult in sight. They were in their element. The mothers sent them up there to keep them safe from predators when they were big enough not to need their mothers' milk. It all worked famously until the earthquake of 2016. The rock falls blocked their access. I believe the road workers corrected that by making a culvert under the road for them to get through, but human visitors aren't welcome. I suppose there is no space on the road for the cars to stop any more. Pity because we humans can learn a great deal from nature.

I smile because the outside lights of my house glimmer in the twilight, and the dogs bark a welcome. They don't like me going off without them, but sometimes I need the space. This evening was one of those times.

Chapter 5

My mother is standing at the door with her hand on one hip and a query on her face. "What's up?" My mother is always straight to the point. She must have read something on my face.

I try for nonchalance because I know I must tell her soon that we must leave tomorrow, and she won't like it. "Nothing. We talked too long on the beach, and that activity made us late for tea. Sorry."

"Amber, I know that look on your face. You are hiding bad news from me."

I try to look unconcerned but serious. "Sorry, Mum. You are right. It is just that Malcolm and I have to go to Christchurch tomorrow. Something has come up." I feel shame at the white lie, but I can hardly say he hates it here, and I can't say I don't want to go back with him. To say all this now would be too shocking.

"Doesn't your work stop for a public holiday?" My father looks directly at Malcolm, expecting him to apologize for the behaviour he spotted on the beach, but Malcolm's face clams up. Funny, for a lawyer, he doesn't have much to say for himself. He merely shakes his head to show his superiority.

I look enthusiastically towards the kitchen to change the subject. "What are we having for tea, Mum? It smells great. I am famished. A few moments on our beach makes me feel like I've been climbing up the cliff or swimming, enough to take the aches and pains of city life out of me anyway." I am babbling, trying to take the attention away from talking about our imminent departure.

"I hope you like crayfish, Malcolm. I managed to buy a good-sized one."

Malcolm shuffles his feet. He is uncomfortable. "It is a good entrée, but I have never had it for the main meal."

Sensing he is not easily placated even though she has no idea what happened on the beach Mum says, "It is a starter, followed by Beef Wellington. Then Pavlova for dessert. No holiday is complete without Pavlova."

She looks pleased with herself if still a bit miffed at our short stay. I feel sick at the idea of upsetting my parents. Although they visited Christchurch last week, I don't come home often. I looked forward to this weekend for ages and was so pleased when the government announced a public holiday for *Matariki*, making it a long weekend. Now, I have gone and ruined it all. My parents don't ask for much, and I wasn't an easy child to bring up. I am an only child so no others to balance out my bad performances.

Mum hurries over to the kitchen area, where the meal is almost ready to go on the table. I race over to help. It is the least I can do.

She glances over at me with one eyebrow raised. "What is going on, darling? Have you and Malcolm fought?"

See what I mean, ever the direct one. I have no way to get around this demand for honesty.

I look down at my feet as I would have as a child. It's amazing how returning home returns one to childhood. "Kind of, well, I suppose it could be called a fight, but it was more one-sided. I think he is jealous of Daniel. He thinks we were lovers of some kind. He doesn't understand that friendship between the sexes can be platonic. He went to a public school in England, all boys. I guess he hasn't learned how to mingle."

Mum nods her head. "He is unusual, but if you love him, we will do our best to welcome him."

Now I look earnestly at her. "I know, Mum, but this reaction is so out of character. I have never seen him like this before. Truthfully, I was scared and glad Dad came along when he did. I was so sure he was the one. Now, I don't know. Perhaps I should send him off in the morning, and I will stay for the weekend."

Mum's eyes are gently evaluating me. Her look pierces my heart. "You do what you think is best. You know we would love you to stay for the weekend. We can take you to the bus or the train if he takes the car when he goes."

My mind races. "I'll try to tell Malcolm, but not until tomorrow morning. I don't want this day to upset me further. Malcolm won't want me to stay, but that should be my decision. I used to be so decisive. I don't know what's happened. Lately, all I seem to do is worry about not upsetting Malcolm and ignoring what I want. I don't even visit my girlfriends anymore. That is, I visit when it is convenient to Malcolm."

Mum looks sad, but she tries to stay positive. "Before making a life decision, you must know it is right, not just a convenient one. But come on, cheer up. We have a meal to celebrate."

Dad opened two bottles of wine, one – a Spy Valley Sauvignon Blanc – to have with the crayfish, and the other – also a Spy Valley Pinot Noir – to have with the Beef Wellington. My parents know I love Spy Valley wines. I'm unsure if it is because the wine is excellent or because the owners are such admirable people with their winery in the valley where there used to be an infamous spy station – big white ball over all the antennae, secret workers, that kind of thing. It was part of the Five Eyes program with the Americans, Canadians, Australians and the UK. Most of us thought it made us a nuclear target when we had tried so hard to be nuclear-free. Well, anyway, it has gone. I suppose new technology has taken over the same function. It hardly matters because the wine is outstanding. I can't stop smiling while Dad pours us a glass each and watch Malcolm's surprise at the name on the bottle.

"Why would anyone want to call their wine Spy Valley?" The way Malcolm asks borders on the impolite, not that Malcolm is worried.

Dad just laughs. "The winery is in a valley with that name." He stops there, obviously wanting Malcolm to stew in his thoughts.

"It's a great wine," I say cheerily. "I think even you will like it." I am a bit shocked at my last remark. I am not used to sparring with Malcolm. He looks daggers at me. That look gives me one answer to my scrutiny of Malcolm's change in temperament. I suspect it isn't so much that he has changed, but that I have. I am at home here on my turf and with my parents. I feel a strength I thought I had lost. Whatever I decide, it has to be good for me because even Malcolm would not enjoy living with someone who despises him.

What an odd thought. I thought I loved him, and now I think I despise him. I am completely muddled. How can my feelings change so quickly? It possibly says more about me than him. Surely love is forever, no matter what?

"Well, what is your answer to that?" Malcolm looks straight at me, making me feel like a naughty child caught daydreaming. I was daydreaming, but that doesn't make me an imbecile.

I try to look interested. "I'm sorry, I was off with the fairies. What did you say?"

"It doesn't matter. You have been distracted by that person next door ever since we arrived. It's a good thing we leave tomorrow."

I sit stunned because it is the first time Malcolm agrees to leave in the morning. In a way, it relieves me. It's clear what he wants, and with each moment, it is clearer what I want. My parents both have their heads down, eating the last of the Beef Wellington.

Mum stands up and begins to clear away the empty plates. "We had better have Pavlova before it is too late."

Somewhere deep down, I wonder too late for what? I stand up and help clear the table. It pleases me that we have no dessert wine. I feel a little woozy from two glasses. Malcolm had much more.

"Do you enjoy the wine?" I know my face looks cheeky. I can't help it. I believe he wants to decry the wine but can't. It is prize-winning, after all.

Malcolm only nods, which gives the impression of making a great effort.

Walking towards the kitchen counter, I am startled by a loud noise.

"What's that?" I shout, looking around. It sounded like something big had fallen nearby. While we were eating, a wind arose with blasts of strong gusts, nothing we hadn't experienced before, so we ignored the sounds. But now this crash sounds ominous.

"I'll go and look." Dad, ever the action man, already has on his raincoat and reaches for a large torch we keep by the door in case of emergencies.

I stand quickly ready to do whatever Dad wants. "I'll come with you,' I say, but he shakes his head.

"I want to evaluate the scene, and then I will return for your help if need be. I suspect it is nothing that can't wait for the morning."

I look towards Malcolm, expecting him to go too, but he sits like a stone statue, gazing at the fire, looking for a message. No help there, I thought. Suddenly, he stands staring around the room, wondering what he is doing here. He looks blankly at me, as if there is nothing of concern outside. Then, Malcolm announces, "Come on, I am going to bed. It is too dark to do anything outside."

My parents both nod in unison. I can't believe what I am seeing. And yet, I have the oddest feeling that if I disagree with him, he will hurt me. I don't want to follow him up to bed.

For once, I don't jump to his command. I am starting to understand what got me into this fix in the first place. "I will come along later once I know what has happened outside."

He nods and walks smartly out of the room down the corridor. The temperature seems to rise several degrees as he moves further away. Then, the negative atmosphere in the room whooshes away as the bedroom door closes. The three of us collapse into laughter at the release of tension. What has just happened?

Chapter 6

While Amber and her parents worry about Malcolm and his attitude, George, Dan's brother, is on the phone with Dan about the *Matariki* festivities. "Dan, if this wind keeps up, we probably won't make it tomorrow. We will have to postpone it for next weekend. It won't matter that it isn't actually the first day the stars rise. We will just be a bit late, that is all."

George is my eldest brother and frequently thinks he has to organise me.

Now, he is worrying about nothing worth stressing about because I feel sure the wind will die down before morning. I have to admit it is strong, much more than predicted. However, it is only the tail end of a cyclone. How bad can that be? But even the dogs are whimpering to come into the house. They usually like to be out in the wind. Perhaps I should listen to them.

"George, I have to let the dogs into the porch. They are crying. You might be right. I'll check the weather reports, and expect you and your family when you arrive. Don't worry."

George creates the impression of being happy enough with my response. I leave it at that. All the family is looking forward to the celebration of our first *Matariki* festival throughout Aotearoa.

That's New Zealand, in case you don't know, the land of the long white cloud and the land trying its best to love Maoridom.

I look affectionately at my dogs and call, "Get in behind, Bess, Jock, and Mick. You would think the world is coming to an end."

I pat the dogs, careful to pat each one the same. They have been with me for a long time and refuse to share me. It's high time they learned. Excellent sheepdogs, though. I can't complain. They save my legs on the high climbs up to the tops of the hills, looking for wayward lambs. Now, they settle down in their beds. Yes, they have indoor beds, well on the porch anyway, and their kennels outside. Spoilt, some say, but they are always there for me, more than I can say for some people.

Shit, what was that? It sounds like a tree has come down at the Jenson's. I need to see what has happened in case there is damage to their house. I pull on my waterproof thermal jacket but don't take time to put on the bibbed over-trousers. I shouldn't be out too long, but I need gumboots. This pair is non-slip, specially lined to keep out the cold. Couldn't be better. I rush out to the cliff to the place where I can see the next-door house. It has fairy lights around the decks, just like Christmas, so easy to see if anything is wrong. The dogs come with me, no stopping these panting pups – well, it is some years since they were pups, but I still think of them as young things. Tonight, they crowd around me, trying to ensure my safety.

I know my face belies my thoughts, but I tell the dogs, "It's all right, boys. No worries. It is just a stormy night that will pass by the morning."

I hope my voice reassures them. We reach my spot on the cliff where I have a good view of next door. All looks fine, but a large shadow is looming at the back. The old Macrocarpa tree must have blown over. It's a good thing it is so far from the house. It is much too dark to do much about it now. The bright side is that it will give them more than enough wood for next winter. This situation is not a bad problem compared to it hitting the house. What a good thing it is only that old tree.

My dogs dance around trying to get my attention. I am confused and shout, "Whoa! The wind is no problem, mates. Come here. What is the matter with you? Do you want to go and play? No! You want me to investigate the sheep? They know better than me how to hunker down in a storm. Shit! What rain! Where did that come from? It is just pelting down."

What a good thing I pulled my hood up before leaving the house, but water is still trickling down my neck. Nothing is safe from this downpour. It must stop soon, or George will be quite right; no *Matariki* celebrations this year because the ground will be too wet.

"All right, all right. I am here, ready and waiting, boys. What is your problem?"

I try to look where they are standing, but their shadows hide whatever it is. Finally, I am beside them on the side of a steep hill, not that sensible in this weather.

My face breaks out into a smile. "Oh! A newborn lamb is struggling to stand, and there is no sign of its mother. Poor thing."

This lamb is born prematurely. I wouldn't have expected one so soon. The storm must have given the mother a shock. She probably doesn't know what happened, but I can't find her in this weather.

I grin at the dogs wanting them to be relieved that all is fine. "Boys, we will have a look in the morning."

I pick up the lamb and snuggle it inside my jacket. It is freezing outside.

I rub my hands together to warm them up while telling the boys, "Okay mates, time to head home."

The boys and I, plus the newborn lamb, are almost blown back to the steps of my house. The dogs scamper ahead of me, looking for a treat. I suppose I should give them one. They came out in the wind and rain to help. It's not their fault there is nothing to do. They found the lamb, and that is a big thing. I smile, thinking of their surprise because they will not expect a reward despite looking for it.

Nearing the house, a gust of wind nearly blows me over. I am shocked. I haven't felt the wind this strong since the last time I went to Wellington with its reputation for strong winds. It is not usually this bad here. I should listen to the radio to find out what is going on, hoping that my parents are managing to sleep through it all.

For some reason, unbeknown to me, my thoughts slip to Amber. I wonder how she likes this wind. The old Amber would laugh, but this new one, the one who *kowtows* to her man; that one, goodness knows. What happened to her? What kind of madman has changed her into a zombie? I shake my head, thinking I am being a bit harsh, but he certainly isn't my kind of man, nor is he the old Amber's type of person. Perhaps I didn't know her at all. I only thought I did.

I leap up the steps, two at a time, hurrying to get the lamb into the house and out of the wind and the rain.

I grin at the lamb, "Lucky for you, Lucy Lamb, we've all eaten. I can spend time with you. You are not the first lamb I have nursed. I'm not keen on the regular feeds, but if I want you to live, I must find a bottle, sterilise it, make up a formula, and feed you. I don't want you to like the warmth of the house too much. Perhaps one of the dogs will let you sleep with him on the porch. That should work."

While I am telling the lamb the lay of the land, I struggle to put all the necessaries together with one hand; quite an act. I wonder if human babies cause this much trouble. I suppose they do, perhaps more. Fleetingly, I think Mum could help, but then I remember all the work she has done already for the festivities. No need to wake her. The boys and I can cope.

I pull the lamb comfortably into the crook of my arm. "There, there. This concoction is what you want." The lamb sucks greedily, making such loud noises it attracts the dogs; not every day a lamb comes into the house. It doesn't take long before the lamb's stomach becomes full, and for her to be much warmer. Lucy falls asleep almost instantaneously. I put her down with Bess. Bess's mothering instincts are great, so I don't think she will mind. She is smiling up at me. Her eyes are bright, and her mouth curls smile-like. I feel sure she approves. Fleetingly, I wonder why I call the three of them 'boys' when Bess is so obviously a girl. It is okay to call them mates because it might mean either.

The dogs settle into their beds on the porch once again. I make sure they are happy and find them treats. All three thump their tails in unison, realising they will receive a treat. I smile, give each one a reassuring pat, and then tromp back to the door to take off and hang up my wet weather gear. The best investment I have ever made.

Once inside the kitchen, I turn the radio on to the National Station. I should check Marlborough Marine Station. Their weather report will be the latest. To my surprise, the ferries from Wellington to Picton have stopped, that is both companies. This is unusual. The Interislander usually stops if the Strait is too lumpy for the passengers, but Bluebridge not so often. The weather in the Strait is usually worse than here, so difficult to tell the conditions out there. The older Interislander ferries are having trouble with the Strait at the moment, even on a good day. They needed replacing some years ago. Whoever thought it would be clever to put the Railways in charge of the ferries? What does a railway company know about the sea, especially given that the Cook Strait has such a bad reputation, one of the worst straits in the world, so they say? We used to have such special ferries designed for our conditions. I suppose the government cut back on what they would pay for them. This attitude is silly because so many tourists use these ferries, to say nothing of the lifeline they provide for the South Island. It is part of State Highway 1, the road that comes from Auckland all the way to Invercargill in the south. We would be cut off from food, building materials, and most goods necessary for life if they didn't sail. Oh well, I can still use my launch if I need anything from Picton or even the North Island, that is, if it isn't too big.

It is probably time to call it a night. I slip past my parents sleeping soundly. No need to wake them about the storm. Time enough in the morning. It will blow itself out at some time or another. I am pleased I reroofed the house last year. This storm would have taken the old roof right off. What a cheery thought to sleep on. I smile, wondering what I would do if the roof disappeared.

I am knackered. I must have some sleep. I walk to my bedroom and get ready for bed. I set the alarm to wake me in four hours. Lucy will need a feed then, I am sure. Tomorrow is another day, and hopefully, I will speak to Amber. A young Amber is my last thought. Her cheeky grin peeps at me as she thinks of something outrageous. A silly grin washes over my face as I slip off to sleep.

Chapter 7

After Malcolm leaves in a huff, Mum, Dad, and I sit around talking. The storm increases in intensity. Now the rain is so hard, we can hear it drumming on the roof - through solar panels, roofing, insulation and whatever the ceiling material is - quite an effort. It is unusual. Dad walks out on the deck to have a look. He has on his all-weather gear and stomps down to where we heard the noise.

He shouts, "It's the old tree at the back. We can't do anything about it until morning. It isn't hurting the house. Come and see, the rain is falling straight down. The wind has forgotten to blow. Oh no, here it comes again. The rain is pouring sideways now. Amber, I don't think either of you will be going anywhere tomorrow."

Mum nods in agreement, almost in relief. "We will just have to convince Malcolm we are good people."

I look askance. "Mum, I think it is past that point. I don't even want to go into the bedroom with him. I saw something evil about him. I have never seen him look like that before. Goodness knows what happened to him. He is usually so kind, considerate and thoughtful. That is how he seems to me."

Dad has come inside and now stands with his back to the fire, rubbing his hands behind him. He looks serious.

"I couldn't agree more that you should be careful. I think you should sleep in the guest room tonight because I don't trust him."

Mum looks torn between being a good hostess and protecting me, so I try to make her feel better. "I might just sit up all night. It is impossible to sleep with how I feel anyway. We should watch the news to find out what's happening."

Dad picks up the remote to turn on the TV. I think it will be lucky if we get any reception, especially with the strength of the wind. The dish must be having a terrible time up there on the roof. He turns the station to the late news. There is a pixelated picture, and the sound quality isn't good enough to make out the words. He picks up the emergency radio. We have had one at the ready ever since the Christchurch earthquakes. Those shakes made us wake up to preparedness. Sometimes, I think it is overkill, but tonight I see the point. So much for a joyous *Matariki*. We listen intently.

Dad feels the need to explain the radio commentary to Mum and me. "They say to expect gusts of 110 kilometres per hour or stronger. I think they are being kind. That last whomp, felt like it shifted the house!"

Dad sounds excited, more than worried, but Mum is circumspect.

"We should pack a go bag, just in case. Dan, next door, will take us to safety in his boat."

I look towards Mum in surprise. "It doesn't seem too bad, although a go bag is a good idea."

Then I gulp. All my things are in my room, the same place where Malcolm is currently sleeping. I have little desire to creep in there. I will have to make do with my all-weather gear. It is parked on the deck, hanging up to dry after my last foray into the rain. Fortunately, my backpack with my money and other essential items is on the couch. It might even have a toothbrush in it with a bit of luck. Sometimes, a bit of slovenliness goes a long way. Mum told me to put it away a while ago. Now, I am pleased it is still here.

All the wonderful smells of dinner have dissipated, but the spark of the log fire and a whiff of smoke lingers in the room. We have a heat pump, but we prefer the warmth of the fire, and there is plenty of fuel outside, just for the gathering. It is July, and the weather is cold. Heat is essential.

Mum brings me a pillow and a sleeping bag. She has given up on trying to get me to sleep with Malcolm.

She sighs, "It is past my bedtime, and we will need all our wits about us in the morning, dear." With that and a kiss on my cheek, she leaves the room. Dad raises his eyebrow and looks quizzically at me.

"Are you going to be okay out here by yourself, Amber? Our room is close enough to hear if you need anything."

His meaning is clear. He has no belief in Malcolm's kind-heartedness, but I suspect he did not like him when he first met him. I should note that Dad is a good reader of personalities. Something I frequently fail to notice. I should pay attention to his comments in the future.

I try to make my face look encouraging. "Don't worry, Dad. I will sleep comfortably. The logs on the fire will last all night."

He nods. I know this isn't what he means, but he is not a man to belabour issues. He expects me to call if I need help. With that cheery thought, I say good night to him and cuddle into the sleeping bag. There is almost an eerie silence outside - a gap in the storm.

I toss and turn, trying to go to sleep, but I am unable to rest. I could blame the storm. It is ramping up again, and odd noises come from within and outside of the house. However, I can't shake the feeling of foreboding, which has nothing to do with the storm or the house. I have no idea what I am thinking. Surely, Malcolm wouldn't do anything to harm me. He loves me, or so he says. There I go again, not accepting what I have believed for the past year. Deep down, I have a worry that I refuse to acknowledge because Malcolm is usually charming, and all are in his thrall. In the past, I felt lucky he was with me. I have never known him to be jealous; besides, other people have shown me attention, not just Daniel. He hasn't even laid eyes on Dan. What is he on about?

Perhaps I talk about him too much. That might be the issue. I can correct that, but do I want to change?

I begin to think of the me before Malcolm. I made all my own decisions, owned a flat, and had a good job. Sure, I rented the flat out when I was overseas, but that paid off the mortgage. It was almost freehold when I returned home. I still have the job but seem incapable of making decisions, and somehow, Malcolm has finagled control of my finances, and I no longer have a flat. Why did I let that happen? Did I think I would lose him if I spoke up? In my more honest moments, I acknowledge that the fear of losing Malcolm has outweighed my desire for money. I thought, what did it matter if he controlled the finances? It would benefit both of us in the end, no matter what. Now, I am beginning to realise the fallacy of that belief. A sneaky thought enters my mind as I think of Daniel. I believe none of this would have happened if I had been with him. Why did I let our friendship lapse? I shake my head, having no immediate answer.

My mind goes around and around, almost making me dizzy. As I drift off, a loud explosive sound wakes up the whole house. Mum and Dad rush out of their room, and even Malcolm comes blearily out.

We hear a grinding, sickening sound like some monster pushing its way down the hill.

"It can't be this side of the hill because it is not prone to landslides, and there are no other houses. I wonder if it is the cottage over the ridge. I am not sure if the owners are here this weekend. I will ring to find out," I say, having no idea why I think the sound is a house moving.

Dad, taking control, leaps to the phone. "Oh, dash? No reception. Perhaps the landline works."

He lifts the receiver, but his eyes tell us all we need to know. There is no reception there either.

Mum queries, rather unnecessarily, "What should we do?" My mother's eyes have gone round and large. She is thinking the worst.

Malcolm looks at her arrogantly, "We should not do anything without light. We will have to wait until morning. It is only an hour away." Malcolm looks serious, standing very straight, expecting everyone to organise around him.

Dad grabs the torch. "I'll go along the track to see what I can see." He says this nonchalantly.

"I'm coming too," I say rather quickly, then I remember Mum will be alone with Malcolm. Why this bothers me, I am not sure.

Dad says sternly, although he is not good at harshness. "No. You are going to stay here to look after your mother. You can come if you like, Malcolm."

Malcolm shakes his head. "It is futile going out there in the dark in this weather. A tree could fall on us or even the hill, and then, where would we be?"

Dad rolls his eyes and shakes his head in disbelief. "If I am not back in twenty minutes, go next door and ask Daniel for help. He will not be afraid to go out. Someone could be hurt."

Malcolm looks surprised. "You don't even know if it is a house, let alone if anyone is staying in it. Why risk your life?"

My father's face looks like thunder, but he only says, "Because it is the right thing to do," he says and marches out of the room.

I know I should help him, but I also know I should stay with Mum. I decide I should do what Dad says. After all, if something happens to him, the idea of leaving her alone with Malcolm is unthinkable.

Chapter 8

I look around, having no idea what woke me up. It isn't the alarm. It would still be ringing, and the dogs are barking loudly. My first thoughts are about the lamb. She must be frightened with the dogs so close to her. I hurry out of bed and pull on yesterday's clothes. They are handy on the floor next to the bed. Then I hear it.

What on earth! I rush out to the porch and pick up Lucy to cuddle her.

I look severely at the dogs. "Mates, you must stop the noise. Your barking isn't helping."

The three of them hang their heads immediately. They know they have done something naughty, but was it honestly bad? They must have been trying to warn me. The sound is not close enough to threaten us. It is over the ridge at Kirsty's old place, but I don't think anyone is there this weekend. I know she rents it out occasionally, but there was no sign of activity yesterday, and besides, she usually tells me in case they need help.

It is still inky black outside. Thankfully, the rain has eased. Well, it isn't pelting down in sheets. I pull on my oilskin, thinking it might offer better protection. My thermal jacket is warmer, but the oilskin will cover me from my head to my knees and has a good hood. I remove it, deciding to wear my woollen sweater Mum made. It is a natural fleece. She spun the yarn and mixed brown with white wool. It is almost waterproof by itself. But I decide I still need my oilskin and long gumboots. My head begins to clear, and I wonder if I should feed Lucy before heading out. Perhaps Bess should stay with her while Jock and Mick come with me. Pity Bess can't hold a bottle. I left everything ready last night, thinking I would be half-asleep when Lucy needed her night feed, so it would be only a matter of mixing the formula and heating it in the microwave before putting it in the bottle. Her eyes perk up as she watches me prepare her meal. She already knows the food is for her. Smart girl. I hold her close as I feed her, drop the bottle in the work sink and tell Bess to stay. She looks upset until she understands her job is to look after Lucy. She settles down in her bed to make room for Lucy. I smile and say, "Good girl. You are such a good dog."

Just then, Mum and Dad walk in hazy eyed. Dad smiles at me, "I'll just get my parka, Son."

"No need, Dad. We can't do anything tonight. All I want is to ensure that no one is out there needing help."

I don't want Dad out there with his legs the way they are, but I nod in reassurance. I am glad he has offered. "Both of you go back to bed. We'll talk about it in the morning."

Mum looks relieved. She must be imagining him getting caught up in something horrendous. "Come on Dad. We can sleep to make sure we are fit to help in the morning.

Mercifully, Dad nods, and they both turn towards the bedrooms.

I grab the brightest torch I have. This one can shine across a football field.

I shout at the dogs because it is critical they stay together. "Get in behind, Mick and Jock. We have work to do." The sickening noise sounds like something huge is sliding down the hill. It reminds me of the sound the hills made when I was in Christchurch during a terrible earthquake, like an unworldly beast growling, but it isn't quite the same. I wonder again if it is the house. If so, there is nothing to do except to confirm no one is in it.

I stride over the top of the ridge with the dogs close at my side. They know what I expect. I want to stop them from running off into unknown danger. Slipping down the other side, I spot another torchlight. Good thing I came. Whoever it is will be disoriented.

"Hello," I yell with all my strength. The wind is still gusting furiously but has lost some of its puff. I hope that is a good sign. The person rushes over towards me. I hear a welcoming voice; one I know well.

"Oh hi, Dan. Glad you came. I came over the hill from our place to see the house disappear into the trees below. I think it will slide all the way to the beach. I couldn't see any sign of activity inside, no lights, nothing like that, but I think it is worth checking it out just in case."

I nod. "My thoughts exactly, but the hill might come down now that the house has wiped out all those trees." I flash my light around. Despite its great strength, I can't see much beyond the crashed trees.

We pick our way carefully down to the fallen trees and stop. I can't see very far because some trees still stand tall, but I have never seen the likes of this before. There is a pathway carved out going down.

I feel my face stretch into a look of astonishment. "It is almost like it used the tree trunks for skids. Mr Jenson, I can't remember a storm this strong."

Mr Jenson nods. His mouth is open, although it will not help. "Nor have I Dan; nor have I. By the way, it is high time you called me Jon. You have known me all your life. Jon, it is."

I nod and almost shake his hand as I greet him for the first time this night. My reaction shows me that I am more shocked than I want to let on. "Jon, it is then," I say formally and begin to laugh. It releases the tension, particularly because Mr Jenson grins and then laughs.

"Let's go down over there, or perhaps we need to go back over my hill and down the path to the beach. That way, if this side of the hill collapses …"

"We won't be here for it," Jon finishes my thought.

My dogs need guidance. "Mates, *haere mai*,[6] come here. We are going this way." I whistle at them to make sure they follow the command. When I use Māori commands, they respond immediately, as if it is more serious, and in this instance, it is. Both have wandered off, sniffing around the fallen trees and could get into danger. It is a good thing I decided on the long way around. Jon and I could have been in peril going where the dogs were.

Puffing and panting, we four arrive on the beach in record time. The waves crash loudly but then become deafening as we round the point. This point can be tricky at the best of times because the waves come directly in from the Straits, and tonight, they look ready to fight all of us.

Mr Jenson's voice sounds strained. "I think we should stay close together, Dan. You might manage okay, but I'm not so young anymore."

I look quizzically at him. "You are very fit, but I agree. Mates, *haere mai, kia tere*.[7]" The dogs respond well. Tonight, I don't want them to make any mistakes. We don't have to go far to discover the sight of our lives. A shadow of a house rests comfortably on the beach. What a turn-up for the books!

I motion to Jon. "I will let the mates go carefully over there to find out if anyone is about. They are lighter than us and will bark if we are needed."

---

[6] Haere mai – Come here, in Māori. It is also a greeting.
[7] Kia tere – Hurry up, in Māori.

Jon nods, and we watch the dogs walk sedately up to the house and begin to sniff. I haven't trained them for this, but they are used to finding lost sheep. I suspect they understand my meaning. They know people live in houses. Soon, they disappear around the other side of the house. I can hear faint conversational yelping. It is clear they are involved, and we wait.

It takes the dogs about half an hour to sniff everywhere they think is necessary, and by then, there is a faint outline of the sun trying to show through the black clouds. It won't have much chance to shine. It will be lucky if it can throw a milky glare until the day is well underway. In the storm's hiatus, both Jon and I sense that if people are in the house, they are either dead or unconscious because there is no movement. Even the house appears happy with its position on the beach. Eventually, they come racing back. They look pleased with themselves. I pat them both, confirming they know how happy I am with them.

There is relief in Jon's voice as he says, "I think we can go home until the light is good enough to inspect the house."

I agree with Jon. "Come to my place for coffee and breakfast, and you can ring Mrs Jenson to let her know you are okay."

Jon looks a bit disgruntled. "If I am Jon, then my wife is Julie to you. Have you got that straight?"

He sounds annoyed at me, and I have to smile. "Sorry, I am not thinking straight. Perhaps you can ask Julie, Amber, and her boyfriend for breakfast."

"I think our phones are out. I will have to go over there, but I appreciate the offer. Julie will have breakfast ready for me when I get home. I will return once I have had breakfast, talked to them, and decide what we are doing. We have to find out how much damage this storm has done."

"That's for sure, and I don't think it is over yet." I point to a pile of ugly black clouds amassing on the horizon. "Whatever that is, it will hit us soon. I'll ring civil defence to tell them about the house. Maybe they can tell us something about the roads and other damage."

"Dan, how will you do that if your phones are out?"

I smile. "I invested in one of those satellite phones meant to work in all weathers, just in case something like this happened. Living alone does that to you. I have to be careful so that even if my phones are out, I can still call for help. I put an antenna on the roof for it to work in the house. I should have told you, but I thought I would never need it."

Jon's eyes shine, understanding how critical this revelation is while thinking it is something Malcolm would never have considered, not in a thousand years. "I didn't think I would ever see the day when a house would slide all the way to the beach. What a ride?"

Reaching my steps, we shake hands to thank each other for the support. Seeing Jon so full of life makes me sad for my father. He left the farm because his arthritis made it difficult for him to walk.

I am glad he didn't try to come to help. I would have been worried the whole time. In truth, I know he couldn't walk in these conditions. I suppose he knows it too. I turn toward Jon. He waves farewell as he turns his torch back to full to trudge off to his home across the bay. My feet want to turn to follow him home, but I climb upwards to home, my home without Amber.

Chapter 9

"I hope your father is safe, Amber?" Mum says in a small voice.

Mum and I wait anxiously for Dad to return. The weather is minimally better, but we aren't out in it. The rain has almost stopped for the time being. The horrendous noise we heard from over the hill has stopped; that is the crashing and an almost human sound. No idea what that was. I am glad nothing more is coming from that direction. It doesn't help my apprehension.

Malcolm returned to bed as soon as Dad left. It relieves me because I am sure I cannot be polite to him. He should have gone with Dad. Neither Mum nor I like the thought of Dad being out there alone. What kind of man is Malcolm? Not the sort I thought him to be. He can speak at a conference and hold people in his hands, but he can't do the work essential for human survival. Not much good, given our changing environment.

The smile on Mum's face didn't quite reach her eyes, "I'll make us some coffee, darling. If I am doing something, I might not worry so much." Mum looks bright, but I can feel the aura of apprehension emanating from her. I don't know what she will do if anything happens to Dad. I guess that is the downside of a long and happy marriage; one is unhappy when the other isn't there. Of course, this time Dad is in danger, but I can't imagine anything happening to him. I sometimes worry about what will happen when one or the other dies and who would cope best. Now, this event is horrifying, yet nothing has happened to him.

I shake myself out of these unhappy thoughts. "Yes, coffee might be good for both of us. I will turn on the radio again. Now that it is almost dawn, there might be more positive news."

Just then, I hear Dad stomping up the steps to the deck. The rustle of his wet weather gear indicates he is taking it off. He arrives inside in his socks, smiling from ear to ear. Something good must have happened.

My mother relaxes quickly with Dad's return. "You look happy, dear."

Mother seldom asks him where he has been; even in this chaotic time, she is still reluctant to come out and ask what he saw out there, and yet she must be as anxious as me.

Dad becomes animated as he explains events. "We saw the strangest sight over the hill. You know Kirsty's old place. Well, it managed to slide right down the hill to the beach. It is sitting there resting in a homely kind of way. We didn't go inside because it was probably unstable. We will have a look when it is lighter."

"And just who is *we*?" I say like I am a parent asking an errant child.

Dad looks at me with a smile. "Daniel and I came out about the same time. He had two of his dogs with him, and they explored the house for us just in case someone was inside. They didn't find anything unusual, but we still need to look on the off chance the dogs were wrong."

I frown because I am still puzzled by this response. "But it doesn't account for the big smile on your face."

Dad comes over and cuddles me. "I was just thinking how well Dan and I worked together. He is thoughtful about his dogs and talks to them like friends."

Mum smiles enthusiastically, and I begin feeling they have practised this speech, or something like it. They are trying to tell me Dan is a much better option than Malcolm. I wonder, once again, why I didn't choose to come home more often after I went to university overseas. There never seemed to be the time, and Mum and Dad always greeted me at the airport whenever I arrived back. They were living in Christchurch then. It is only recently that they moved permanently to the Sounds. Still, I could have made the effort to see Dan. I guess I thought he wasn't interested because he didn't contact me.

Dad faces me and looks into my eyes. "Dan is not only kind to his animals; he always remembers his parents and is lovely to us." Dad has a silly grin on his face, and they both stand back, looking very smug. It is as if they are saying, 'look what is at home, not away'. I know they don't like Malcolm but this recent carry-on has entrenched that feeling.

I can't resist challenging, "Are you trying to tell me that I should look next door rather than my present situation?" I ask very directly.

Mum would never admit to such a thing. "Oh no, dear. The choice is yours. We happen to love Dan because he is always there for us." Mum's eyes are sparkling with a faint glint of amusement. She knows she has made her point.

But Dad continues, "Do you know he has a satellite phone that he generously offered us to use. He says we can contact anyone we want? When he learned our phones were out, he offered his immediately. What a man!"

They are making a comparison, and I can't stop thinking Dan was out in the storm while Malcolm snuggled up in my bed. What kind of a man is that? And there is the temper he displayed yesterday afternoon on the beach. In the rush of finding a house so close to us sliding away, I brushed aside my trepidation about yesterday. But I know they have a point.

I try to cover my thoughts with, "Dan probably isn't the least bit interested in me. He must have plenty of lady friends in town." I say defensively, although, at the same time, I hope I am wrong.

But I want to push down any feelings bubbling inside me to concentrate on what I should do about Malcolm. Do I want to return to Christchurch with him? I certainly didn't want anything to do with him last night. Then, I can't just hide out here and pretend nothing happened. I have to ask him what he wants. I must ask him about his jealousy towards Daniel. After all, he doesn't know him. Where has his suspicion come from? A guilty thought enters my brain. I suspect I waxed lyrical about Daniel when we were driving here. I felt a little excited at possibly seeing my old playmate, but I certainly didn't imply we had an affair. The idea is just madness. We were both too young and innocent for anything so adult. I blush, remembering a kiss we shared the last Christmas we spent here before we went to uni. It was so sweet, gentle and innocent. It made me feel extraordinary and very much like a woman. I didn't tell Malcolm such details. It was private between me and Daniel, not to be shared. Possibly, my eagerness to visit Daniel caused his temper. If that is the case, we must discuss it to put it behind us.

By this time, Mum is in the kitchen making breakfast, Dad is showering to bring warmth into his body, and Malcolm reappears without a smiley face.

I walk up to him, making sure I look unconcerned. "Did you have a good sleep?"

Malcolm almost turns on me. He responds angrily, "How do you expect me to sleep with such a storm and all that noise? You said this place was peaceful. It hasn't shown itself to be quiet in any way."

His eyes look deeply angry. It is obvious he hasn't recovered from yesterday.

His face is screwed up in a way that reminds me of a squashed prune. I want to laugh but his actions are so serious. "You sound as though you want to remain for the rest of the weekend. That's good," I say carefully.

He looks surprised. "Where did you get that idea? No, I have packed, and I packed your things too. We should take off straight after breakfast." His look brooks no objection.

Despite the look, I say, "I am not certain I am going anywhere today. There is probably cleaning up to do outside, and I want to help my parents. Would you consider staying to help?" I am annoyed at the tentativeness of my voice.

I know by his face that he has no intention of staying. I have never seen him so obviously commanding, expecting I will bow to his every whim.

"No, we will both leave within the hour." He orders, giving no other option. I am shocked. Who does he think he is? This is my place and my holiday. If he doesn't like it, he can leave. I feel my body tremor as if a cold wind has rushed through it. It is the first time I have thought for myself for moons. Thinking it, however, is not the same thing as taking action.

Dad enters the room, fresh out of the shower, rubbing his hair dry. "I don't think you will be going anywhere today, not by road. I would be surprised if the road is open. There were landslides or dropouts after the last big storm, and it didn't carry nearly the impact of last night. It will be too dangerous on the road. You could call the water taxi or perhaps the mail boat. We will have to ask Dan next door to ring to find out. Our phones are out."

Malcolm's face darkens further. "I will not ask that man anything. Surely, you have your own vessel to take us back to Picton?"

I am stunned at his impoliteness. He is not the man I have known for the last few years. He is a monster. Someone out of a horror movie. I shiver once more, not from cold but from shock. I wonder if I am stupefied because of the storm, or is this all Malcolm? Perhaps Malcolm is in shock. Last night was not the most pleasant weatherwise, but that does not excuse his behaviour.

I try to keep my voice even. "I will organise the water taxi for us," I say, not meaning I would go on it, but to appease Malcolm and guarantee he leaves us in peace.

His lips turn up in a sneer. "Oh, so you are going to run across to your boyfriend, are you?"

I look aghast.

Just then, a cold breeze comes from a door on the deck, and Daniel enters in time to hear the remark. He looks from Malcolm to me in confusion.

"Nice to meet you mate. I am Dan." He holds out his hand for Malcolm to shake. Malcolm doesn't return the gesture. "I have brought the phone down so you can ring whomever you want."

Malcolm looks uncertain for the first time. Maybe he grasps this is a serious situation, and this may be his only way out. However, he responds, "No mate! We will take the car." He turns and begins to head for the bedroom.

Dan looks at him as though he is a complete idiot, but his words are gentler. "I wouldn't do that if I was you. There are several dropouts on the main road, so goodness knows what our road into here is like." But Daniel is speaking into thin air. Malcolm has already left the room. There is nothing I can do. I stand there, looking helpless. I feel completely lost.

Chapter 10

I am in Amber Jenson's house deciding what we will do. I am certain of one thing, that is that I want Amber's boyfriend out of here. He feels dangerous, dangerous to Amber, so I take the time to ring the water taxi. I feel pleased I had the foresight to buy a satellite phone, but the phone rings and rings. The line is busy. It is unsurprising, given how many people must be trying to leave before the storm hits again.

"Sorry, mate," I say, a bit insincerely to Malcolm. "You will have to wait. I can't take you by boat because I must check my stock, and we still need to investigate the house on the beach." Deep inside me, I am annoyed at explaining anything to him. If he is a man, he should offer to help.

Amber perks up. "Mum and I will check your sheep if you don't mind us using your horses. You and Dad could check the house, but be careful because it will be dangerous to go inside. Maybe you can look through the windows. Even being that close isn't sensible."

Amber's face clears as she makes her pronouncement in earnest. This statement sounds more like the old Amber, taking charge and organising us. I am unsure what I think about this.

These days, I'm used to making my own decisions, besides she repeats much of what I have already said. I'm happy she isn't being wimpy like yesterday. She doesn't glance at Malcolm. It's a good thing because he is quietly fuming. I try the water taxi once more.

My eyes look into the near distance, trying to ignore the idea of Malcolm. "Hi, this is Daniel." ….. Yes, that's me. We have a guest who needs to return to Christchurch, and the road is most certainly impassable." In the background, I hear Malcolm mutter, 'Two guests.' I ignore his grumbling. "You think you can reach here around four p.m. this afternoon, all things being equal? ….. That's good. We will be waiting for you. Just let us know if there are any changes." I click off and look for Malcolm to tell him the good news but he is nowhere to be seen.

I look surprised. "What happened to Malcolm?" I ask, looking around.

Amber looks at me. "He grumped off that way. Not sure what he is doing. We need to get on with it because there is no knowing how long the break in the weather will last."

I smile at her. I hope she is resigned to letting Malcolm go. The relief on her parent's faces is palpable. They must be thinking the same as I am about him.

"Okay," I say, "Let's go!"

The four of us head outside towards my place. Somehow, it feels just right, as if this was a normal gathering. Jock and Mick sit waiting patiently at the foot of the steps. They sniff the air, confirming all is well in our world. They are such good dogs. I am so proud of them.

I see Amber looking around as if she is missing something. "Don't you have three dogs. Where is the other one?" Amber calls.

I smile. That is the old Amber, worried about everyone. "She is at home looking after Lucy. She is the first thing on the agenda. I must find Lucy's mother and hope they bond. I can't leave it too long, or the mother will reject her."

Amber jogs up beside me. It feels unbelievably natural to have her at my side. "I didn't know you had a lamb. Was it born last night?"

I grin at her, feeling pleased she understands. "Got it in one, and the mother was nowhere in sight. I took it inside for warmth and to feed it. I don't like animals dying unnecessarily."

"How like you," she says with a beam. I have an impression she wants to put her arm through mine. Maybe it is my active imagination because she doesn't move any closer. "So, did you stay up all night with her, or did you transfer duties to your mother?"

I rest back on my haunches. "No, Bess did the mothering duty. Mum has enough to cope with, what with cooking and keeping Dad entertained. Bess is still on the job now. Bess must be wondering where I am. An exceptional dog, she had no complaints when I left her behind and took Mick and Jock this morning. She loves coming out with us. It is quite a sacrifice on her part to look after Lucy."

Just then, our arms bump, and an electric shock explodes. What is that all about? I turn towards Amber for her reaction, but she is concentrating on the rough ground and probably hasn't noticed.

At the house, I pick up Lucy and let Bess out while I shout out to my parents what I am doing. Lucy is so happy to be outside jumping and rushing at Jock and Mick. We all walk across the hill to the paddock where I found Lucy last night to discover if her mother is around. Much to my joy, a sheep bleats pitifully near where I found Lucy. I pop Lucy down, and to my relief, she heads straight for the sheep. The sheep immediately stops bleating and welcomes her wee one. Lucy's tail is wagging so fast that it is at risk of falling off. Finally, they settle, and Lucy takes her first drink from her mother. Big grins spread over our faces. It is a miraculous sight amid all this bedlam.

Jon says, "We must hurry to Kirsty's house because it could all collapse and then we will have no hope of finding anything."

I nod, and Amber and her mother say their goodbyes, dashing off to saddle the horses for what could be a long day. Jon and I may have drawn the best straw this day.

In the end, it doesn't take long to survey the house. We peer in all the windows, and I tiptoe into the darkest parts. We find no one is inside, no stray person or animal. I called Kirsty last night after I saw the house, but she has not yet responded. The civil defence says we should leave the house once we investigate to confirm no one is inside. There will be time enough to deal with it once the weather is good enough for an insurance inspection. I take photos, inside and out, to help Kirsty. I know what these insurance people can be like. They might say that vandals destroyed it or some such nonsense to wiggle out of paying for the whole thing. The house is munted[8] - a right off, with no possibility of repair. I can't imagine trying to repair it. Besides, the section is on the top of the hill. I think this is DOC land. The Department of Conservation won't take kindly to suddenly having a building on its land, especially in its present condition.

Jon joins in. "The section has had it too," he says breaking into my musing. "It's not just the house that came down last night. The whole hill moved. Probably it is still unstable."

I nod thoughtfully. "My house is built on rock and concreted into it. I now understand how critical that design is because of this catastrophe."

Jon responds thoughtfully, "Ours too. I worried about earthquakes when we built, but the builder insisted it was the best house site on the property. Now, I agree. There is no slope behind looming over it and a good stretch of flat land in front. It might move in an earthquake, but not in this weather. It survived the 2016 Kaikoura earthquakes, so I am not too bothered."

---

[8] Munted – a common term for completely broken or unusable. It came into popular use during the Christchurch earthquakes of 2010-12.

I know my eyes lose their shine as I worry about Kirsty. "Yes. Poor Kirsty. She relies on the income to supplement her pension. I wonder what she will do." I look thoughtfully at Jon. Jon shows just as much apprehension. "Perhaps we should invite her over after the weather improves.

"Good idea, Dan. I wonder how the girls are faring."

I am unconcerned because I am sure they know what to do, but I have a nasty feeling about Malcolm. "We must go to your house to guarantee Malcolm takes the water taxi when it arrives. We don't want him trying to take off in the car."

We walk companionably back to the Jenson's place. It takes us less than a minute to notice Amber's car has gone. We look anxiously at each other. "What has that silly fool done now!"

I feel the anger rising in me. I try to stop it, but nothing helps.

We walk around to the car park just in case it is simply hiding behind something, but no luck. Then a very bedraggled Malcolm arrives, limping up the path. I can't stop myself from grinning. He is mud from head to toe. What on earth has he done?

I'm sure my eyes show distrust, but I try to mask the feeling. "Nice to see you, Malcolm. Can we help in any way?"

My offer of help, infuriates him. His bedraggledness disappears, and the Malcolm I saw on the beach turns up. He seems to be able to change in an instance.

Malcolm responds showing his arrogant self. "There's not much you can do. Why do you keep your road in such a state? I almost killed myself. The car slid into the mud, and I couldn't get it out. Besides, there is a large slip around the next corner, so there is no way out that way."

I feel a bit smug. "I tried to tell you that earlier. I have to clear that slip most winters after some rain. It must be worse than usual after last night's storm. And you needn't think I will clear it quickly because more rain is coming, and that hill may still move. I will do it once it has dried out somewhat."

Malcolm is open-mouthed. He is about to say something, but Jon puts his spoke in. "If you had waited, you would have heard the water taxi is coming to collect you at four p.m."

Malcolm is petulant, just like a child. "What is the use of that? We still won't have a car."

I feel like I am his father trying to make things better. "Jon and I will get the car, but it is too big for the taxi. It will have to wait until a barge can take it to Picton."

Malcolm looks confused. "How can it reach a barge?"

Now, I am genuinely angry. "We will drive it to the beach and move it onto the barge. Simple."

Both Jon and I stomp off to the house. We know we need to use my truck to pull the car out of whatever mess Malcolm has made, but not just yet. I need a coffee.

Jon calls out to Malcolm, "You should take that hose over there to hose the worst of the mud off you, then go and have a shower. You will get sick standing around in that gear."

Malcolm looks offended. He points to the hose in horror. "You expect me to have a cold shower with that first?"

We both nod in unison. We treat him exactly like an errant child, and he knows it. He stomps off inside. I shake my head. "I suppose we will have to clean up in and outside after him."

Jon agrees, but then he begins to smile. The smile becomes a giggle, and before we know it, we are rolling around on the deck, laughing fit to bust, making spectacles of ourselves. You would think we are small children found out in some ignominious plan.

When we calm down, I shout to Jon, "Julie and Amber are not yet back, so let's go and collect that car, Jon!" I don't want to upset our enjoyment, but the evenings come quickly at this time of year, and the car should be collected and cleaned before more damage occurs.

Jon nods his agreement, and we leave to pick up my truck. Not long after, we find the car sitting, as we suspected, in a ditch.

My face bursts into a grin. "Lucky, he slid in here. I'm sure there will be a landslide around the corner just as he said."

Jon jogged to the corner and nodded his head.

Jon looks flabbergasted. "It's not too bad, but he would have probably gone over the side if he had tried to go around the corner. There is insufficient space for the car to pass without riding over part of the slip." Jon shakes his head. "He is such a fool. He should have listened to us."

I look exasperated as I think of Malcolm's actions. "I don't think he listens to anyone, even himself, the way he is acting." My mind is racing because I am annoyed at Amber for falling for such a twit. I can see he is handsome, but that's about it.

I wave to Jon. "Jon, if you sit in the car to guide it once I get it moving, I'll attach the come-along underneath and get the truck to do the work."

Jon and I work well together. He is happy to be guided by me, despite his age. He didn't come from a farm but is willing to try anything.

The come-along pulls tight, and the car moves slowly out of the ditch. Jon keeps the wheels straight, which makes the process easy. Pop and the car is suddenly out on the road in all its muddy glory. I leap out of the truck to go to shake Jon's hand. We both laugh, remembering a muddy Malcolm struggling to pull the car out without help.

I am pleased the removal wasn't too difficult. "Don't know how he expected to recover it. It wasn't stuck too bad, but it gave my truck a run for its money." I laugh, and Jon slaps my back. We are still seeing the vision of a very muddy Malcolm.

Meanwhile, the sheep have been regarding us seriously. Their looks increase our hilarity. I wonder what they thought of Malcolm.

Chapter 11

It takes Mum and me much longer than expected to check all the sheep, but I cannot complain because Daniel's sheep are all in the closest paddocks to the homestead. The scenery is to die for with its tall hills - some would say mountains, green pastures and ravines complete with native bush and the fresh smell of the wet tussock grass. I remember the dawn chorus of my youth. The birds woke us up chatting to each other, some screeching 'good morning,' while others are more cautious. I had forgotten how I missed this place, the peaceful feel, the sounds of nature, frequently not soothing but somehow comforting. I know I am lucky I can return anytime. I guess, I had taken its existence for granted.

We are shocked at how much destruction there is around the farm. Hills have fallen into ravines, and gullies gush with water, the water we would love in summer. At this time of year, there is nowhere for it to go except to flood unsuspecting pastures and upset sheep. The sheep are pleased to see us, but we have no extra food for them. Indeed, there is no need. The pastures are lush with ryegrass, white clover, and other grasses. There are fescues, cocksfoot, timothy, plantain and chicory popping up in the paddocks where the ewes are grazing. Lucerne is growing well where the sheep will go after weaning. They should be happy souls, especially as their location is high above all the water-soaked paddocks around them.

A frown crosses my mother's face. "Amber, you can't expect them to be happy despite the pasture." Mum is reading my thoughts. "I would hate to stand around in last night's rain. It might have penetrated their thick coats."

My response is thoughtless. "Next month, the sheep might have had more to worry about. The shearing season will be in full swing. Then they will shiver without their coats."

My mum looks upset at me. Her mouth is open, and her eyes flash. "Amber! When did you become so cold?"

I have upset Mum. I think back to what I just said. She is right. "I am sorry, Mum. I wasn't thinking about the sheep. I am so worried about what to do with Malcolm. He isn't the same man I thought I knew. It is possible he was always like this, but I didn't notice. I just acquiesced to all his requests to keep the peace because most things aren't that important. I don't care which movie I view or program on the TV I watch, unless they are extremely violent. Then I object, but mostly insignificant things are unimportant. I care about my friends, and I think he has deliberately kept me away from them." I add this last bit without thinking. It is an idea on the brink of my mind, forming into reality.

The look on my mother's face is a picture. "This is terrible, darling. But it doesn't mean you take out your angsts on unsuspecting animals."

I lower my head, hit by a deep feeling of shame. I begin to talk to the sheep. "I am sorry sheep. I envy your freedom. Last night must have been terrible. It was bad enough inside in the warmth." Needless to say, the sheep take no notice. They keep eating as if nothing unusual happened.

I turn to my mother. "Thank you for calling me out on this. I was out of line. Please make sure I never do it again."

Mum isn't mollified. "You must do that for yourself. I won't be by your side all your life."

I can feel the worry lines deepening on my forehead. "I agree, Mum, but I don't know how to tell Malcolm I don't want to return with him. I am afraid he will act violently." I add this last bit tentatively. It is an idea that has been growing in my mind ever since I saw that terrible glint, the one that looked like he could kill me.

This bought a quick look from Mum. "Has he hit you?"

I feel my shoulders fall back in shock. "No, Mum. Nothing like that. It is just that on the beach, he had this look in his eye, and I have seen it since. It is a kind of madness burning in him. I might be the cause. Maybe on our drive here, I said too much about Daniel and painted him like some amazing Superman. If I was more sensitive to his feelings, his reaction might not have happened."

Mum shook her head. Her eyes glitter, annoyed at the thought. "He is an adult, Amber, and you talked about your childhood friendship. You can't blame yourself for his jealousy. If he is jealous of your youthful relationships, how much more he must be of your friends? I think the man is sick." Mum looks directly into my eyes, "But you don't have to fix him. It is up to him."

This statement is clear. Mum knows I would think I should help him. I suspect she means I must solve my own problems. She is not speaking about Malcolm only. But I can't risk him hurting my parents. This is my problem. I think I will return to Picton with Malcolm, then tell him I am not going any further. I will ask for time off from work. I have accumulated lots of holidays and I can work from here on anything urgent.

I tell Mum my thoughts, but she is unhappy at the very idea of my going anywhere with Malcolm. We ride in silence on our way home. The weather is still threatening the continuation of the storm, and I wonder if the water taxi will come.

Once we return the horses, we hose them down and brush them until they shine. We check their feed and walk silently back to our house. Nearing the deck, a strange sight meets our eyes. My father and Daniel are lying there, laughing their heads off. What could be so funny? Mum and I stand ogling them in amazement.

Dad is the first to notice us. He pokes Daniel in the side and points towards us. They both sit up, holding their sides as if preventing them from falling apart. "Glad you have returned. Was all well?" Dad speaks weakly. He still lacked breath from laughing.

Daniel is visibly trying to stop laughing. "Thank you for checking my sheep. How are they? Do they need anything?" Daniel changes quickly from hilarity to serious interest in his animals.

My mother assesses the situation and grasps Daniel's change of subject. "All is well, Dan. You have nothing to be concerned about. You must have moved them before the storm to the close paddocks."

Daniel looks at Mum and agrees. "Yes. We had a fair warning a storm was coming, but not this size. I suppose there is much work to do once the weather calms."

Mum agrees. "Many slips in places where you would expect to find them, some flooding, but it isn't so bad because the gullies are coping with the water even if it floods some paddocks. It should all drain away. The slips are the main problem. But what is so funny?"

Dad and Daniel look guiltily at each other. "It was just how Malcolm looked when he returned from crashing your car, Amber. Dan and I couldn't help taking the Mickey out of him. We thought he should shower with the hose before going inside." This statement brought more raucous laughter from both of them.

Dan readily agrees. "You should have seen the sight of him, mud from head to foot. I don't know how he did it."

"Malcolm crashed my car? How bad is the damage?" I almost shout.

They both look guilty again. "We haven't gone to get your car yet. He didn't look hurt, so I hope it isn't so bad. Maybe he slipped into a ditch driving too fast. He said it drove into the mud all by itself, not his responsibility. There's plenty of mud about, that's for sure." They both begin laughing again.

All I can think about is the floor inside the house and the potential damage to my car. Once again, I feel guilty for introducing Malcolm to my family. As if matters could not get any worse, the skies darken threateningly. Pessimistically, I think the water taxi will not reach us today. I must clean the floor, shower and change my clothes, ready for any eventuality.

I try to shake the guilt out of me to decide on a safe course of action. "I will go inside and clean up before I step into the shower," I say almost primly, hoping this will allay some of my guilt.

Mum's face changes to sympathy as she says, "We can all clean up any mess, darling."

I know by the 'darling' that Mum has forgiven my earlier *faux pas*. I feel relieved, but I still haven't resolved 'the go or not to go' situation. The coward in me hopes the water taxi will not come until tomorrow. A little sparkle in me winks because tomorrow is *Matariki*, and I dearly want to spend this *Matariki* with my parents.

Chapter 12

My father and Daniel return the car and go inside to clean themselves.

Mum and I clean the car but Malcolm sulks inside, and I quietly fume. He should be out here helping us. I am uneasy about what Malcolm is doing because my backpack is there, standing beside his bag on the mat near the door, as if ready to make a race to leave. When I saw him earlier, he did not even peek at me when I tried to say I wanted to stay for *Matariki*, especially seeing it is so close. In frustration, I give up worrying because I can hear Mum washing my car already. I go out to join her.

We wash the car in silence, but it feels good and companionable. "It doesn't look too bad this side," Mum says.

I nod in agreement. "It is okay this side too; a few scratches, but that is to be expected if he went in a ditch. The insurance should cover it." I stop washing. "I should have taken photos before we washed it. Damn. They will never believe me."

Mum looks amused. "I am sure they will understand. They must know about the storm. Take some photos now, just in case. They will show the before and potentially the after, so all isn't lost."

I take out my phone and click away, ensuring the shadows show how deep the mud is. I giggle. "It looks like we have been playing mud pies, similar to when I was a child."

Mum smiles, and her eyes twinkle. "You were such a mischief, into everything. Trillions of times I had to hose you down before you entered the house. I suppose Dan was the same, mud all over. No wonder he suggested Malcolm hose himself."

I giggle at the memory of Dan and me, but also at the thought of Malcolm's face when offered such an indignity. "We did get up to some things, didn't we? But we always had a fabulous time."

Mum reprimands me. "You didn't do the wash in those days." Mum pretends annoyance, but I know she enjoys the memory.

I look towards Mum hoping for guidance. "What am I to do, Mum? Malcolm isn't talking to me, so it is impossible to discuss not returning with him."

"What will be, will be," Mum says unhelpfully.

I glance at my watch while I finish taking photos. My phone still has no bars.

I screw up my nose as a new thought comes to me. "It's way past the time for the water taxi to be here. Malcolm will be too scared to go on board once the sun is down, what with the waves and not knowing the area. Perhaps I should ring."

Mum puts down the hose. "Finish the car, and then we can ask Dan to put in a call. The taxi must be stretched with holidaymakers trying to get back to Picton, to say nothing of the people who must get there, the sick or injured. Such people must be their priority. Earlier, I noticed a helicopter flying across the ridge. Perhaps something urgent is happening over there, and look. Here comes the beginning of the rain again."

The rain starts to make splodgy giant blobs, and at the same time, I hear the faint sound of an outboard. It doesn't sound like the water taxi. It must be a local. I hope it is because anyone else would be silly to be out in this weather. The sound increases.

"Oh, we have a visitor," Mum notes. "No, Dan is out on the dock. He must know them. Oh, it is his relatives arriving for *Matariki*. We should have known they would come no matter the weather."

My face clears at the thought that there might be a way to get rid of Malcolm early. "Perhaps they will take Malcolm with them when they leave," I say hopefully.

Mum smiles. "I think they are here for two nights. They will greet *Matariki* at sunrise."

I feel my eyes flash at the thought that I might miss *Matariki*. "That does it. I want to stay. I have never celebrated *Matariki*." I hurry to finish my side of the car, thinking I can polish it in the morning. "I will ask Daniel if I can use his phone to cancel the taxi and worry about Malcolm later."

Hurrying away, I see Mum's eyes crinkle with the beginnings of a smile. None of us want Malcolm here spoiling our festivities, but it might be the best solution to a sticky problem.

Rushing inside, I find Dad sitting comfortably by the fire. There is no sign of Malcolm. He must be in the bedroom. Good, I think. He can stay there all night if he likes. I realise Daniel isn't there either. I temporarily forget he is on the dock greeting his family. Without speaking to Dad, and remembering where Daniel is, I race outside to catch him before he goes home.

Impulsively, I shout, "Daniel, do you mind if I use your phone," I am calling from the steps leading down to the dock.

He stands ready to hug his grandmother, and a shadow of exasperation dashes across his face. I have forgotten how critical protocol is to this Māori family, especially with *Matariki* just around the corner. I should let him greet his family.

My face much show my annoyance at not reading the situation. "Sorry. I didn't mean to interrupt. I wasn't thinking. I want to cancel the water taxi because I want to celebrate *Matariki*. There is not much chance to view the stars in the city." I babble, never mind that there will probably be cloud cover, so no stars. "Perhaps someone needs the taxi more than us tonight."

Daniel hands me his phone without a word. I can tell he is upset.

His face is closed. "The number is already on speed dial." His voice sounds tight.

I wave weakly at his family, hoping they will understand. They seem faintly amused by this exchange, and then I find myself in the middle of hugs from all of them. They haven't seen me for years, and I am struck dumb by the warmth of their greeting. How could I forget how thoughtful they all are? I am excited but too anxious about the taxi. I hope it will not turn into the bay while we chat.

A deep voice I know well sounds close to my ear. "Just push here. The company will answer if it's not too busy." Daniel gives me the gentle look he used in the past when I had done something stupid. It makes my heart race, much to my surprise. We look awkwardly at each other, which only amuses his family more.

I push the speed dial, and it goes straight to the taxi office. "Hello," I say, hesitant about how to begin to say we don't want the taxi, especially if it is already on its way. "Hello. Amber Jenson here. Has the taxi already left to pick us up? ….. A smile spreads across my face. ….. "It hasn't, well, good. I wonder if we can cancel today and rebook for tomorrow. …… Tomorrow, you have no space for the two of us? Oh, I am sorry. ….. But you will put us on the waitlist. Only one of us has to return tomorrow. ….. I can stay until you have space. ….. You have space for one in the middle of the afternoon? ….. Great! ….. Malcolm will take the space for sure. No problem. Thank you."

I give the phone back, looking much relieved. Malcolm can go tomorrow, and I can go sometime later. He will have to accept there is no room for me. How do I get myself into such muddles?

Daniel reads my thoughts. "You seem to attract turmoil, but you always did, not always of your making, but then again sometimes ….."

He smiles down at me, and for the first time, I see how handsome he is. For some reason, I want to hit him playfully in response to his remark. I catch myself just in time. What am I doing? My boyfriend is inside being obnoxious, and I am out here flirting. Is that what I am doing, flirting with Daniel? I understand what he means because my actions are causing my problems. It is all because I am acting like a teenager. Straightening up to my full height, I say with as much dignity as I can muster, "I had better tell Malcolm he will be leaving sometime tomorrow."

Without dwelling on the consequences, I turn on my heel and return to the house before I can say something I may regret. I have made enough trouble for one day, and I still have to find the right words so Malcolm will leave without fuss. There seems to be a shortage of sensible words for this purpose. This situation will resolve itself, given time, I hope.

Chapter 13

Amber's interruption annoys me because she knows greetings are rituals, but I am secretly amused that she thinks she can bowl up and ask for help despite this. The old Amber is in there somewhere. She must let Malcolm loose because he is a detrimental influence. Well, he is just bad, period.

I bring myself back to the present with a jolt. "Sorry, I missed that, Grandma." My thoughts are so deep that I am unaware Grandma is talking.

Grandma has a look in her eye that tells me she has been scheming. "I was just saying it is lovely for you that young Amber has arrived home after all these years. She hasn't changed a bit, still beautiful." Grandmother has a sparkle in her eye, a sparkle I know well.

I make sure she is clear on the situation. "Her boyfriend is with her, Grandma," I say before she has any ideas. Grandma loves to match-make. She is as bad as my mother. My mind whirls at the thought of marriage and makes me scan the visitors to discover if there is a likely lamb to the slaughter among them.

My grandma anticipates my thoughts. "We didn't ask Amy because the weather is unpredictable, and I thought she would be uncomfortable." Goodness knows who Amy is, but the lack of whoever it is pleases Grandma. She has a scheme in mind. I suspect it involves Amber. "Is this boyfriend of Amber's a serious situation or just a passing fancy?"

Got it in one. Grandma knew before she arrived that Amber was home.

"Grandma, Amber's life is her affair. You must not meddle." I sound grumpy.

Grandma's eyes continue to sparkle. "What me, meddle?"

"You, Grandma meddle? What a thought?" I cannot help but grin. She is such a minx despite her age, well probably because of it. She is like a fine wine, becoming wilier with age.

Dad pulls me in for a *hongi* and a quick hug. "It's hard to imagine your grandma doing any such thing."

Dad is smiling broadly. My brothers and their wives join in the hilarity. The kids are just impatient. They want to run up quickly to my house because they think I have better computer games than at their homes. Besides, their hours are unrestricted here, except they must play outside during the day. We all relent, however, when the weather is dreadful, like today.

I can feel the first spots of the return of the rain as I shout, "We had better hurry. This rain isn't going to let up any time soon." I pick up someone's bag. The others take the hint, and we all rush towards my house. My expectations for a family *Matariki* disappeared with the onset of the weather, and now I am unprepared. The fire needs lighting, the food cooked, and the beds made. However, Mum has ignored my pessimism and has been cooking furiously since she and Dad arrived. Dad has cut the wood and arranged the fire, but I must do something. The beds are no problem because they all know where they can sleep and will make their beds themselves. Then, we will all muck in to enhance the feast, a feast large enough to warm our hearts and bodies.

Grandma, the matriarch, orders the kids to organise themselves before they are allowed to play. They will be responsible for cleaning up after dinner. We prefer that the adults make the food on occasions like this. It is less complicated. They are responsible for making their own beds. I smile, remembering my excitement on such family occasions when I was a child.

Dad broke into my thoughts, "There is no point putting a *hāngī*[9] down tomorrow. The ground is too wet, and this storm looks set in for the duration. We'll have to do with roast meat and vegetables. Your mother made sure we had lots of *Kūmara*[10] and *pūhā*[11]. It's impossible to have a feast without them, better for us than that *Pākehā*[12] potato and green vegetables."

One of my brothers, Ian, looks at Dad in surprise. "You sound a bit racist, Dad. What is this? Only Māori food is any good for us?"

We understand Dad is joking, but he can't help himself. "Just because you are a *Pākehā* medical doctor, you think you know

---

[9] Hāngī – an earth oven common in Polynesia.
[10] Kūmara – a sweet potato.
[11] Pūhā - green vegetable.
[12] Pākehā – Non-Māori or New Zealander usually of European descent.

everything. Many times *pūhā* has saved you when you had a sore stomach. It's, what do they call it today, a whole food. I think *kumara* might be as well, son."

Dad's eyes dance while he says this. He expects a response, but my brother only says, "You might be right about that, Dad."

Dad chuckles, "Both *kūmara* and *pūhā* are excellent for our health. I didn't get this strong living on potatoes and salad." He ignores his pain as much as possible because it annoys him how much it slows him down.

We all love teasing each other. It tests the strength of our minds.

Dad looks keenly at me. "Have you been out surveying your sheep today, son?" He is always worried about the sheep, especially at this time of year when the ewes are pregnant. They are so vulnerable when the weather is inclement.

I respond uncomfortably, "Actually, Amber and her mother went to check on them. Her father and I were occupied by more weighty things." I try to say Amber's name nonchalantly, but I can tell by the look on Mum's face that she detects a hidden feeling that flicks at my heart when I say her name.

Mum's eyes crinkle at the corners. "Oh, Amber did that, did she? Why would she mind the sheep if she is so involved with her boyfriend?" She knows she has hit a mark. I don't know how to get her to understand. Dad sits there with his eyebrows raised.

I try to tell them the situation. "Mum, it wasn't like that. Her father and I had to examine Kirsty's house. It slid down the hill last night. We had no idea what condition it was in or if anyone was in it, so Amber and her Mum suggested they examine the sheep. They are both experienced." I end lamely, "At the time, it seemed like a good idea." Then I brightened up, "Jon and I had to collect Amber's car, so that took time."

Mum is tickled pink. "What did Amber do to her car that meant you had to rescue it?"

I shake my head in exasperation. "It wasn't Amber. It was her boyfriend. He decided to hightail it out of here because of all the rain last night. You know what the road must be like! Well, he got himself lost in a ditch. Lucky a landslide didn't fall on him."

My brothers, who have been standing around listening, Mum and Dad, laugh at my annoyance and the situation. My brother George chortles, "By the sound of it, you don't like this man. He sounds a bit of a fool."

I have three brothers, George, Ian and Mike. Two are married, which is a perpetual irritation for me. The issue is not that they are married. I feel irritated because my mother uses this to excuse her trying to find me a wife at every opportunity. She does the same for Mike but he doesn't mind as much as I do.

I respond to George without thinking. "Yes, he is an irritating, pompous ass. I don't know what she sees in him. I suppose he is out of his comfort zone. He was born in London, so is used to city life. These wide-open spaces are all a bit much for him."

Brother Mike asks, "What happened to the car?"

A giggle tries to escape from deep within me as I say, "It's not too bad, a few scratches. Malcolm managed to slide it into a ditch while driving too fast. Quite lucky, because just around the corner was the usual landslide, and he would have hit it or tried to avoid it and gone over the edge. That would have given us much more trouble." My eyes lose focus remembering the scene, while I think of the consequences if he were hurt, or worse. He could have died.

A commotion erupts on the porch. The kids are playing with the dogs, and one accidentally stands on Jock's toes. He isn't the least bit pleased and shows his exasperation.

I leap into action. "I had better sort that out before Jock decides the answer might be to nip. He is a good dog but not used to so much attention." Walking towards the porch, I shout, "Kids, you must be careful with my dogs. They like you but in small doses. Why don't you get out a board game, snakes and ladders, cards, something like that? The boys would like to play with you in the morning, eh mates? See, the dogs are nodding."

I smile while the littlest ones watch the dogs closely, looking for the nodding. "I like Monopoly, Uncle Dan," my eldest nephew says.

I slow down to explain. I must remember they are just kids. "It might be a bit hard for some of your cousins. Remember, they are younger than you. They haven't had as much time to learn. Dinner won't be long, so choose something that will not take all night. Maybe you older ones can play a harder game, but make sure you choose something for the young ones. How about Jenga?"

They are excellent kids and play well together, but sometimes things get out of hand. There is a surplus of adults around to straighten them out, so no real worries. Poor things; they think they are making their own choices. I remember it well. Usually, it was Dad who would sort us out. Now there are Grandma, Dad, Mum and the six of us young adults including my brother's wives. Quite a group from a young child's perspective. They all pat each dog, say their goodbyes and trot happily inside. I make sure the dogs have enough water and food for the night.

"Sleep well. I think it will be a rough night. Listen to that wind. Don't let it bother you," I tell the dogs, shutting the door to re-enter the house with a relaxed sigh. They are good dogs and will not overreact to changes in the weather. My chest swells as I think what a lucky man I am to have such loyal dogs and a thoughtful family.

Chapter 14

I am using Daniel's phone with some trepidation. A worried expression escapes even though I try to hide it. I don't want Malcolm to think I am using Daniel's phone to be near Dan. I hope he will stay put and not see me using the satellite phone. I need to sort out the pick up by the water taxi. My nose screws up as I make myself clear.

The phone call made, the next item on the agenda is to tell Malcolm the result before he does anything disastrous. It worries me to think what he will be like in the morning. He will feel like a fish out of water, knowing no one and getting up at dawn. Rising that early in the morning won't suit him. If he likes, he can stay in bed and miss the fun, but it is more crucial how I explain the water taxi situation to him.

Instead of planning, I rush inside to find that Mum and Dad are already preparing dinner for us all. Guilt clutters my mind because I should be here helping, not racing around trying to fix taxis because I want to attend the festivities in the morning.

I am sure there is guilt plastered all over my face as I ask, "What can I do to help, Mum?" I say, trying to look enthusiastic. "Where's Malcolm?"

Mum looks up from checking the roast in the oven, "He is still in your room. I asked him to come to the fire, but he prefers to read lying on the bed." Mum is disgruntled. "He is waiting for the taxi. I told him it might not come tonight because of emergencies."

A sigh of relief escapes my mouth. Mum's statement warns Malcolm that things might be different from his preference. "I will see if I can entice him to come for a glass of wine."

I dash down the corridor, forgetting my offer to help with the food. A glance at my parents shows me neither is happy with me, or perhaps it is with Malcolm. It is hard to tell. I put that aside, readying myself for a battle with Malcolm, preparing to be non-confrontational, if that is possible.

I can't remember when I became so cautious. I know I didn't used to be. Maybe it was when I went to university in the States. It was a shock to the system. The university was great, and I felt like a kid walking into Willie Wonka's factory. There were so many courses, so much on offer, and I could even choose courses for grading by writing papers and take-home finals, or ones with timed examinations. I preferred the take-home finals system. I have never been good under exam pressure. The system suited me just fine, so my marks were great. But I remember times when I asked questions in class when no one else was asking. That took courage but my need to know outweighed my embarrassment. I don't think it was the States that changed me. I have to admit it was Malcolm.

I met Malcolm at a conference. He was confident and handsome. I was overjoyed when he came to coffee with me and my friends. I can feel the butterflies in my stomach as I walked with him with the eyes of other women on us. They appeared to be saying, 'How could a girl like that be with him?' I didn't know the answer because I was walking on air. Now, he is ordering me around, and I follow without question. I suspect I did it from the first day I met him. He seemed just so special.

Tapping quietly on the door before entering, I am immediately annoyed at myself. It is my room, after all. Why am I knocking? Malcolm looks up from reading. The look on his face does not make me feel any better.

Malcolm thunders, "It's about time you came. I thought the taxi would never arrive."

Oh dear! I sigh. "I'm sorry to say the taxi cannot come until tomorrow. There are some elderly people who have priority, and others needing help. We come a long way down their list tonight."

Malcolm looks horrified. "What can be more important than getting me back to civilization? Did you tell them my work is critical and I must be there on Monday morning? No, I suppose not. You want to stay here to make google eyes at your boyfriend."

My blood boils. It is all I can do to hold back the sharp comment which festers in my head. I speak tightly, "No change was possible, and Daniel has nothing to do with my decisions.

They say they can take you in the middle of the afternoon tomorrow. They have space for just one."

Malcolm looks daggers at me. "That's convenient for you. What bothers me is why you insist on calling him Daniel. Your whole family calls him Dan. What is it with you?"

He appears to miss my comment that only he will leave tomorrow. Well, I have said it. It is up to him to listen. Much to my surprise I say, "It is no business of yours what I call him. I used to call him Danny, but he is all grown up now, and that name is a diminutive. And, if you must know, calling him Dan seems much too familiar. Now, are you satisfied? I don't understand you. You didn't used to be this obnoxious. Mum and Dad would like you to come to have a wine before dinner. Do you think you can do that and not spoil their evening, even if you want to spoil mine?"

My anger is so great that I want to stomp away and leave him to stew without dinner. He must read my thoughts because a shadow of a smile slips across his face. This smile brings no great joy to my heart. Rather, there is something in the pit of my stomach that turns over. A feeling is emanating from his body that has nothing to do with the physical. I think he is evil. How could I not know this before tonight?

He opens his mouth to speak. I wait breathlessly, wondering what will come out. "I will come and be charming. You won't like your parents enjoying my company, not one little bit. I will make them love me. Then, we will talk when we leave tomorrow." He waves his hand imperiously. This statement sounds ominous to me. Which part of not going, does he not understand?

Not a sound slips out of my mouth as he stretches out his long legs to leap off the bed and straightens his clothes to look almost respectable. He even stops to comb his hair. 'Ugh', almost slips out of my mouth at the action. I decide not to repeat that he is the only one leaving tomorrow. It can wait. Tonight is here and now, and I must manage it without dispute. I walk out the open door and then gasp. Mum and Dad must have heard our exchange because they are standing near the corridor looking surprised. His good behaviour won't fool them. He has shown his true colours.

When Malcolm settles himself by the fireplace like the Lord of the Manor, Dad hands him a glass of red wine. "I hope you like it. It is the best red of the Spy Valley wines. We love it."

Malcolm swirls the wine like a wine taster, sniffs it and takes a small sip. "Excellent." He says knowingly. I admit his knowledge is okay, but he is not a great connoisseur.

My Dad, ever the gentleman, comments, "Glad you like it, son. A good read on a night like this warms the heart." Dad smiles. He is playing the game of the exemplary host. Thank goodness for that. I don't know what I would have done if he had chosen another route.

Mum and I help ourselves to glasses of wine, but I can't help but notice Malcolm bristles at the familiarity of Dad's language. 'Son' is not a name he values. It is too demeaning in his eyes. He fails to see it as a gesture of friendly acceptance of him as a person. I settle beside Mum on the couch. Dad sits in the other armchair beside the fire where Mum usually sits. I feel irritated at Malcolm's presumption that he can sit in Dad's seat, but then I remember he can't know that it is Dad's place. I must pull myself together, or I will spoil everything for my parents.

The conversation is stilted, and so Dad clicks on the TV. It springs into life. "I went up on the roof and straightened the dish. Hopefully, it will last for tonight," he says, shrugging his shoulders as if to accentuate the difficulties caused by the weather.

We all look appreciatively at the box and wait for any news of Marlborough. Much to my surprise, we lead the News. The main road around the Sounds from Picton to Havelock is out. The slips, particularly the under-cuttings, are too bad for emergency repairs. It may be weeks before repairs happen. We must use sea access in the meantime. There is no other way out.

I speak loudly, possibly louder than is essential. "No wonder the water taxi is so busy," I say, hoping something will penetrate Malcolm's mind. "Pity my car is here. It will be days before a barge will come here. They will want to help those people with real problems."

"Look, darling," my mother looks concerned. "The road from Picton to the south is in a mess again too. Even if your car was in Picton, you would have to go home through the West Coast, the long way around. That trip will add hours to the travel. You will be best to fly. I suppose the planes are full too, especially because people will have come here for the long weekend."

Mum is trying to make Malcolm understand the extent of our situation. He doesn't look convinced.

Malcolm mumbles, "Lucky you have those tickets on the taxi for tomorrow. But, how will we travel to Christchurch?" I could shake him. He hasn't got the picture at all. I borrowed Daniel's phone, not only to book the ferry, but to ensure Malcolm goes as far away from me as possible.

I try to close my face from showing my true feelings. "I booked you on a flight out of Blenheim. The shuttle will be at the water taxi wharf, waiting to take you to the airport. I think you can manage to get a taxi once you are in Christchurch when you arrive back. No worries." The look on Malcolm's face shows me the penny has finally dropped.

Malcolm is spluttering in shock. "You are not coming with me," he shouts in surprise.

I hold myself together and speak primly, as if I am a Victorian school teacher. "I told you in the bedroom that there is only one space left on the water taxi all tomorrow. I thought you would appreciate it. I can take it if you like, and you can stay here." I speak sweetly, trying not to laugh out loud. It is not my preferred mode of voice.

Mum intervenes, "Tea is about to be served, then we can resolve this matter later."

Malcolm changes instantly to the polite, charming man he wants to project. "What a good idea. Food is always good for the soul."

I feel sick at the sounds of his gracious behaviour, but I'm sure this does not fool Mum and Dad. I help Mum bring the food to the table, and we sit down as the wind screeches deafeningly.

Dad's face belies his comment. "I hope no sailor is out in that," Dad says, guaranteeing the topic is changed.

That thought crossed my mind too. The problem is, if it is too stormy for sailors, then the water taxi won't come. I desperately want it to arrive. It would have been great if it had arrived tonight, but that is now impossible. The wind seems to ratchet up a notch as I reflect on Malcolm. My thoughts of him jumble up with the sounds of the storm, the creaking of the trees, and the splattering of the rain. I must clear my thought channel of anything concerning Malcolm to something positive. I don't want to spoil Mum's meal.

Chapter 15

The night continues, and the atmosphere in the house does not improve.

The wind tonight is as bad as last night's storm, but, so far, no more trees have blown down around our house. I wonder why storms at night always seem worse than during the day. I suppose it is the thought of being out in the cold and unable to see clearly. The poor sheep don't have the option of wandering in and out. They are there no matter what. They must be having a terrible time. I hope no more babies are born tonight. It is too early for them and too cold. Besides, I don't want to think of Daniel, out there in this weather.

Mum, Dad and I sit around the fire and natter. Malcolm's presence makes us more reserved. Our conversation remains stilted until Malcolm decides it is time for bed. I look up at him and say I will be in when I am ready. I will not let him bully me into going to bed at a time that suits him. He is still on good behaviour and so says nothing but smiles with a piercing look behind his eye. A shiver runs down my back. It feels ominous, just like the weather.

The three of us de-stress as he leaves the room.

I hate how this visit has turned out, and I wonder where I will sleep tonight. The worry is quashed by Mum when she says she has made up the bed in the spare room. "I expect it used. I don't want all my good work going for nothing."

Dad looks at me quizzically. "What are you going to do, lass? You can't return with him tomorrow, certainly not in his present temperament. There is no knowing what will happen. The serious question is, what will happen when you return to Christchurch? If you want us to come with you, we will. We have business there soon, so it will fit in with our time. You will not be taking us out of our way. Besides, if you take your car, I think you should have someone follow you because we don't know if your car is okay. Mud might have filtered into goodness knows where. It can splash in the most unlikely places."

I think about what they both say but shake my head. "It is my problem. I don't want you involved. It is up to me to sort this out. I will ask for time off work and stay here while I sort out what to do, that is if you don't mind. Things might be clearer in the morning."

Mum pats my knee. "You know we are here for you. You don't have to ask."

I know this, but they brought me up to face my problems, and this issue certainly tests my ability. Do I want to be controlled all my life, or do I want to be on my own? Alone in a big city seems a bleak future. When things are good, Malcolm is excellent company. He is a bit like the little girl with the curl in the middle of her forehead, when she was good, she was very, very good, and when she was bad, she was horrid. This nursery rhyme is him right down to the ground.

I remember living alone before I met Malcolm and not having anyone to tell my deepest secrets. I thought Malcolm was a good listener, but if I think about it, he seldom remembered anything I said. I just glossed over his not knowing something because I felt I was less important than him. He just let me talk, and it all washed over him. Now, I wonder why he wanted to live with me. Was it because I made life so easy and I looked good on his arm? Is that all a girl is worth? What a dreadful thought, yet I suspect the idea has some truth.

It can be very frustrating living alone. Yes, that is the word, frustrating. People thought I was lonely when I lived independently, but the lack of immediate human response is an issue. Even a dog can replace that feeling of aloneness. But it is the lack of someone to share a thought or a disaster at work. That is, simple things. Being alone is one thing. The feeling of loneliness is another. To my surprise, I have to admit I have felt lonely in recent months living with Malcolm. I thought it was a phase in which he didn't want to listen or perhaps pressure from his work. I was happy to give him a pass, but now I wonder if he really wants a doll and not a person. Sharing should be part of the human psyche. I take a sip of my wine, thinking I am becoming maudlin.

Suddenly, I acknowledge that I am being as thoughtless as Malcolm. I turn towards my parents and ask earnestly, "I hope you don't mind my staying on for a few days?"

Mother looks shocked. "Why would we mind? We love having you. We don't want to interfere in your life, that is all. It is yours to live, but we don't like seeing you hurt. How can we help?"

I smile. I know Mum wants to help. She has told me many times, but my thoughts are so scrambled. I have no skills for this kind of thing. I must be alone to mull over my thoughts, so I say, "If you don't mind, I will go to bed now. I didn't sleep much last night, and I hope to get up before the sun in the morning. I want to watch *Matariki* rise to make a wish."

The thought of sitting on the hill watching the stars rise makes a smile reach my eyes. Mum and Dad are happy because they observe my body unclench as I talk about the morning.

Mum smiles. "We hope to be there too, up on the ridge. The view of the sky will be hopeless if this storm keeps up." Mum gets up and hugs me.

Dad continues, "Yes, but we will know it is there, even if clouds cover the stars. It relaxes us just to think about them high up in the sky, watching all of us. We might be lucky. Who knows? The storm might break."

They both laugh. Mum says, "It's not what the weather forecast says, but it's possible. Forecasting has never been the forecaster's strongest point in these shaky isles."

We all laugh. Better reporting methods have improved reporting reliability, but our wind-swept country has unreliable weather. I go to the sink, get a glass of water and say goodnight while they rise to turn in for the night too. I move quickly to ready myself for bed.

After I clean my teeth and wash myself, I stumble out of the bathroom and fall into the bed, ready to drop off to sleep instantaneously. My body is aching with exhaustion, but my mind wants to replay my last conversation with Malcolm. The trees outside moan in agreement with my thoughts. I can't help comparing Malcolm with Daniel. The one is so arrogant, whereas the other is kind, thoughtful and forgiving. Why didn't I come home more frequently through the years? I might have avoided the present situation, of course, if Daniel *was* interested. He didn't come down to Dunedin at all while we were at 'varsity, but he was far away in the North Island, and I could have come here to the Sounds. I have no idea why I didn't. I was involved with my new life, studying, meeting friends with similar interests, wanting to know all about the world. The Sounds seemed far away from all that. Daniel must like living alone; otherwise, he would have married ages ago. We were childhood friends, but that is different from adulthood. Now, we are such different people with different experiences. He loves the outdoors and farming. I love city life and the outdoors too, it is true. Would I like to live out here all the time? It can be isolating, but it is only a short trip across the water on a good day to Picton. Wellington is only a short plane ride away. It is not 'the back of beyond' like some Australian stations. Here, is positively overrun with people compared to there. I find myself drifting off with this pleasant thought.

Suddenly, deep in my subconscious while I am dreaming. Something surreal is happening. I feel a presence in the room, but who can it be? I brush the thought aside in my dream state, but then I hear breathing close to my ear. It has a tangible quality with a raspy quality to it that I have only heard in Malcolm. Surely, he isn't in the room. I know I dropped off to sleep. This feeling must be a dream because he was sound asleep when I peeped in on my way to bed. But someone is definitely in the room because that sound is too human for it to be a dream. I try to open my eyes, but they are heavy with sleep. The floorboards near me creak. I feel, rather than see, a shadow moving across the room. I sit up and shake my head. I want to know if I am awake or in a dream.

"It's only me," a familiar voice, whispers. "I thought I would come to find out how you are, given you didn't want to disturb me by coming into my room."

I bristle because first of all, the room Malcolm sleeps in is mine, and secondly, I didn't want to see him last night, and I certainly don't want to see him now, so why is he here?

I have difficulty keeping the annoyance out of my voice. "What are you doing awake at this time of night?" I glance at the clock and find it is past three o'clock. "Why are you sneaking around?

We can talk in the morning." I try to sound authoritative, but it comes out submissive. Why does he do this to me?

"I want to sleep with you. It is impossible to sleep by myself," he says petulantly.

I turn over and put my back towards him. "I need to go to sleep. I will be up in a couple of hours. I have set the alarm."

There is a surprise in his voice. "Why have you done that? I thought you said the taxi would be coming in the middle of the afternoon."

My fingers ball up because my whole body wants to punch him. "I have already told you it is *Matariki* tomorrow, well now, today, and I want to celebrate it even if you do not. Just go back to bed."

I sense he continues to walk towards me.

He spits out a strange laugh. "You still want that boyfriend of yours after all you have done to me. I will not leave you here. You will come back with me no matter what. I will tell the taxi driver to take us both."

I don't say anything. I cannot think what I can say to change Malcolm's mind. He has no idea how things work around here. Perhaps he has Sound's Fever, a fever caused by isolation, but that is impossible because it usually sets in after seclusion for a long time. He has barely been here a day.

Now, he slides under the bedclothes and wiggles himself close to me. I move to the edge of the bed. If I move much further, I will fall out. I don't want to make a noise. Mum and Dad need their sleep. We have caused them too much trouble since we arrived.

His cold hands grip around my waist, trying to turn me around. I resist.

I try to make my voice sound commanding even though I am whispering. "Malcolm, you must go," I try to say with strength, but it comes out as a murmur.

He giggles somewhere down in his throat. I am sure he is out of his mind. I think his eyes even flash as his strength increases. Suddenly Malcolm is right beside me, and I have nowhere to move. I try to shrink myself into a small ball. It is all I can do to protect myself.

Chapter 16

Julie Jenson awakes from a sound sleep, uncertain about what has awakened her. She thinks it is the wind, but whatever the sound, it isn't a particularly loud noise. *But it was enough to disturb my sleep anyway.* She looks across at Jon, whom she expects to be sleeping soundly, but is surprised to see he is awake too.

"You heard the noise then," he asks, but it isn't a question. It is a strong statement.

She nods, "But I don't know what I heard. Something unusual woke me, maybe the wind."

Jon glances at her questioningly. "You didn't hear it?"

"Hear what?" Julie's mind is drowsy with sleep. She isn't up to processing much.

Jon's voice sounds anxious. "The cry that came from the direction of the spare room."

Julie is suddenly wide awake. "You mean where Amber is sleeping? Is she in trouble? But how can that be? She is alone in that room. Perhaps she had a nightmare and called out in her sleep."

Chagrin crosses Jon's face. "Of course. That idea wasn't on my radar. I am on edge because of that Malcolm fellow. He is not to my liking. I hope she has the strength to leave him. There is something unhealthy about him. I am uncertain what it is. It would be good for her and us if she stays here for a while. She hasn't acted like herself since she came home, too quiet. It's not like her. She is usually free with her opinions, even if it is impossible to agree with all of them. It means she is thinking for herself."

Julie frowns. "I have noticed that too. Some men have that effect on their women. They want to own them. I didn't ever imagine Amber would fall for that type of person, but I suspect he charmed her. You saw him tonight. When he first came into the room, he was quite a different man from the one we first met. He was trying to impress us for some reason, but he dislikes us. I feel sure of it."

Jon puts an arm around his wife's shoulder. "It is not us he dislikes. He is in love with himself, so is unable to deal with anything or anyone that takes the shine away from him. That is what I think, for what it is worth."

The parents sit up straight again because another sound penetrates their bedroom, but this sound is more like a struggle. It takes some of the doubt away.

Julie takes Jon's hand and looks at him carefully. "The problem is, perhaps they could be making love. Some people are noisy. How can we tell if he is hurting her? I thought we soundproofed our walls when we built this house, Jon, but their lovemaking might be more active than ours. They may have made up, and you know what happens at such times."

Jon's hand is resting against his cheek as he taps his nose. "It's possible, Julie, but the noise sounds more like a struggle. Perhaps we should make a cup of tea, taking care to be noisy when we pass the spare room. If it is a fight, Amber might call out. Now, she might be trying to be quiet not to wake us. Silly girl, I would rather she saves herself than worries about us. Of course, we still don't know if she is in trouble."

Julie doesn't need any more suggestions. She shoots out of bed, pulls her dressing gown and slippers on then starts for the door.

Jon calls anxiously, "Wait for me. I don't want you to get into trouble." Jon takes a little longer to get ready but is soon at the bedroom door, waiting for Julie to open it.

They walk down the corridor without speaking, but they walk purposefully. If anyone is awake in the spare room, they will hear. When they pass the room, they are surprised because the door is open a crack. Both try to spy inside but can see nothing. It is too dark. At that moment, the wind increases its decibels and eliminates all but the loudest sounds. They imagine they hear a faint noise that could have been someone saying 'help,' but it could have been the wind. Jon and Julie look at each other with raised eyebrows, then rustle down the corridor to the kitchen, wanting to make their presence felt. Jon puts the kettle on and pulls out cups and saucers, not attempting to be quiet.

Julie looks quizzically up at Jon. "It must be obvious to them what we are doing," Julie says quietly. She can't speak naturally, even though she wishes they would hear her in the spare room. She has a small hope that Amber is sound asleep and that she and Jon have overactive imaginations.

A surprising gleam comes into Jon's eyes. "Perhaps we should make breakfast. We will have been up in an hour anyway, and the smell of bacon and toast will penetrate that room."

Now, Julie almost smirks. "Oh Jon, what a good idea. We are up now, so breakfast is perfect. Bacon and eggs on toast are just what the doctor ordered."

Jon gives Julie a high five. "Julie, you sound like a school kid let out for the holidays."

Julie's face brightens up. "I feel like one, too. Possibly, the spirit of *Matariki* - remembering all the family, the living and those that have gone before - is penetrating the house." Then she grasps the bench. "What is that? It sounds more like a struggle. We must discover if she needs help. The suspense is killing me. What should we do?"

Jon reminds Julie, "It is our home, Julie. We have a right to know what is going on in it. I will go right in and ask Amber what is happening." But Jon doesn't move. He sits rooted to the stool, listening.

Julie walks around to his side of the kitchen island to take his hand. "We must try. Let's listen closer to the door. We can do this together."

Jon looks uncertain. "It would be terrible to lose the trust of our only daughter. She wants to deal with this herself. We would be meddling."

Julie moves closer to Jon. "I don't think she will think it is meddling. I think she needs our help. Come, we can do it."

They move towards the spare room. Amber's voice rings out clearly. "Leave me alone. I don't want this. We can deal with our relationship in the morning."

Malcolm laughs, "You would like that, wouldn't you when your boyfriend is there to save you? There is no saving you from this. You are mine, and I will take what is mine."

Amber's voice is muffled but sounds frightened. "Malcolm, let me go. You are hurting me."

Malcolm commands. "If you cry any louder, I will have to put the pillow over your face to stop you from being heard." An ugly grinding sound, almost a growl, emanates from the room.

"That does it," Jon whispers. He pushes open the door while flicking on the light switch.

A shocking sight meets the parents' eyes. Malcolm has Amber in a chokehold that could well crush her windpipe. He is lying almost on top of her. She cannot move.

It is Jon's turn to be commanding. "You get out of this room immediately," Jon says. "No one treats anyone in my house that way, especially not my daughter. Leave!" He almost screams this last word. He is no longer trying to be a good host. "You can stay in her room until it is time for you to catch the taxi. You are lucky we are not calling the police."

Malcolm laughs. "Call the police! They will not come, especially in this weather. You don't know your daughter. She loves rough sex."

Julie is too shocked to speak, but Jon continues, "I distinctly heard her telling you to stop. That statement is all the evidence I need, and it will certainly be enough for the police. Don't think you can get away with rape just because you are a lawyer."

Jon is red in the face and ready to hit the man. Malcolm relaxes his hold on Amber enough for her to wiggle away from him and roll out of bed.

Malcolm is sneering as if he holds all the aces. "You will have a hard time proving rape. The police will need sperm for that, and embarrassingly in this circumstance, I couldn't complete the action. Amber loves it so much she isn't the least bit scared."

It is all Jon can do to hold himself back from hitting the man. "Oh, so you need fear to have your way with her?" Jon looks disgusted. "I am not going to talk about this further. I want you out of this room, now." Jon points towards the door.

Malcolm moves leisurely out of the bed. Passing near Jon, he remarks, "This is not the end, old man. I have more moves; you will see. Your daughter is mine, not yours."

Jon points directly at the door once again. It is all he can do to stop himself from hitting the guy as he walks past. When Malcolm goes, Julie closes the door with a sigh.

Julie looks sympathetically at Amber. "We don't have to talk about this, Amber, but I think your father and I need some explanation. It can wait until after the ceremony up the hill today. We are cooking breakfast. A good cup of tea will do you wonders." She brushes a curl off Amber's forehead and squeezes her hand to show nothing is her fault. It is a familiar action from Amber's childhood. She wants to reassure Amber.

Amber takes her mother in her arms, "I am so sorry, Mum. I don't know this man anymore. He is frightening."

Her father puts his arms around both of them. This move releases the tension, and they all start to cry.

Chapter 17

I have forgotten the calming effect of mothering. Well, actually, both my parents take turns to help me find my way back from the shock of recent events. My first reaction to Malcolm's attack was anger, then just quickly morphed into feeling responsible for his actions. Now, I am ashamed.

Mum, always looking on the positive side of things, says, "You have nothing to be ashamed of, darling. You didn't know he was a monster, and even if you did know, you would not be responsible for his actions."

My mother still has her arm around my shoulder, while Dad sits quietly beside me on the other side.

We are still in the spare bedroom, sitting on the edge of the bed because I haven't yet found the strength to stand. I feel Mum wants to move us out to the breakfast bar to eat because this morning might be a long affair up on the hill. The storm has died down; therefore, we might have a chance for a ceremony outside. I hope the clouds clear. I feel, irrationally, that if we can glimpse the stars, things will not be so bad because the stars will brush all the evil away.

I position my legs at an angle that should make them work so I can stand, but I can't quite make my body go upright. It is not responding as it should.

My father's face looks like thunder. It is so unlike him that I begin to shake as he says, "Your neck is red, Amber." Dad sounds angry. "We must take photos now and then retake them later when the bruising comes out, in case we need to call the police. We may have difficulty getting him onto the water taxi. He hasn't shown great compliance with anything so far."

Mum dashes out to get her phone, returning with it all ready to shoot.

I can't think clearly. I have no idea what course of action to take. All I know is that I don't want to see Malcolm every again.

I try to pull myself together and say the first thing that comes into my head. "I should have a shower first. I don't need to look like the wreck of the Hesperus." I pull my nightie around me.

Dad looks carefully at me. He is not as angry as he was but is still upset. "No, you should remain just as you are, but your mother can take the photos. I will go and prepare breakfast. Julie, make sure you take photos of any other bruising on her body and then send the photos to me to make two copies. You never know what he will do. He may try to take your phone." He dashes out the door and closes it quietly.

Mum examines me thoroughly, noting other bruises, then clicks away. "We should do the same tomorrow because those bruises will be darker then, "she says, echoing Dad's words.

I feel like a train wreck. The photo session is unhelpful. It raises the level of my anxiety because it is so undignified. I understand its importance, but that does not remove my shame. I feel terrible.

Mum tries to placate me while at the same time ensuring we all address the seriousness of my situation. "I'm sorry, darling, but I agree with your father. It is better to have the photos than not. We don't know what this day will bring. He is lucky we haven't rung the police." She puts her right hand to her lips. "Sorry, dear. We decided without asking you. Do you want us to call the police? We will if it is best for you. In the heat of the moment, neither of us wanted the extra attention."

My heart goes out to my mother. She is only doing what she thinks is best for me. "Mum, it is okay. You did the right thing. I don't want the extra attention either. It is bad enough that Malcolm is acting like a bully. Hundreds of questions from the police will make it worse."

Mum is all business now. "I'm glad you agree with our thinking. Let's go into our bedroom. You can use the shower in the *ensuite* while I find some clothes for you."

The practicality of the moment helps clarify my thoughts. "Mum, I think Malcolm left my backpack in the lounge. It will have clean clothes in it." I manage a weak smile for the first time.

It is great to be talking about something ordinary. I can cope with simple thoughts, nothing complex. Fancy, his desire to make me go with him is becoming a favourable move for me, a little one. Because of his obsession, I have my clothes. I breathe a sigh of relief. Thank goodness for my parents.

Mum goes to get my backpack while I head into the shower. The hot water soothes my skin. I wash my hair; goodness knows why. I just have to get the smell of him off me. Fortunately, Mum has a hairdryer.

When I enter the bedroom, Mum looks at me appraisingly. "You look much better. You must wear a scarf around that neck if you don't want questions, but the rest of you is like yourself." She looks very pleased. "Now, it is my turn. Dad will delay breakfast until we all shower and are ready for the day."

I hug her before she disappears into the *ensuite*.

When I reach the breakfast area, Dad is chomping at the bit. "What took you so long? But I see you are a new woman. You took time to wash your hair."

I am surprised my dad notices how I look. Before my shower he seemed more interested in what to do with Malcolm, or that is how it looked to me. "Is it that obvious?" I say with a frown. "Mum is showering now. I hope I have left all in order." A smile sneaks out as I look at him. I see the worry on his face, but it makes me feel safe; something I couldn't imagine I would feel ever again.

Dad looks at me appraisingly as a wisecrack slips out of his mouth. "You looked like you were wearing a bush. Now, it's a tamed bush, much better. I like it either way."

He must have thought about what his words might sound like to me because he clarifies his statement. A warm feeling rushes through my body because of his caring nature. I wonder what I ever saw in Malcolm. He is nothing like Dad. Malcolm has no sensitivity, all good looks and brash actions. I must have been mad. I sigh and sit on a stool to sip the proffered coffee.

Dad was productive while I was off getting rid of the traces of Malcolm off my body. I shake, because I can still feel him much to my annoyance, but Dad's voice calms me. "I made both tea and coffee. I think you prefer coffee. Mum and I like tea. Something for everyone." He clinks his cup with mine as if we are toasting. "It is all up from here, dear."

"I hope so," I say like I still have to conform to Malcolm's wishes and am worried about not going to Picton with him today. I have no idea how he imagines I want to go with him or that I will do as he asks after this morning's efforts. How much more evidence do I need to show me that he is a monster?

This thought makes me think of Malcolm and I begin to wonder what he is doing and morphs into the idea that I should offer him something to eat. Good manners have been drilled into me, and Malcolm is still my guest no matter the circumstances. If I could clear my thoughts, I doubt I would have said what I say next. "I will make something for Malcolm and take it into him."

This comment brings an immediate strong objection. "No, you are not to do that, Amber," Dad says sternly. "He can make his own once we leave." There is a finality in his voice that makes me realise I am being stupid. If I go in there, he will think he has won, and it will be all on once again. It is just so hard to give up the control he seems to have over my actions. I will have to learn. It's not as if he is the only man in the world.

Dad and I discuss what I can do if I remain at home. He makes it sound easy, almost as if getting Malcolm to Picton is the least of my worries. Looking at the bigger picture of life, I suppose it is. Life after Malcolm may not be easy, but I still have my job. Foolishly, I sold my apartment so Malcolm and I could live together, and somehow, my earnings have paid for the mortgage. How I will get that back is beyond me. I suppose I must cut my losses and start again. I am young and have many years to save up for living quarters. It is not the end of the world.

Dad's face is serious. "I hope you know that the law says he will have to give you half the value of the apartment. Of course, that doesn't include the mortgage." Dad reads my thoughts.

I screw my face up, worried. "The problem is we are not married. I think that only counts for married couples."

To my surprise, Dad looks a bit relieved. "Good thing I mentioned it then. The law changed back in the 1990s. If you have been living together for three years, in law, it is like a marriage. I think you meet that threshold. Goodness knows how you have lasted so long. He is very controlling."

I breathe a sigh of relief. "Well. That's one problem solved, then." I say it as brightly as possible while thinking that means asking him to settle our finances. He won't like that, not one bit. Maybe a miracle will happen.

Mum bounces into the room, looking expectantly at us, knowing we love her. She always enters a room this way, and people respond. It is hard not to react to such a lively nature. People wonder where my personality comes from because I am very direct but enthusiastic and usually positive. I think it might be from Mum, although Dad is usually more direct.

Dad notices Mum's arrival, looking fresh as a daisy. "There's tea in the teapot if you want, or perhaps you will join Amber in coffee this morning. It's time for my shower," Dad says as he leaves with a flourish.

Mum and I both agree to wait while Dad has his shower. It is a special breakfast, after all. Dad returns in a flash, looking shiny clean, and dressed for the weather. He organises the bacon and eggs while Mum is in charge of toast. When we sit down again, we all notice the silence. The wind has stopped its fury, and the clouds are beginning to scatter into puffs and patches of cumulus.

Mum looks at Dad and me as if we are both children. "Hurry up. We don't want to miss the show. I made some cookies for the children. They will need something to keep them going."

I look affectionately at my parents. "Mum, Daniel's family will have organised something for them."

Mum has the strangest look on her face. A look that says I have forgotten something critical. She all but wags her finger at me. "We must contribute, darling. Have you forgotten everything while you have been away?"

I gulp. I know we must take something, but there is a bulging picnic basket by the door, and I assumed that was it. I thought that was our contribution. I don't seem to be able to say anything unless I put my foot in it. So now, I am uncomfortable. I should have remembered. Mum and Dad want to take more than what is essential. It is their contribution to the celebrations. I feel small, like a child unable to act sensitively. I am much too old to be acting this way. I know Daniel's family will not expect us to bring anything, but they would never come here without presenting us with something, no matter how insignificant. I had only thought of the immediate picture. Life is for giving as well as receiving. I know this, but somehow my brain is not processing anything properly.

Dad takes my hand. "It's all right, dear. None of us feel we have grown up despite our years. There is so much to learn, so much to do, and so many questions to answer. Life is a puzzle for us all. We make the best path we can."

I give him a grateful grin and then say, "Well, come on then. Let's get the festivities started."

I dash for the door without thinking about the basket of food. I want to be out of the house as far away from Malcolm as possible.

Chapter 18

Mum, Dad and I slip and slide, going over the path up the hill, to the point where I am glad of my gumboots. The steps help, but it is still very muddy. I smile as the clouds clear further and the stars twinkle. A deep sigh seeps up from my gut as I relax. I want to see Daniel's family because they were always kind to me. Of course, I am fooling myself. I really want to see Daniel. As we draw near, their laughter floats towards us in ever-increasing volume.

A tall young man calls out to us with a familiar voice. "*Kia ora,* stranger."

"It can't be Ian, is it?" I say in surprise. "You are so tall," I remember Ian as the shortest of us all when we played together. He is also the youngest.

He looks surprised. "I hope so. At twenty-six, I would be a shorty if I were still the size I was when you last saw me." He grins at my embarrassment.

I try to cover my discomfort although I am sure it shows on my face. "I guess. We forget people grow up when we are away. I know your age, but the image in my head is still Ian the smart Alec, Daniel's baby brother."

Ian tries to appear stunned. "Who me, a smart Alec? Who would have thought it? Come on over. Mum and Dad are waiting to greet you." And indeed, Daniel's family is almost in a line from the father and mother down to the littlest. "We thought we should welcome you back formally, hoping you might stay. But where is that big boyfriend of yours, I have heard so much about?"

I feel ashamed, but Mum pipes up, "He is too tired to wake up at this hour of the day. We left him to sleep and come over if he wants."

I look gratefully at Mum. She squeezes my hand. I feel Dad behind me with his hand on my shoulder, making me feel safe. I go over to the line for introductions to those who do not know me. Some *hongi*, some give me a hug and a kiss. Daniel bear hugs me as he whispers, "I'm glad that Malcolm isn't here to spoil the fun." He frowns, looking down at me. "Something has happened, hasn't it? You must talk with me later."

With that thought, he releases me and darts away behind his brothers. I am surprised that he can still read me as well as he did when we were children. I brush aside the thought and concentrate on the gathering around me.

After the introductions, we begin to talk all at once.

Daniel's father calls us all to attention with a loud resonant voice. "*Taihoa, taihoa,*[13]" He notes, "We have all day, so let's talk one at a time."

---

[13] Taihoa – Slow down or be cautious.

I almost put my hand up as I ask, "If I may be first? I need to know where to look for the *Matariki* stars." I look shyly around the group.

Once more, all begin to explain at once. I regard this family in wonderment. I have missed their friendly banter, open discussion and loud explanations. Why have I stayed away so long? I know the answer to this question but find it difficult to explain, even to myself. Studying, the excitement of a city, then later overseas, and meeting Malcolm, are reasons. But they pale into insignificance with this family's warmth. I want to cry, not because I am sad, but because of lost time and my bone headedness. I know I have the right to live my life my way, but family and friends are essential. I am learning the hard way. Perhaps we all do.

At that moment, Daniel's Dad takes me by the hand and sits me on a long seat conveniently placed for viewing the sky. "They are just rising over there in the east. See Orion's belt, then look right at that pyramid-shaped group, the face of Taurus; well, go a little further right, and you will see *Matariki*. That big shiny one in the middle is my favourite, the one I wish on every year. It is not exactly in the middle. It kind of begins with that sail-like shape. The actual start of the New Year is during the first full moon, but we like to welcome in the stars. *Matariki* may be new to the *Pakeha*, but we Māori have welcomed its rise every New Year for as long as I can remember."

I look out at the conflagration of points of light in the sky and am confused by a thought, but I say, "Of course, this is the Māori New Year. It is so strange that we are just beginning to celebrate it when we acknowledge Chinese New Year. And, we should change Guy Fawkes Day to Parihaka Day too. The attack on Parihaka Pa occurred on the same date but in a different century. It is of greater interest to us than blowing up the British Parliament."

Daniel's Dad's face wrinkles into a smile as he pats me on the shoulder. "*Kei te pai, kei te pai*[14], all in the fullness of time, little Amber."

I feel delighted to be here. "First, I am shocked at how much Ian has grown, and now you call me little. Granted I am not the tallest in the family, but I have grown up too, just like Ian."

His eyes gleam, "You will always be our little Amber to us, the one the boys treated like their sister. You are still that person to us."

This pronouncement brings tears to my eyes. I turn away to contemplate the stars before I let the side down and bawl. It is an emotional roller coaster that threatens to zap all my resolve. Such stirring thoughts, but I don't want to break down in front of this family, especially after the earlier events this morning. I might not be able to stop crying.

---

[14] Kei te pai – All is good at the moment. Here, it implies that we can wait.

Fortunately, Daniel's mum points out it is time for *karakia*[15], prayers, and the ceremony for the day. I need this singing, speeches and the thoughts that go with it. This type of singing comes right from the heart. I am sure I have forgotten the prayers in Māori, but I hope I can remember some of the *waiata*[16], the songs we sang when we were young.

We pray and sing so loud that the hills reverberate with the harmonies, and we choose stars to wish on. I have all but forgotten Malcolm, but Daniel is staying uncharacteristically away from me. Does he think I will poison him? And yet, his greeting was so warm. He did say we should talk later. I had a deep warmth inside me when he was there. He is special to me, but perhaps I am not to him. After all this time, of course, I am not. He has other interests, other loves, and other things to do. I must stop mooning around. I still have to do something about Malcolm.

The children can't wait for the end of the ceremony because of the games organised for them. There is even a competition about who can make the best animals. They use homemade play dough for the little ones and clay for the older children. They are very excited and want to do their best. It will be a long day with much eating, laughing and story-telling.

Mum and Dad are having a good time, talking to everyone. I have never had my mother's ability to chat with anyone. Mum can

---

[15] Karakia – Prayers.
[16] Waiata – song.

go into a room where she doesn't know a soul, and when she leaves, she not only knows most of their names, but she introduces different ones to people they should know. It's something to watch, but now she moves happily among friends.

I notice Dad tap her on the shoulder and whisper something in her ear; then he disappears quickly towards our house. I am curious. I hope he isn't going to check on Malcolm, especially by himself.

I go over to Mum and ask, "Where is Dad going? I hope it is not because of Malcolm."

Mum's mouth opens, shaped like an 'O'. "No, not Malcolm. He forgot to pick up the cookies I made for the little ones. He wants to collect them now before all the games begin. Otherwise, they will go to waste."

My watch tells me it is hardly six o'clock. Surely, Malcolm will be asleep. "Okay, I will stop worrying."

Mum looks amused. "Your father knows how to take care of himself. All will be well, darling. You go and talk to Daniel."

I can't help but laugh. Mum is still match-making. She has Daniel's mother's match-making disease. Turning to retrace my steps as fast as possible, I stumble but somehow manage to catch myself, before I fall. I see Daniel's look of surprise at my effort. He is watching me from afar. How I wish he would come closer. Then I remember Malcolm.

I really must get my act together. I can't continue to think about Daniel when Malcolm is still in the picture. I must be brave and tell Malcolm it is all over. That is what I will do. I must do it before he leaves on the water taxi later today.

Chapter 19

I feel content that Amber's family and my own are all here for *Matariki*. Despite the storm, it makes the world feel perfect. I gaze out towards the *Matariki* constellation, wishing for the impossible. Every year, I have sat on this spot to wish for Amber's return, but I didn't expect her to come, boyfriend and all. That is a definite spoke in my ambitions but I should have visited her in Christchurch or wherever she was. For some reason, it was never the right time. I just expected she would return at Christmas or some other holiday, and we would take up where we left off. We never did have an understanding of any kind, but I know her family and mine thought we were a match. I have not been interested in any other person, and I didn't foresee her to be either; a bit foolish. What did I expect her to do? Should she understand I am waiting for her without me saying anything?

Here I am again wishing on a star, only this time I hope that if Malcolm is the one for her, he treats her well. I sigh and take a look around. The children are enjoying their games. Mum and Dad are thrilled to have all of us together. My brothers and their wives natter, happily to one another. Amber is off in the distance, talking with her mother. Julie is comforting Amber about something.

I am sure something happened last night to Amber, but what exactly, I have no idea. I hope all is well with Malcolm, but strange, he isn't here. Perhaps not. He is an oddball and would find us a bit confronting dealing with us all at once. We are a tight group, hard to break into if you are not outgoing. He doesn't like me, that is for sure. So, there is that angle. Mind you, the feeling is returned with warts on. It's time I went to talk with Amber. Mother will be over if I don't act soon.

I walk over, ignoring the rush of young ones trying to get me interested in playing with them, as I move surreptitiously closer to Amber.

I have no idea how to open the conversation. It has been so long. "Hi there! I hope you are enjoying the day?" I say rather stiffly. But what else should I say when I have hardly talked with her in the past ten years?

Amber looks as though she has been crying. "I am having a great time, thank you. Nice to see you," she says, almost shyly. Her head is down, so I am unable to see her eyes. I feel rather than know she is unhappy.

I notice Julie scooting away. She has just spotted my mother. I think it is an excuse to give Amber and me space.

I am surprised when I look closely at Amber's face. She doesn't look the least bit happy. "You don't look so thrilled to be here. Are those tears? You didn't use to cry for no reason."

Amber studies her feet. She moves them gently around, embarrassed. "I cried because your father is so kind to me. He reminds me of how close we all were when children, and I have been trying to decide why I haven't returned sooner."

I am relieved, if that is all it is. "You should have. I don't know why you didn't want to see us," I say, thinking this conversation isn't going how I want it to, although what direction I want it to go in is a mystery.

She points out a log we used to sit on many years ago. "Let's go and sit there for old time's sake."

I nod, not knowing where this will lead. That log is special to me, and I guarantee it will stay here for many years. Now it is decaying a bit, but I don't think the *Huhu*[17] bugs have damaged it too much. As children, we used to hunt these fat white bugs that turned into quite frightening beetles. The grub tastes like condensed milk; well, as long as you don't eat the head. Eating that part of them ruins the whole effect.

 We sit about a foot apart. I feel like I am in the school playground, wanting to sit next to my girl but afraid a teacher will tell us off. In this case, I think the authorities – our parents – would cheer us on.

---

[17] Huhu Bug is a long-horned beetle, endemic to New Zealand.

I don't know her interests these days, nor if she wants to talk with me at all. I am determined to try, however. "What have you been up to all these years, Amb?" I hesitate. My pet name for her falls out of my mouth. "Sorry, I should call you Amber now." My face flashes a grin. I am embarrassed.

Her face lights up. It warms my heart. "You can call me Amb. And if you want to know what I have been doing, I keep doing nothing in particular it seems. So, not much different from when I was a child, but I hope with more style." Her eyes smile. She remembers our good times, I hope.

I want to put this meeting on a friendship footing. "Well then, you should call me Danny, just like before. I am not this formal man called Daniel. The sheep would laugh to say nothing of my dogs. They don't stand on ceremony."

I hear a giggle escape Amber's solemn face. "That puts me in my place, Danny. I don't know who Daniel is either, the boy next door who turned into a man."

I look dubious. "Not a prince? I thought I would change into a prince."

Now Amber is laughing outright. Her mother looks across, wondering what all the hilarity is about. She looks relieved. So, there is a problem. Why else would she look relieved at Amber's laugh? I bet it is that malicious Malcolm. He is the evil prince, if ever there was one.

This is a subject I want to open up, but am not sure if it will scare Amber away. I hope not because I persist. "How did you two meet?" I say without bashing around the bushes.

Amber's face closes up. I have said the wrong thing. "I am sorry. I didn't mean to pry."

She looks at me quickly. "You haven't upset me, no, not at all. It is an obvious question. We met at a conference. It was just like any other conference, boring. Malcolm was the only interesting thing in sight. That must have been the problem."

I consider what she is saying. "Why is it a problem? You must love him, or else you wouldn't have brought him here."

Amber's head drops down almost to her knees. "I know now it is a mistake. He is not the man I thought he was, but that is my problem. I will deal with it before the water taxi arrives this afternoon."

I feel uncomfortable and have no idea how to respond. All I want to do is to put my arms around her to comfort her. She is distressed. My mind flips as I try to work out how to respond. While I am trying to figure it out, Amber's mother arrives.

Mrs Jenson's eyes show a deep hurt, as if something has already happened to cause her to worry. "Amber, I am worried about your father. He went to the house, but he's been gone too long. Where can he be?" The words tumble out as she looks at the two of us, possibly wondering what we are discussing.

Amber is quick to offer help. I am pleased because this is exactly as the old Amber would have acted. "Don't worry, Mum. I'll go across to find out what is going on. Maybe he made breakfast for Malcolm. It could be something that simple. Don't think the worst."

Amber hugs her mother. I note, neither Amber's mother or I believe what Amber says. Malcolm must have done something in the night. I wonder what it could have been, but then I don't have any right to interfere.

Despite my thoughts, I find myself saying, "Can I help?" Then I state, "I will go with you in case you need help."

Amber looks horrified. "Oh no. That would be a red rag to Malcolm's bull. He will slaughter us."

I laugh. "That bully would not have a chance in a fight with me."

Amber is deeply concerned. It pulls at my heart strings as she says, "I don't mean a physical fight. I mean verbally. He already has decided you are my boyfriend, and the thought of it sends him crazy." She looks terrified.

I don't know what to do because I don't have enough information. I want to ask what happened, but think that won't help. "I don't want to make things worse, but if Malcolm is so jealous, someone should go with you."

Julie says, "He is right, darling. You can't go over there without protection. Think of last night. You don't need anything like that again. I hope he hasn't hurt your father."

Julie has the same frightened look Amber has, which gives me a bright idea. "If I make things worse, how about George? He has won boxing competitions and is a lawyer, so he knows how to use words and will protect you. I think he can read a situation."

Amber shifts around. "I don't want to make things worse. I have already caused enough trouble bringing him here."

Julie speaks up. "She always did have a guilt complex, even as a little girl when she caused the problems for real. I am afraid, Dan, that Amber is worse now. She is not responsible for any of Malcolm's actions, but she believes she is responsible for the man. She doesn't believe her father or me." Julie shakes her head in frustration.

My mind is finally in gear, thinking through all possibilities. "I have a better idea. I will ask Ian to go over in ten minutes if you are not back. That way, you can have delayed help, and if help isn't needed, there is no need for anyone to know. Ian is an experienced fighter, and he won't go in all guns blazing like George. He will be diplomatic."

Amber looks more enthusiastic. "I think that might work. Okay, give me ten minutes. I will run across and check. Ten minutes should be plenty of time."

Amber hugs her mother, waves to me and runs off.

Julie Jenson turns to me with a worried frown, "I am not happy with waiting, Dan. You didn't see what we saw."

I take her hand, "Don't worry. I have no intention of waiting ten minutes. Let me go to get Ian. We will both go across. No problem."

Julie breaks into tears. I am stunned at this reaction. She must be very worried about Amber. "You must go. I can deal with myself." She manages a weak smile.

I leave to find Ian to give him his duties. Thoughts of Mrs Jenson's distress are filling my mind as I race around trying to locate that wayward brother of mine. I spy him in the middle of a game with the young ones.

"Ian," I call trying to show urgency while not upsetting the wee ones.

"What?" he says unhelpfully.

"I need your arm, if you don't mind. It will only be for a short time kids. He will be back to you in no time."

Ian has a question mark on his face, but the penny seems to have dropped. He comes quickly as I indicate the path to the Jenson's house.

Chapter 20

Ian and I walk smartly over to the Jenson's home, sticking to the grassy slopes because the path is too muddy. A Morepork breaks the silence. I think it is out a bit late in the morning. They are usually well asleep by now. Something must have kept it awake, possibly the quiet after the storm, but my thoughts are darker. Amber's home looks ominous as if dark clouds have settled on it.

I urge Ian on, not that he is walking slowly, "Hurry up, Ian. Something has happened in the house."

Ian looks balefully at me. He is in no mood to rush, but he speeds up, perhaps because of the urgency in my voice. Then we stop near the deck.

Ian looks inquiringly at me, wanting to know what I am thinking. I almost laugh because he has reverted to his childhood look when he didn't know what to do. I whisper although it sounds as loud as a gull screeching, "We need to look in the windows to spot if all is in order. Amber won't like us jumping in when she hopes to manage things alone."

Ian agrees and quietly makes his way to the left side of the house. There is a problem with checking the house this way because the deck surrounds all the windows, and some have curtains drawn. I indicate that I will go to the right. Ian nods and moves silently on. I want to creep onto the deck, but know it is a silly thought because it probably creaks. Irrelevantly, I wonder why I haven't noticed the deck sounds before. I have been here often enough. I listen attentively, and I am sure I can hear someone crying, not loud, more like sniffling. It must be Amber because it doesn't sound like a man. Then Amber says, "What have you done to him? There is so much blood. You must be insane if you believe you can get away with hurting my father."

I creep back to where I can see Ian and beckon him to come to me. His movements are quiet. He may live in town these days, but he hasn't forgotten his hunting skills.

He stands beside me and looks up keenly, waiting for an explanation. I say, "Malcolm has done something to Amber's father. She is in there weeping, saying there is a lot of blood. Whatever has happened, it doesn't sound good. I didn't think to bring a weapon with me because the thought of violence of any nature hadn't entered my head."

Ian looks at me, wondering if I was born under a pumpkin or perhaps, I am a country bumpkin for real, which I suppose I am. "Big brother, you still have much to learn about human nature. We are not all good. I have learned that to my disadvantage. I didn't bring a gun, but I have a knife."

I am horrified. Why did he think to carry a weapon? "Well, I hope you won't use it. We are both big men and should be able to overpower Malcolm without bloodshed."

Ian grips my shoulder and looks intently into my eyes. "If I need to use the knife, I will. I learned more from my time in the army than I did hunting out here. Of course, I also became a medic, which took me to medical school. I was lucky."

I am irrationally irritated at Ian's remark. "Lucky or not, we have to decide whether to enter and how to enter," I say sharply.

Ian grins lackadaisically. "You have already decided to enter, big brother. It is only the how that we need to decide. I say we march right up to the door and open it. Surprise is a great weapon."

I knew my brother had experience in hot parts of the globe, but only now do I appreciate the significance of that experience. My heart swells with gratitude that he is my brother and that I had the sense to ask him for help. I think about his idea and see I have no better one, so I agree.

I hope my voice doesn't reflect the longing I feel. "Yes, you go first. Malcolm is not the least bit thrilled with me. Seeing me will set him on edge before we can survey the scene." I want to rush in and grab Amber, but sensibility takes control. "We must have a signal for me to know when to come."

Ian holds up his index finger and raises his hand. "If I do this, come immediately, don't wait. If I slap my leg, it means to wait."

I flick my hand up to show I understand. "I can do that, and if neither of these things happen when you enter the place, I will come."

He nods, and I stand back to let him march noisily up to the door and open it alone.

A voice I have come to know and dislike says, "Who are you, and what are you doing here?"

Ian smiles from the doorway, "I thought I would come and invite you to our *Matariki* festivities. You are the only person missing out."

Ian's eyes survey the scene. I wonder what he sees. As a precaution, I call the police and describe what little I can see. They say they had better come before it escalates into something more serious. Before putting the phone away, I ring the water taxi too.

Amber calls, "Ah, Ian, so nice to see you. Yes, we should all go to *Matariki*, but we must do something to help my father first. He has lost a lot of blood." She sounds like she is trying to stay calm and yet cannot believe what she is saying.

Ian remains at the door but says, "I can see the problem. I should be able to deal with that quickly."

Malcolm must have agreed for Ian to enter because he begins to stride inside, but not before he raises his index finger as a signal to me, although oddly, he slaps his thigh. I take this to mean to come in carefully. He has seen something he is unhappy about.

I run up the steps to the deck and clatter across it noisily, which is not easy in gumboots, shouting, "Ian, Ian, Dad wants us at the house pronto." By this time, I am across the deck and at the door. I hope my noisy arrival will give Ian some space to take action. Malcolm should be distracted by my presence.

I see Malcolm as I enter the room. He is standing tall with a rifle in his hand. He has a carving knife beside him on a table. Ian uses the time my surprise entrance provides to good effect. He is now beside Jon Jenson, telling Amber what he needs to help her father. He ignores Malcolm despite Malcolm's egotistical stance.

My entrance is effective because Malcolm's eyes are on me. "You, I thought you would have the sense to stay away and let me deal with my problems. I suppose you want to act like a knight on a white charger, out to save your girlfriend. Well, let me tell you, she is mine. She has always been mine and will remain so no matter what."

I have no response to this. What do you say to a madman? I don't feel like getting shot or knifed, for that matter. Well, not today at any rate. And yet, at the moment, I am out of options.

While I watch, Amber brings Ian a pile of towels and fills a basin with warm water for John's wounds. My role in distracting Malcolm is clear. How to do that and not get shot is the question. I am sure I can attract his attention, but the consequences may not be to my liking. I can see Ian's rationale in bringing the knife.

I decide that talking is the best thing. "I don't want to take Amber away from you. I am pleased she has found someone she loves. We were just kids, best friends certainly, but children, that is all. You can have her."

Amber shoots me an angry look. If looks could kill, that one surely would. My face wrinkles into a smile which I don't feel. "You see, Amber isn't the least bit interested in me," I said this last bit to cover the rather harsh comment I made before.

Malcolm shifts on his feet as if weighing my words. His gun now points to the floor rather than at me. Well, one thing is going in the right direction.

Malcolm's eyes look cold, so cold it makes my insides shudder. Of course, it might be the rain and wet clothes, but I don't think so. He looks pure evil. "I know what you believe. It is written all over your face. Your smart words don't have a ring of truth. You forget I am a lawyer, but I was in interrogations in the army. I can read a liar quicker than anyone. That's why I win cases."

My left eyebrow rises involuntarily. "I suppose it takes one to know one."

Out of the corner of my eye, I note that Ian is pleased with his rapid cleaning of Jon's wounds but unhappy with something else. I am unable to tell what that is. His index finger goes up and circles. He wants me to keep talking. Well, that I can do. I open my mouth and proceed as dispassionately as possible. "So, how are you finding the Sounds? Clean air and open spaces are good for the soul. It must be better than any city."

Malcolm scoffs. His hands wave around a bit, but he doesn't seem distracted with the gun and the knife nearby. "You have no idea about living in a city." I have to take that as the truth, because it is. I have never lived in a city, even when at uni. The campus was in a small town. "The culture, the atmosphere, the theatre, the arts, your open spaces cannot compare. And you want a girl like Amber to live out here?" He tut-tuts, appearing to think the concept is beyond him.

I move one leg forward, resting comfortably on the back one while watching Malcolm warily. "The first thing is that Amber is a woman, not a girl, and it is possible to have all that culture while living here. Wellington is just a short trip away."

He laughs sarcastically. "You call that a city? It's not a patch on London, Paris or New York." Because he wants to put me down, he becomes more interested in me than what is happening to Amber. He is fully engaged in our discussion. Ian moves Amber behind the kitchen island, which places him at Malcolm's back. The only fly in the ointment is Amber's father. He lies where he fell in the middle of the lounge. If I move the two-seater sofa towards Jon while walking in, I hope it will afford him some cover. I push the sofa forward while I move towards Malcolm as Ian sneaks up behind him. The tension in the room increases. I might look confident, but I am unsure where this will take us. Malcolm is on the edge of reality. One wrong move and someone else will get hurt. Besides, he still holds the rifle and has a knife close beside him.

Chapter 21

My immediate reaction to Ian turning up at the door is annoyance. It is hardly five minutes since I left, yet here he is. Perhaps my timing is wrong, but it isn't long. My second reaction is relief. He is a doctor, and I certainly need one. My father is lying on the floor covered in blood, and this maniac, who I think is the love of my life, is waving a gun around and has already cut my father with a carving knife. He didn't even use his own knife. He had to use ours. For some reason, this fact outrages me further.

What on earth is Ian doing, hanging around the door like a schoolboy asking Malcolm for permission to enter? Why doesn't he march in here and take charge? Of course, the gun might be one reason, but I am sure Malcolm has no idea how to use it. See how he holds it like in cowboy movies – hip height. He couldn't shoot a hole in a bus if such a vehicle chose to join our party at this moment. My mind is shattered. Of course, I am not being useful sitting on my buttocks, crying. Pull yourself together, girl! You are no use to anyone like this. It feels like months since I came here, yet it must be only a few minutes, maybe longer.

I dry my eyes and look expectantly at Ian. I don't know what to say to Malcolm. I seem to be able to inflame him no matter what I say. But what is Ian doing asking Malcolm to the festivities, ignoring the reality around him? He must be able to view my father from his position. What is the matter with the man? Oh, I think I get it. He is trying to distract him so he won't get hurt. I hope he is thinking of my father.

Oh no! To my horror, I see Danny lurking near the door. What is he doing here? I watch his arrival with trepidation. Malcolm is bound to be upset just at the sight of him. Is Danny trying to aggravate Malcolm? I thought I knew these brothers, but apparently, I don't. Nevertheless, I am the one who doesn't understand, because I begin to see logic in his actions. Danny is distracting Malcolm deliberately so Ian can reach my father. It works! Amazing! These brothers know a thing or two.

"Amber, Amber, listen!" My attention returns to Ian whispering desperately at me while I have been off with the fairies. Malcolm's attention focuses on Danny. Malcolm's skin colouring has changed to a pale puce. I am sure he is very angry.

I try to focus. "Yes?" I query, but he puts his hand to his lips to tell me to whisper. I sit straighter to indicate I am attending.

He murmurs, "I need you to bring me some towels, hot water, Savlon or some other skin antibacterial stuff, and any other first aid things you can manage."

I nod, "The laundry is open, and I should be able to find those things in there, but running water will alert Malcolm."

A flick of annoyance passes over Ian's face. "We will worry about that if he reacts. Now is the time to fix your father."

I respond quickly, feeling hurt at the tone of his voice, but then, I suppose I deserve it. I stand carefully, but not to my full height. I want the kitchen bench to protect me where possible and scurry towards the door. Once in the laundry, I stand and search for the requested items. Hunting around, I find some germicidal lotion and a first aid kit. I hope it has bandages and other medical things. I put everything together in a bundle held together by a towel. Then, I run hot water into a bucket. It's not the cleanest, but it is easier to bring than going to the kitchen for a basin. Speed is more important. I gather everything together and creep back to Ian and my father.

Ian has taken the time to rip Dad's clothes open and expose the wound. It is one long gash with blood still bubbling out. He looks more concerned about Dad's head than the cut, and for the first time, I notice a bruise turning into an egg shape on the side of his head. What did Malcolm do? I watch Ian for an explanation.

He looks anxious, but he whispers, "Don't worry. It will be okay once he is in hospital. I will clean his wound. You have done a great job."

I feel stupidly grateful for the compliment, which makes me understand how much I need positive support. Ian works quickly with one eye on Malcolm. When finished, he turns to me, "I want you behind the bench where you must stay with your head down.

I can't move your father right now, but I don't think Malcolm is thinking of him. You, go now."

I scuttle away quickly and sit on the tiles coiled to spring up and defend myself. It dawns on me that this is the first sane action I have accomplished since bringing Malcolm home. He hurt me badly, but that is no excuse for inaction. I used to be so good at it.

I watch Ian slink behind me and then on towards Malcolm's back. I see Ian and Danny's plan unfolding, but Malcolm has a rifle and a large knife near him. Worse yet, Danny has pushed the couch towards my father and is marching up to Malcolm calmly, despite the gun, not thinking of the danger. Childishly, I want to cover my ears and shut my eyes, but I know that is fear. I control my infantile reaction. I must stay alert in case there is something I can do to help.

Ian holds his hand up, index finger pointing skywards. It is a signal because Danny leaps forward and grabs the gun while Ian grabs Malcolm from behind, but not before Danny hits Malcolm with his fist. Malcolm hardly moves despite the impact. He stands stock still. He must be in shock. He must think of himself as invincible with the rifle and knife. But he is no match for these two country boys. They have him on the floor, not giving him a chance to struggle.

Ian yells at me and gets my attention. "Amber, get some tea towels or tape, anything we can tie his arms so he can't move."

I need no further request. I find the tea towels, PVC tape and scissors and race over. Danny and Ian work together to tie him up.

Danny shouts urgently, "Make sure to tie his legs so he can't move."

Ian looks exasperated. "We must be careful not to cut off the circulation. We don't want a dead man on our hands."

Malcolm enters the conversation, having assessed the situation. "No, you don't want to do that, mate. It would play nicely into the court case I plan."

The thought tickles my fancy. "Malcolm, you won't be planning any court case if you are dead. I thought you weren't stupid."

The look in Malcolm's eyes did nothing to ease my fear of him. "I haven't finished with you yet, girl! We have a long way to go."

This comment stuns me. "What do you mean, a long way to go? You can't expect I will stay with you after you raped me, almost killed my father, and now threaten my good friends with a rifle? I keep hoping the old Malcolm will return, but that is impossible. I suppose you were always this man. I didn't see it, or worse, ignored it." I want to stamp my foot in exasperation at this statement, but I don't.

I look up to view two shaken faces. "Malcolm raped you? It's a good thing I didn't know that before I hit him. I held back, afraid I might do him permanent damage. Now, I wish I hadn't." Danny looks upset.

I go over and take his hand. A warm shock courses through my body as we touch. Does Danny feel it too? I don't think so by his reaction. "I don't think that would have helped me. I like the thought but not the action. This altercation is all my fault. I put him out of his comfort zone by bringing him here. The open spaces, the storm, the feeling of being trapped have all contributed to his actions."

Danny hugs me. He doesn't hold back. "You are partly right, but I saw you and him fight on the beach before the storm."

The hug makes me feel warm and fuzzy, but also guilty because Malcolm is right there. He is my boyfriend. I feel I must defend him, though goodness knows why. My voice sounds more like a little girl. "True," I say, "But that doesn't discount his isolation. We all know each other. He knows no one."

Ian counters this with, "I think you will find he has done this before. It would explain why a lawyer of his calibre, who loves big cities, has taken to a small country with a population smaller than many cities in larger countries. I wondered that when I first heard about him."

Malcolm smirks despite his condition. "I'm glad you know I am a great lawyer. I will contact the police once I am out of here. They will be interested to hear my story."

Now, it is Danny's turn to laugh. "We have already called the police. They will be here shortly. We cancelled the water taxi. They were quite relieved because they were so busy. The police are not that happy with you either. It is all they need, given the people in distress because of the storm."

Malcolm sneered, "It hardly matters what tale you tell them because they will believe me before you."

Danny pulls himself to his full height, "What do you mean by that? We are from here, and the evidence is strongly against you."

Malcolm almost snorts his retort. "Ha, that is all the evidence you have? Nothing more substantial than that you are from here? I can reconstruct the case in my favour, and as for you, lassie, you needn't think you can get my money. First, you will not leave me, and even if you succeed, all our possessions are mine." His face shines with triumph.

Ian enters the conversation. "Our brother George is a good lawyer. He is your match. I will get him over so Amber can make a statement today." He turns to me and continues, "The law says you must receive half the house. It is a minimum."

Malcolm guffaws, "I am mortgaging the house to the hilt on Monday. You can have half the mortgage if you like." He smiles almost sweetly at me.

I am flabbergasted. "But why would you go to such trouble?"

Danny continues his line of thought. "Don't worry Amb; George will know how to avoid such a situation."

While the discussion about my welfare continues, Ian returns to my father. He crouches beside him, putting his fingers under my father's chin. Malcolm, Daniel and I watch, not knowing what will happen.

I realise there are more critical matters here than my finances. I must focus on the broader issues. I wish my mind would stop jumping around so I can grasp what is really happening. It had seemed a wonderful idea to come and celebrate the Māori New Year with Mum and Dad. Now, I wish I had left things alone and had forgotten about my childhood and what a wonderful place this was. I feel consciously withdrawing into an imaginary ball, just like a little child who has broken a rule.

Chapter 22

Jon's reaction to my brother's touch is remarkable because his eyes flutter and slowly open, regaining consciousness.

Jon stars around at us gawking at him. "What, what happened?" Jon stutters.

Ian sits comfortably on the floor, smiling at him. "I woke you up, Mr Jenson. You have a bad hit on the head, and a knife cut down your side. No, don't move," Ian says while Jon tries to rise. "I don't want you up yet. You need to get oriented and let nature take its course. That bump needs attention. We will get you to the hospital as quickly as possible."

Jon looks alarmed. "I don't need to go to a hospital. I can lie down on the bed. It will settle in a short time. Too much trouble to get me to Blenheim. There is the trip across the bay, then the nearly 30-kilometre drive from Picton to Blenheim. No, I am fine here, and you should be calling me Jon anyway." He flops back on the floor, exhausted.

Ian laughs. "There is not much wrong with your thinking. That is good news, but I want to take you to hospital. The trip is already organized, and it will upset things more if you don't go."

He says this last bit almost like a warning to a recalcitrant child. He has done this before.

Ian continues, "I am not sure how many of us can go, but I think we must tell Mrs Jenson because she will want to be with you."

Amber pipes up, "And me. I want to be with him too. I don't know who can be with Malcolm, but it isn't me." Amber is sitting on the couch, uncharacteristically biting her nails.

Ian and I glance at each other as I say, "I think the police will see to him when they get here. He is not our worry anymore." The thought of which makes me smile. "And one of us must go to tell Amber's mother. Perhaps you should go, Amber. You will be able to tell her better than us. Tell my father, too, so he and the family will not worry and can go on with the festivities."

Ian has all of us under his thumb. My little brother is all grown up and I am only just realizing. He is impressive, which makes me happy to be his brother.

Amber nods, running and shouting as she makes for the door, "Dad, I will be back before you know it," and rushes out.

Ian and I watch her disappear into the early morning light. I feel a twinge of sadness that Amber didn't acknowledge me as she left. Silly, I know, but I feel part of me just ran away without a word. I remonstrate with myself. Amber may love it out here, but there is no way she wants to spend her life here. Malcolm is right about that. She loves the city too much. There is not much use for an archaeologist on a farm. I must stop thinking about her. I should focus on the job at hand.

I turn my attention to Malcolm. He is struggling to loosen his bonds. "No point in wasting your energy. Ian's work is excellent, better than I could have done. Perhaps we should sit you on the couch. It would be more comfortable than the floor."

Malcolm scoffs at me, "And why would you consider my comfort? You think you will get my girl because you are sure the police will keep me. Let me tell you, it will be unusual for them to hold me for any time, even if they charge me, which I don't think they will. It is not usual to hold someone of my standing, and they will listen to my explanation." He sneers at me in a way which makes my stomach turn over.

Ian stops tending to Jon and looks up. "I am curious to know how you think you can get out of a charge of rape and physical assault? The evidence is clear."

Malcolm smiles almost beatifically, except there is something malicious under the smile. "How can you lay a charge of rape with no semen? She showed no fear, and that reaction had an odd effect on me." He looks annoyed and yet content at the same time. One would think the case was closed.

Ian's eyebrows rise. "You need fear to complete your act? I am surprised because you must have had sex with Amber before, and I doubt you used coercion. I wonder why this time is different. Oh, I know. You think she is leaving you, so you need a different type of control. In the past, you curbed what she did through limiting her friendships, what she did, where she went, and I suspect even controlled her money, but this time, none of those things will work."

Malcom's eyes look like slits. "You think you are so smart. You cannot prove anything you have said. That is the point. The police will consider it a tiff between two lovers, not rape."

While I listen to this explanation, the hair on the back of my neck rises. "Then, how can you explain what you did to Jon? He didn't bump into a table by himself or cut his side. You did that all by yourself."

He surprises me by grinning. "It is all self-defence. He mistook a situation and came at me with that knife. I managed to take it from him and accidentally cut his side. I pushed him away to stop him from hurting me, and he hit his head on the kitchen island when he fell. None of it is my fault."

I feel anxiety rising in me because it is almost plausible. The only witnesses to Jon's event are the perpetrator and the victim. I am glad I took photos of Jon when I first came in. I hope the forensics will confirm Ian's and my story. Be that as it may, we are about to face the police. I can hear a large vessel coming up to our dock.

Ian is frowning as he indicates he will go to meet them. "Don't worry, big brother. We have got this."

Amber and her mother rush in, and Ian lingers to speak with Julie while the hoped-for boat arrives. My father and George are not far behind. I am pleased to see them both but worry about the children.

I try not to sound over-anxious, but I don't think I succeed. "I hope this isn't ruining the children's *Matariki* fun." My worried looks says it all.

Dad looks at me with a twinkle in his eye. "They are fascinated. They think it is a CSI program come to Marlborough Sounds. It was all I could do to make them stay at your place to continue their games. The seriousness of it all has not sunk in. They are fine, and their mothers intend to keep it that way."

George moves across to Amber and says something quietly to her. I guess what it must be, but something in me pulls at my heartstrings as I wish she didn't have to go. Amber's head has dropped almost to her knees, then she stands, pulls her shoulders back and walks out of the room. I watch her walking with George to the spare room to discuss her legal situation. I would love to be a fly on the wall but resist the temptation to follow.

Malcolm looks at me knowingly. It is a look that infuriates me. "What do you think they will talk about? Money or sex, which one?" His voice is almost a snarl. Ian walks towards the door and turns his back in disgust at Malcolm's words.

Before I have time to answer Malcolm, a voice calls from the door, "Knock, knock. Is this the Jenson house?"

Two officers stand there waiting for an invitation. Jon answers. He pushes himself onto his arms and is sitting in an uncomfortable position. "Yes, this is my home. I think you best talk with these two neighbours of mine. I was out for the count. They know more than me."

The older of the two police responds, "If that is what you want." They enter the room, shaking hands with Ian because he is the nearest. The two officers introduce themselves to us while their eyes swivel around the room, taking everything in. They are not in the mood for small talk. It must be a busy time for them. We are not the only ones requesting assistance in this weather.

Officer Boyd, the older of the two, says, "We will talk with each of you but in a room alone. Officer McBride will stay in here. One person is tied up, I see, so he won't be a problem, but just because McBride is a woman, don't be fooled. She knows how to handle herself." This latter is said to Ian and me.

Jon sits up to show he is not badly hurt which is not at all true. We all know this but he also wants to be helpful. "You can use our bedroom, second door on the right. No problem." He lies back down with a glance at Ian, expecting a doctor's order from Ian to behave himself. He smiles as he lies down again grimacing in obvious pain. It doesn't stop him from taking in all the proceedings.

Ian and I look towards the door. "Do you have a medic from St John's with you because this man needs to go to hospital? Oh, I should introduce myself." We all introduce ourselves, even Malcolm, to make things speedy. Ian worries about the time it will take for Jon to reach help. He knows how critical it is for Jon to be on the water before the gale decides to return. The surges from the storm's last efforts have not yet died down, and they will be disturbing enough.

Malcolm grunts. He tries to bring the attention to himself. I think he likes the limelight. Well, he can have it all as far as I am concerned. He wines, "It's okay for Mr Jenson, but how about me? These ties are cutting off my circulation. I should be released, especially because I have done nothing wrong."

The police glance at Ian and me, but we retain blank faces. We have no idea which way this will go. Then Jon speaks in a faint voice. "I think you should interview Ian and Daniel before interviewing Malcolm. Malcolm is the one who is responsible for my state. This place is my house. He is a guest here. Make up your minds about releasing him after the interviews." Jon sighs. It takes much out of him to give this much information. He lies down again.

Both police confer quietly, and then, with a decision made, they call Ian first.

Chapter 23

In the spare bedroom, I sit quietly on the edge of a chair while George sits on the bed taking out a notebook and phone. I am agonised at the thought of going over Malcolm's recent actions. It makes me feel so stupid.

George smiles confidently at me as if this will be no trouble at all. He is tall, as strong as Danny, but a slightly darker shade of brown. His tousled dark brown hair is uncombed today, and his bright brown eyes continue to shine encouragingly at me while I feel my shoulders curving in, trying to make me disappear. He is dressed casually in jeans and a natural wool jersey. He looks more like a farmer than a lawyer, but it is a holiday, not a fashion parade. What do I expect?

I don't know what he expects from me. A formal interview with a lawyer is daunting, especially about such personal matters. It doesn't help that I have known George most of my life. It might even be harder because he is like a brother.

George smiles at me. "This shouldn't be scary. All I need to know is what happened here, and if you wish to leave Malcolm. Of course, I need to know what possessions you consider yours and which his. This information will help me decide what we should do. We will discuss the attempted rape in detail later when we have more time."

I frown as I feel my stomach doing conniptions. "I don't mind talking with you, but I hate thinking about what happened and how stupid I am not recognising what kind of man Malcolm is."

George looks earnestly at me. His voice is gentle as he speaks, "None of us knows everything about another person, especially one we think we love. Malcolm is the kind of person with several faces - one for you, one for your friends, and so on. He is a chameleon. Such people are hard to know, and you are possibly the last person to have any idea what he is thinking. Let's start with this weekend and work backwards. I wish to record this because we need a statement of your intent before Malcolm makes big changes to your joint finances."

I nod and tell him about the fight on the beach, then ramble on to what happened when I was trying to sleep. It isn't easy. George has to prompt me to go on when I become emotional. The prompting helps because it stops me from lapsing into despair at the impact on my woeful circumstances.

I begin again, "I can't imagine when I became so thoughtless. I used to be decisive, knew where I was going, and took charge of my affairs. Now I don't know what to do about my belongings or what direction to take in life. I am such a wimp."

George can't help a smile crossing his otherwise serious face. "Wimp is not how I would describe you. The strong person I knew when you were little is still there. She is simply lying in wait to be activated. It is not your fault Malcolm is an arch manipulator. He trained in manipulation and negative communication for his job, but perhaps he was always that way. Now, where are we?"

I think about George's perspective of my circumstances and sigh. "I was about to tell you how my finances became so muddled."

George sits at attention, all ears, "Good. Let's hear it then," George is now in professional mode.

I look down at my feet, which seem to have a will of their own. They pull up, not wishing to be placed firmly on the ground where they should be. "Malcolm's charisma, outgoing nature, and command of most subjects overawed me. He possibly had me from the very beginning. I seemed to melt into him and thought he knew what was best. Thus, I agreed to sell my place and put the proceeds into the down payment on the apartment. He put the same amount in for a down payment. For some reason, it was my place to pay off the mortgage, which I did as quickly as possible by saving anything possible from my salary. I don't know whose idea it was. It just happened. Then I paid for most of the furniture because Malcolm's money was invested in this and that, or so he said. It meant I had no savings for retirement because there was nothing left over for a fund."

While I expound on the pros and cons of living with Malcolm, we hear a kerfuffle in the lounge.

George becomes more serious. "The police and medics must have arrived. We must hurry. I need to know if Malcolm has a retirement fund?"

I nod, realising once again how silly I have been not continuing my retirement fund. Now, Malcolm's finances are unhurt, but mine are in a mess. On a visit to a stockbroker a couple of years ago my stocks and bonds were converted to his name. I tried to stop this change of ownership by returning to see the stockbroker, but he said I must get Malcolm to sign a form. This explanation didn't sit well with me because he changed my name on my shares in front of me, and I didn't sign anything. The idea was to consolidate our funds to have more to reinvest. Of course, this system only benefits me if I stay with Malcolm."

George is unhappy as he says, "You can only receive fifty per cent of the proceeds from the apartment, and fifty per cent of any joint assets."

I interrupt. "I don't want a shit fight over money, and Malcolm will turn any such discussion into one. I will be happy with half of the apartment. It will be a good down payment on a new place, and I am young. I can pay off a mortgage. I have done it before, so it is possible to do it again." I sit back, feeling relieved, but hope I am not being rude.

George asks me a few more questions before saying, "I can run across to Dan's house to transfer this to his computer, tidy it up, and then print it out for you to sign. You must sign it this weekend. He will be unable to do anything to your finances before Monday."

I sigh as I think out loud, "The only fly in the ointment is I want to accompany my father to the hospital, and goodness knows when I will return."

George settles back as he puts his notebook and phone away with a satisfying smile. "That won't be a problem but I will need your email. Can you receive emails on your phone?" I nod. "Good. I can send it to you no matter where you are. Then, all you have to do is read it carefully, correct anything that is incorrect, print it out, initial each page and sign where it tells you to, scan it and resend it. No problem."

I am aghast. My mind is racing wondering how such a thing can be accomplished. "I will be at a hospital. I don't think Wairau Hospital has a business centre."

George laughs outright. "I am sure they won't have one, but if you ask nicely, they will help. If not, ring me, and I can arrange to have my secretary come with a computer and printer. Problem solved."

A frazzled feeling settles over me. "Now, I am disturbing some poor unsuspecting secretary, all because I can't recognise an idiot when I see one. It isn't fair to bother her on her holiday."

George's eyes glint. "What do you mean 'her'? My secretary could be a man." He stands up and reaches over to hug me. "Don't worry, my secretary is perfectly capable of saying no to me without consequences. I am sure she will be delighted to help. It is up to her if she has time. I will pay her, so no problem."

I try to calm down even though, much to my surprise, I wobble as I stand. George helps me, but the room spins. I sit down promptly, feeling disoriented.

George is concerned but not alarmed. "I didn't know I had that effect on you. I thought, only my brother made you quake."

I laugh despite myself. I can feel my head returning to itself as I take deep breaths. "Let's go out to meet the storm."

George opens the door, and we walk into the corridor. Just then, an officer takes Ian towards the bedrooms. My heart races. I hope I haven't caused a problem for Ian. Then I hear an unfamiliar voice, "And just who have we here? I thought I knew how many people were in this house, and here are two more. How many more are there?" The officer sounds annoyed.

George rapidly intervenes. "I am Amber Jenson's lawyer. I needed to interview her about events here before other things crowd her mind. No problems, Officer. We are happy to comply with whatever you need."

This statement and George's non-confrontational manner mollifies the officer somewhat. Officer McBride calls to the other officer, "Officer Boyd, this means the discussion schedule is increased by two, and that man over there needs to get to the hospital." She points to Jon Jenson, who looks affronted he is the subject of such a concept. Malcolm smiles beatifically as if he has everyone on a string, and we are all dancing to his tune. I am infuriated.

Officer McBride opens her mouth to speak again, but Officer Boyd continues, "Perhaps we can limit the meetings to five minutes for each person. We only need contact details and an initial statement – a notebook reference. Then we will require all to come to the station after the weekend to make formal statements."

"That works for me," Officer McBride says enthusiastically.

Officer Boyd states, "I am responsible for all the investigation at this time. This situation is an emergency as it stands right now, so we must treat it as such."

Ian stands impatiently beside my dad, not saying anything. Questions will only slow the process. He looks worried. I gaze around at the others. They look resolute, as if action is out of their hands; that is, all except Malcolm. I sigh because, by the look on his face, he is about to erupt. Then, before my eyes, he turns into the sweet man I first met. The change is so quick I almost missed the first part. I shudder. Why haven't I noticed this change before? Chameleons have nothing on him.

Chapter 24

I stand back while I watch my brother, Ian, care for Jon. The calm of this scene changes when Officer Boyd re-enters the room. He finishes the interviews quickly and then discusses his findings with the other officer. I listen intently.

Boyd checks his notes. "Perhaps they all colluded before our arrival, but I don't think so. They all say more or less the same thing. They agree on the relationship between the boyfriend and Amber, that girl over there. Things haven't been so peachy with them lately, and Malcolm, her boyfriend, didn't want to come out here for the festival season. He is English, so it means nothing to him. Amber thinks the wide-open spaces are too much for him. She thinks that freaked him out, which worsened when he realised the road conditions made them impassable after the storm damage. He likes to be in control, and there is no way he can control how to leave here. He took it out on Amber. The others seem to think he has always been a bully, but Amber only realised it when she came here for the long weekend. We still have to hear his side of the story, but it seems he attempted to rape her. The result is that Amber is about to leave him for good but now looks frightened to go close to him. See how she keeps to the far side of the room, keeping her distance from him. It is hardly possible to be any further away. I think the father came in at the wrong moment, and an altercation occurred."

Officer McBride cannot stop herself from frowning. "You mean, Officer Boyd, that the father came in when the attempted rape was in progress?" Her face changes to shock and her feet tap as she looks up at her boss.

"No, Officer McBride. I didn't mean to imply that, no. He entered the house when that man, Malcolm, was preparing to return to Christchurch. Malcolm organised Amber's things without saying a word to her. It is unclear what happened after that because I haven't heard from the father, but Malcolm held a carving knife and had Mr Jenson's rifle nearby when Jenson entered the room. There was an altercation in which Mr Jenson sustained a nasty cut to his side and, according to the doctor, a more worrying hit to the head. He fell, or was pushed, onto the corner of the kitchen island. The doctor worries that Jenson cracked his skull or the brain has sustained a deep bruise. He wants him examined immediately. Of course, that isn't possible, but he must reach the hospital as soon as we can get him there. It is unclear who began the fight, but the knife and the gun had to be near the boyfriend because Jenson was coming from the celebrations up on the hill."

Officer Boyd taps a pen against his pad, readying himself to continue writing. He speaks in a low voice to Officer McBride and then he takes out his phone as he walks outside. McBride walks closer to us. While on the phone, Boyd jots down notes, then nods to himself, clicks the phone off, returns inside and says something to McBride. He turns to us with an announcement. "I just consulted with CIB, the Criminal Investigations Branch, because of the seriousness of the issues. There is an urgency for Mr Jenson to reach the hospital so we will take photos, but we ask you to preserve the scene when we take everyone to Picton. CIB will come across when they can. It is a busy night."

Jon Jenson calls out rather weakly, "With my wife and me, as well as Amber and Malcolm gone, there is no need for anyone to be here. When we leave, we can lock the place up."

Officer Boyd nods and continues, "Officer McBride, you will take Amber into a bedroom to take photos of her injuries."

My heart goes out to Amber. She shakes. "My mother has already taken photos of me. You won't need to do it again." Amber is quite firm.

Officer Boyd shakes his head. "We can't make you have the photos taken, but it will help us to have our photos. Your mother's photos will not carry the same weight. I hope you are willing. Officer McBride will take care. It is not the first time she has photographed someone."

He avoids saying victim's photos, I am pleased to say. It would have increased Amber's anxiety to be called a victim.

Amber makes up her mind to go and stands up, frowning. "Let's get on with it then."

She leads McBride to the spare room, walks smartly, and shuts the door loudly behind her. My whole being feels for her. I can see her distress.

Boyd continues. "Once we have collected as much evidence as possible, we will take Malcolm to Picton for his formal interview. We will recall all of you within the next two days."

George looks serious almost as if he is questioning a witness during a trial. "Might I ask, what evidence you intend to collect beyond the knife and gun?"

Officer Boyd's face breaks into a grin. "I can tell you are the lawyer in the family. We need the clothes Amber had on during the alleged attempted rape, the tea towels used to tie Malcolm, and any other thing associated with the alleged crimes. I hope there are no objections." He speaks this latter, brooking no resistance. He is used to giving orders. It is part of his daily life.

There is a general noise of agreement from all in the room. All want things to move quickly. Even Malcolm does not object. He sits, grinning like the cat that got the cream.

McBride comes out of the bedroom to take photos of everything possible having finished taking photos of Amber. Officer Boyd continues, "Take the tea towels and tape, off his hands and feet, and ready him for boarding the boat. We don't want him falling into the sea with no way to protect himself. We must be careful with him. When he is on board, I will tell him how we will proceed. I am sure he knows it already, but we don't want to find we haven't warned him of all possibilities."

Officer Boyd does not speak quietly, so Malcolm must have heard. Then, Boyd strides over to Malcolm, and McBride follows. McBride removes the restrictions from his hands and feet while Boyd explains that they intend to take him on the boat. Malcolm is a picture of a perfect gentleman. He is assured and calm. He does not appear to be a man likely to be charged with at least two crimes. Alarm bells are going off in my head as I wonder what he has up his sleeve.

Malcolm uses his best public-school voice to intone clearly, "I appreciate the way you are handling this investigation, Officer. I hope I have time to give my side of events. I am a lawyer." He smiles up at McBride, using all his charm.

The charm offensive does not fool Officer McBride. "In Picton, we will conduct a formal interview where I know the environment will meet your requirements."

With this statement, she returns to Officer Boyd's side. He turns on his heel to face everyone to make an announcement.

Boyd is all business. He has spent enough of his busy day here. "Mr and Mrs Jenson will be coming with us. I need to know if anyone else is coming to Picton. There is an ambulance waiting at the dock, and I wonder if Mrs Jenson will accompany her husband in the ambulance?" Boyd looks at the medic for a response.

The medic's response is quick and to the point. "She can, but no one else. However, it would be better if someone accompanies her in a separate vehicle." The medic looks at all the anxious faces. "She possibly needs support, and we will be too busy with the patient."

"I want to go to the hospital," Amber states emphatically.

Ian, now the doctor with a patient, speaks firmly. "And I wish to accompany my patient, but it would be possible to go by private vehicle," he says. "My car is in the long-term council car park in Picton. I can take Amber and Mrs Jenson. Dan, I think you should stay here, seeing we all came across to see you. Our parents and families need you here right now."

I respond lethargically, "I will stay behind with George, Mike and the family," I say, even though my heart is with Amber.

Then my father shouts his approval from near the door as I agree with Ian that I should remain. My responsibility is to my nieces and nephews. They should have an exciting festival.

Officer Boyd, very much in command, declares, "Then it's arranged. We will take care of Malcolm on the boat, and the medic will care for Mr Jenson until he reaches the hospital. Amber, you and Ian can mind your Mum. Once we are in Picton, the ambulance will take Mr Jenson to Blenheim. We will take Malcolm, and the doctor will take anyone else who needs a ride."

Ian looks at Amber. "Perhaps you need to get a small bag together for yourself and your Mum and Dad, just in case you don't return today."

Amber points to her bag on the floor but quickly gathers things for her parents to add to their go bag.

Boyd nods approvingly, "Good thinking." Then he pulls Malcolm up by his right armpit and walks him toward the door.

"Hey!" Malcolm begins to struggle. "I can take care of myself unless you wish to charge me, but I am not sure what your charges will be." He leers at the Officer. "That will be interesting."

Officer Boyd sees Malcolm change into the person who frightens Amber. He shakes his head. Malcolm looks like he will continue to react negatively, but without prompting he turns back into an angel.

He stands tall and somehow manages to look elegantly commanding. "I mean, I am happy to walk. No need to hold me." He moves away from Officer Boyd while talking, but Officer McBride moves up on Malcolm's other side. Perhaps they understand he is a devious character.

Officer Boyd seems aware of Malcolm's intentions. "We will not mistreat you. You are in charge of yourself, but we must guarantee you reach the safety of Picton undamaged." It is Boyd's turn to be charming.

Malcolm is non-plussed. For once he is unsure of himself, and Amber looks mystified by his attitude. She shakes her head and runs to gather up her backpack. Then she adds some more things to her parent's go bag.

I must say that I am surprised at Malcolm's changed attitude because I have only seen him at his controlling best.

"Amber," Malcolm turns towards her and speaks as if she is his lacky. "Make sure all our luggage gets onto the boat. I will leave that up to you." He smiles sweetly at her as if nothing is wrong.

Amber stares back at him. I can only imagine what she must be thinking. I watch the police and Malcolm clamber onto the boat with Malcolm's luggage followed by Amber carrying her backpack and parent's go bag. Then the medic and Ian help Jon and Julie. I wander towards my house, not wanting to watch them leave. My father is ahead of me, but not by much. I catch up to him.

He doesn't beat around the bush, "So, you are still in love with her, son?"

I don't know where he gets these ideas. It is clear Amber hasn't separated from Malcolm although I think she is ready to leave, but it isn't as easy as it seems.

"I admire her. She was my best friend while we were young. Now, I have no idea what I think." I feel my face closing up. I don't want Dad to draw me out about Amber.

Dad looks like a cheeky imp. "Well, I certainly know. It is written all over your face. I can't say I blame you. She is a beautiful woman inside and out. Your mother and I would be delighted."

My chin is almost touching my chest. "Dad, I don't think this is the right time."

Dad takes me by the arm and propels me forward. "Son, it is never the right time if you don't make a move. Go to Christchurch with her to help her move out. That would be a nice gesture."

I don't know how many times I have to explain that Malcolm could hurt Amber just because I am within cooee[18]. "Dad, I would enrage Malcolm. He can't stand me even being in her parent's home. What would he be like in Christchurch? Besides, she has to work things out for herself."

Dad looks at me in exasperation. "You can, in the least, make the offer. She can make up her mind whether you go or not. You will never get married if you moon around and don't take action."

I don't know what to say. I know I will have to face my mother over the same issue. She will be worse. I am surprised she wasn't at the Jenson's house organising the two of us together.

I try to keep the irritation out of my voice. "Dad, we should enjoy *Matariki* and not think of such things." I consider walking fast, but I know he is trying to help. I shrug and walk on, listening to the birds, the rustle of the bush, and the crash of waves against the cliff. It calms my nerves. These are the sounds of home.

---

[18] Cooee – or cooey, Australian/New Zealand slang for 'to call'. Here it means, within calling distance.

I explain my misgivings. "Amber wouldn't like living out here all the time. True, she loves it for holidays, but she is used to the city. I am not. This is the big problem."

Dad's eyes pierce mine. "Have you asked her? You are making decisions for her when there is no decision worth making."

I have to agree I haven't asked her. That would mean I declare my interest, and what if I am not really in love with her? I shake my shoulders. But it is silly because I know I love her. I always have. She is the reason why none of my attempts at other relationships have worked. I match them up against her, and they all turn out wanting. Annoyingly, I was content to live alone until all this happened.

Chapter 25

Once down on the dock, I climb on board with my mother. I can feel how tense she is. She must be so worried. She hasn't said a word except to ask me how I am. I am astonished because my dad, her husband, is in much worse shape than me.

Despite the choppy water, the trip across the bay goes without incident. I watch Malcolm from a safe distance. He does not notice that his bag, a small backpack, and the go bag are the only luggage that has made it to the boat. The go bag and the backpack are near me, and I am as far away as possible from Malcolm. I have no intention of having my things anywhere near him. A shiver runs through my body at the thought. None of us speaks as we travel across the Queen Charlotte Sound until we tie up to Town Wharf One in Picton. An ambulance is waiting patiently at the end of the dock. Ian sighs with relief.

"We can rush your father to the hospital, thank goodness," Ian says, trying to cover his anxiety as we help Dad off the boat. I am worried about my father, but Ian seems to be more anxious than any of us. We have all put our faith in him. Perhaps the heaviness of that responsibility is weighing on him, but he is a doctor and must be used to it. I wonder why he is so concerned.

I nod towards him approvingly while reaching down to help Mum climb onto the dock. Her legs are shorter than mine, so it is a bit of a stretch. "Mum, you are coming with Ian and me." I smile at her, hoping my trust in Ian will extend to her. She looks relieved as she gazes at the ambulance, realizing that help will come for Dad soon.

"It won't be long until we know how he is," I whisper encouragingly, having no idea why I am whispering. There is something heavy in the atmosphere. Perhaps it is Malcolm. I know my comment is inane because I know nothing of ambulances and hospitals. Mother probably knows much more. She had me and I required the odd stitch here and there, not always my fault, but I must admit, mostly.

A shadow passes across Mum's face, and then she says, "Yes, I am pleased because I believe head wounds can lead to concussion, and that can lead to dementia. I don't want such an outcome from today's proceedings. All we wanted was a family celebration during this special time of year. As events have turned out, I believe we have something we will remember for the rest of our lives."

I groan. How can I be so shallow? Mum must have been worrying about this ever since she first saw Dad. I have been so caught up in my own emotions to think about how it must affect her. I hadn't given the result of the hit on the head a second thought. He is my dad, and as such, he has always been the guiding light in my life. I tell myself once again that I must stop turning inward and begin to think of everyone else. We have all been impacted by the result of the introduction of Malcolm into my family. I shake myself because there I go again, thinking of me. I must watch the others more carefully.

Then, Mum turns towards me and looks intently into my eyes, "What is the matter, Amber? You are worried about something."

It is true, but I didn't think my thoughts were that transparent. I try to look bright as I cover my thoughts by saying, "I was remembering how I left things with Daniel. He was so good to us about all this, and I didn't even thank him before we left."

Mum's face crinkles up in a smile. It is the first smile I have seen on her face since the drama with Dad began. "If that is all, you don't have to be concerned. He knew the urgency of moving your father onto the boat and probably didn't expect you to notice him. You will have plenty of time to go and thank him when we return home."

My mother's resilience amazes me. I wish to be so together that I can think outside of myself in crises, especially when a crisis affects someone whom I love dearly. At the moment, I am not being very successful at self-management.

I reassure her, but suspect I am really comforting myself. "I should have said something at the time. Danny will remember only how thoughtless I was of his help. Mum, he even risked his life when he entered our house. Malcolm had that rifle trained on him, and Daniel was nonchalant about the whole thing. He acted as if it was every day that a madman with a rifle and a knife were intent on hurting him. Now, I have no idea how long it will be until I see him again because I need to sort my things out in Christchurch first."

My mum hugs me so hard that I have difficulty breathing. "You don't need to do it all at once, dear. Christchurch can wait. All you need is to know that you are well and that things will settle. Your Dad and I are there for you. Don't worry."

My mouth falls open. Here, my father is so sick and may have life-shattering damage, and she is worrying about my well-being. She is consoling me when it should be the other way around. I am an adult and should be able to take responsibility for events. Yet it is me that caused all this stress, just as I did as a child. My mind wanders back towards Danny's soft brown eyes, and I wish he were beside me. I know nothing serious can come from a relationship with him because he is content to live on his farm. He probably has suitable girlfriends to dream about who have lived in the area all their lives.

Ian's voice shakes me back to reality. "Amber, we must hurry. Your mother doesn't need to wait too long before we leave for the hospital. Your father is in the ambulance already. They will leave when the dock gives them clear passage."

I return to the present and notice that the mail boat arrived about the same time as us. Yet another thing has gone unnoticed by me.

There are several passengers whose vehicles clog up the boardwalk behind the dock. Their piles of luggage need to be moved to give the ambulance free passage. I wonder if we should help, but then I notice the owners have it well in hand. They are doing their best to get out of the way.

Ian prods me in the back to draw my attention back to what I should be doing. "If we hurry, we can be at my car in a few minutes. It's in the car park just over there. The traffic should be light, and we can beat the ambulance to the hospital if we leave now. I want to prepare the guys at Accident and Emergency for him." Ian's eyes are pleading with me.

I remonstrate with myself because I am holding up proceedings once again internalising. I notice the police place Malcolm in the back seat of a police car with his bag. There are no flashing lights. I suppose because there is no urgency to get him to the station. He does not even look in my direction. I expected he would yell at me to go with him. Suddenly, I become aware of the flashing ambulance lights. This sight jolts me forward, and I begin to run. I have the backpack on my back and Mum's go bag in my right hand, so I am weighed down somewhat, and then Ian catches up and takes my arm to slow me down.

"Remember your mother. We all need to get to my car, not you alone." I note the slight sound of annoyance in his voice. He thinks I am selfish. I can't blame him.

I blush and say, "I'm sorry. I wasn't thinking," and begin to walk quickly, but not too fast for Mum. She is fit and able and probably can outrun me at this point, but she is also stressed. It is her husband, after all, who needs hospital care. My mind finally focuses when we arrive at Ian's car, which is dusty from sitting on the lot but up to the job of getting us into Blenheim.

My thoughts turn to the hospital. We were all excited when they completed the new hospital, but to me, it resembles a series of Quonset huts, posh ones, but still Quonset huts. Not the corrugated half-circular ones, the wooden ones built as barracks for the army, possibly during World War II. They were at Burnham Military Camp when a friend of mine did her Teaching Probationary Assistant year there. Oh yes, I know a few teachers, not only archaeologists. Teaching is probably more practical, but archaeology is critical because it teaches us history and shows how to prevent remaking our mistakes. We continue to make the same mistakes over and over again. We seem unable to learn from our past. I am not immune to this phenomenon, so I can't talk. See what I have accomplished so far in my life. Here I am, almost thirty years old. I am unmarried and have achieved nothing, nothing other than being compliant.

I shake myself and look around. Ian had succeeded in getting us into his car so he could drive, sometime ago. We are almost in Blenheim, passing row after row of vines all neatly placed. Then, I begin to wonder why my mind is thinking inane thoughts. I guess it is avoidance. I don't want to think about what might be happening to Dad in the ambulance up ahead. When we entered Ian's car, it managed to escape the crowd.

No one in the car wants to talk. We all have our thoughts. We are all worried. Dad's condition is worse than I first thought. How I wish this day had never arrived.

My mind slips back to Danny on the farm, teaching his nieces and nephews about the outdoors, conservation, the animals, the stars, and the whole environmental shebang. Doing that is far more exciting than reading musty old papers in archives here and there. True, I love reading information written at the time of an event. It is different from reading a present-day report about it, with today's interpretation implanted, but it is not the same as the natural world Danny lives in. I can't imagine why I didn't return home frequently after uni. Scared, I suspect; afraid Danny would not want to talk to me the way he did when we were kids. And then there is that electric feeling when we touch. I wonder what causes it and if it is the same for him.

While my mind wanders all over the place, we arrive at the hospital, where Ian is all efficiency, parking his car near the emergency department, guiding us out of the car and towards the entrance where Dad's ambulance is parked. Dad is protesting because he is on a gurney, saying he isn't sick. He can walk. Ian arrives just in time to insist that the gurney is essential. Dad finally complies. Mum and I share a quick smile. We know what Dad is like.

Ian comes across to us. I am pleased that one of us knows what to do. At this point, I have quite decided I am better at being a robot, just following, not making decisions.

Ian is trying to reassure us. "You can accompany the gurney, but will have to wait when he goes for a scan. I hope they hurry up. I will accompany him wherever he goes in the hospital, so don't worry. I will be his patient advocate. They also need me for the details about how he was when I found him. He is in the best of hands."

My mother goes to Dad and gives him a quick kiss on the head. They chat quietly, and I wonder what they are saying. They have been together for many years and shared much. The results of these events must be difficult for them both.

Chapter 26

My father, Ian, George and I arrive at the Police Station at the right time, but I am disappointed because Amber and her mother are still at the hospital. Her father has developed complications because of the hit to his head. I looked forward to seeing Amber here. It is Monday, two days after the altercation, and I miss her.

I feel my body sagging, weighed down with the prospect of the interview, hoping I will say the right things, but also worrying about Amber. "Perhaps we should visit Jon Jenson when we finish here," I say hopefully.

My father guffaws as he slaps a hand on his leg. "He means we should go to see Amber. Once you boys left with your families, he mooned around like a lost sheep."

My brothers all laugh. I cannot see the funny side of it. I watch the three of them enjoying themselves at my expense. "We should all be concerned about her. She suffered a dreadful event, and that scoundrel, Malcolm, he will get off Scot free."

George interjects, "That isn't quite right. He will be charged with attempted rape and assault, both serious charges. That is what the police officer told me would happen when he rang. They have told him he should go to Christchurch to get his affairs in order because they are sure there will be a conviction."

This information does little to help how I feel. I control my urge to shout but say, "You heard what Malcolm said, that they would never keep him, and he will get off both charges if it goes to court."

George grins. "What piffle! The evidence is strong no matter what he says. He may be a lawyer, but that will do nothing to help him."

Not to be outdone, I retort, "It got him out of the police station pretty quickly. They didn't even keep him overnight. He is now a danger to Amber. I hoped she would have been able to go to Christchurch to get her things, then return and sort out the finances from afar before he was on the loose. Now, she will have to face him. You can bet he will change the locks on the apartment to make her ask for his help."

My father's head is swivelling back and forth like at a tennis match. "Boys, we have no idea if he is out. All we know is the police will charge him this morning sometime and that he should go to Christchurch. We don't know if he has been to court yet. It is early, and even if they have arraigned Malcolm, we don't know if he has already gone south. Besides, getting to Christchurch is not easy just now. There are no rental cars available in the area, the direct route south is closed until tomorrow, and the long route is out of the question. He may have managed to get a booking on a plane or a bus. It is possible, but think of all the people he is competing against. The pressure on booking anything is so difficult that some travellers are catching the ferry to Wellington and flying from there. If he had left when he first said he was leaving, then it would have been okay. Amber had booked him on a plane, but that went by-the-by. Things will return to normal in a day or two, but not now!"

The others nod their heads wisely, appearing to know more than me. Of course, they are correct, but my concern is Amber's safety. The idea of him being on the loose makes me fear for Amber's life. I don't think I am being dramatic. Nobody saw what I saw when I entered the Jenson house. I saw the devil in his eyes. He was determined to kill me, but he couldn't think of a way to do it without being caught. I knew I had him, but Malcolm disliked being thwarted.

A question comes to me suddenly. "George, have you investigated Malcolm's background to find out if he has done anything like this before?"

George grins at me. "I was wondering when you would ask. Of course, I accessed the information as soon as I had a reliable computer. That is, one I know is secure."

"Are you saying mine isn't? It has the latest virus software," I say huffily.

George is still smiling. "I mean a computer that is encrypted, forensically secure, like my work one. So, yes, I searched for his name in the London court records, the newspapers and the like and came up with an interesting case. I am not sure if it is him. A man who fits his description, called Malcolm, had a wife who died accidentally about a year before meeting Amber. However, his last name is different. No evidence linked this Malcolm to the scene of the accident, but his wife's relatives said he was very controlling and took charge of her affairs. She was making moves to separate when the accident happened. She hit a tree on a dark rainy night a long way from where they lived. It was her car, and the general belief was she hit a large puddle on the road, which caused her to veer off into the tree. The skid marks and other evidence were consistent with this. Perhaps it isn't Amber's Malcolm, and it does appear to be an accident."

I scowl darkly, "It sounds fishy to me. Was this man a lawyer?"

George nods, in a very agreeable way. "Yes, he certainly was, a barrister none-the-less, and he left for the South Seas soon after with all her money. The relatives chose not to fight it because there were no children and no need for the money. They said they were happy never to see him again."

My mind scrambles up and down while I process this information. I don't want this to be Amber's Malcolm, but if it is him, we must take double care of her. "Is there a photo of him?" I wonder.

My mind is racing. Things are already bad for Amber; she doesn't need anything to add to the disaster that is Malcolm. I must admit somewhere deep inside, I feel pleased at the prospect that Malcolm is much worse than even I imagine.

"There is, and it resembles Amber's Malcolm, except he has a moustache and beard, but it could be someone else." George looks pensive. I would have hoped for a little glee in his voice. "Here, you can look for yourself."

George shows us a photo on his phone of the bearded Malcolm.

It is Dad's turn to scowl. "It sure looks like him to me. We should show it to the police after the consultations."

I am surprised. "Why after?" I ask, secretly pleased that it was Dad who said it was Malcom. If I had, no one would have believed me, biased that's the problem.

Dad looks thoughtful. "I don't know. I think it would not be good to prejudice what we say."

We all nod in agreement. George looks thoughtful. "If possible, I will go last, and then I can present all the information at the end. I am the one who found it and should wear any bias it might cause." George is very serious.

I don't want my brother to take the brunt, but his point is clear. Before the discussion can continue, Officer McBride calls me in. The thought of this interview takes up all my mind because I want to guarantee my information is accurate without showing my true thoughts about Malcolm. I wonder if I can be dispassionate.

Officer McBride conducts the meeting professionally. I find it easy to relax to answer her questions until towards the end when she says, "You harbour resentment towards Malcolm. Is there a reason besides what happened at the Jenson's house?"

I don't know what to say to that question. I am too busy wondering how she read me so easily. "Um, ah, Amber was my best friend growing up. We spent most holidays together," I say rather lamely.

She smiles warmly. "Has the friendship continued? Perhaps your comments are coloured by your feelings for her?"

I am nonplussed. "I don't know what you mean. I have told you all I know as truthfully as possible. If I harbour feelings for Amber, I would still want the truth to come out."

Officer McBride taps her phone and nods. "Thank you. If we need any further information, we will be in touch."

I stand up, shake her hand and leave before I say anything regrettable. I want to ask her many things, especially where Malcolm is, but such a question will put the cat among the pigeons. I walk out and sit beside my father. Ian is going next. Then Dad will be followed by George.

My father raps me on the knee and says, "How did it go, son? You look a bit frazzled."

I try to look reassuring. "I answered every question honestly, but some of it was hearsay. By its very nature, it has to be. I wasn't at the attempted rape. I could only say how Amber looked when I first saw her afterwards. Officer McBride seemed happy with what I said but she asked me if I had feelings for Amber beyond friendship. I didn't know how to respond. Besides, it was my business. I think I said such feelings would not affect how I responded; that I could only tell the truth."

Dad patted me on the knee again and straightened his back. "Too true, son. Don't worry. You will have said all the right things. They have the statement that you made at the Jenson house for comparison. I am sure all is fine."

My body unwinds somewhat as I glance around. It is a tidy police station, small, with a bright reception area; almost too small for us because other people come in with their business. There is a notice on the wall stating for privacy, visitors can move to a secure room. No one makes such a request while we sit there.

George is the last interviewee for us. When he comes out, we are relieved that it is over. "I think we should go to the hospital now to visit Mr Jenson," George says. I sense he wants to talk with us away from the police station, but I am all for going to the hospital as quickly as possible. My brothers and father seem to have the same thought. We all turn to walk out the door in unison.

Chapter 27

Dad, Ian, George and I leave the Police Station, then George insists we meet at a café on the way to Blenheim. I am mystified, but I am sure it is something concerning Amber. I don't know why I think this. I have had a bad feeling about Malcolm ever since entering the Police Station; nothing to do with the police, but something associated with recent events.

All four of us ride in George's car, so he doesn't have to ask us where he should go. I suppose he wants to prepare us. We speed along State Highway One past the Picton airport at Koromiko in silence, then by the Johanneshof Cellars with its German-style wines, and on through the swamp with its dying willow trees looking like some weird Ingmar Bergman film set, then out into the valley where a café sits amid vineyards. The others must be as anxious as me. What on earth does he want to tell us?

We park and enter the brightly lit café empty of people at this hour. A welcoming man rushes out from somewhere. He looks harassed. I suppose his sponge cake must have dropped in the centre or some other annoying thing.

His voice is as polite as his expression. "What can I offer you? We have fresh date scones just out of the oven, cakes, muffins, whatever suits," he beams at us.

I put my hand on the counter and smile, not wanting to burst his eagerness. "A long black coffee will do me."

I look at my father and brothers. I want to get on with whatever it is George has to say. They all agree that coffee is sufficient and order their varieties. I pay for us all, then take mine out to the conservatory we came through when entering. I seat myself at a table for four. The location is more private, away from the flapping ears of the manager. Nothing against him. He looks like a nice man, but I don't want anyone to hear what we have to say.

When we are all seated, Dad says, "Well, out with it. What is so important we have to stop here?"

George clears his throat. "I was the last one consulted."

I look at him curiously. "Well, we all know that," I say grumpily.

George looks at me quickly, then continues, "Officer McBride told me what happened in court this morning." We all stare at him, impatient for him to continue. "Somehow, Malcolm acquired a top defence lawyer, even though we have just had a long weekend. The man he hired is excellent. The police made a strong case for remanding him, but he got bail. The judge bailed Malcolm to Christchurch with a curfew from seven to seven. This timing will allow him to go to work and complete his private business, and his case will not come up for some time. He is forbidden to go near Amber, but Malcolm will be in Christchurch before Amber. The authorities will check on him regularly. He presented himself in court as a delightful man, compliant and unconcerned about the charges. He is sure he will win his case."

Ian looks keenly at George. "He may think so, but the evidence is strong. I am surprised they bailed him. He is a danger to Amber. At least two of us should go with her when she goes for her things. After that, she should return to the Sounds until the trial. I hope she has an understanding boss."

Initially, I am pleased that it is Ian that says this, but then a thought rushes into my brain which makes me frown at Ian. "We can't go making up our minds about what Amber should do. She is a grown woman, not the little girl we all know and love. She wants to look after herself, but I agree she will need help. That man is not to be trusted. How is it possible for a judge not to see through him?"

Dad straightens up and looks at me intently. "Son, he probably did, but he has to work with the material in front of him. If Malcolm's lawyer guarantees his behaviour, he has little option but to allow him bail."

We all shift uncomfortably in our seats. I wonder what society we are becoming. It certainly isn't the caring one our last female Prime Minister advocated. Then I realised I had spoken for Amber, the very thing she didn't want. She might be happy with George or

Ian accompanying her to Christchurch. Who am I to deny her this help? I rub my head in frustration. All I want to do is to protect her, but how can I do that now she is an adult?

Life was so much simpler when I was a child. I almost chuckle, remembering how we fought on the lawn and giggled as we ran after each other as if chasing bandits. I remember one horrifying occasion when she chased me with a *Huhu* bug, an ugly beetle that bites. We were so innocent.

My thoughts are interrupted by Ian. "I think we should visit Mr Jenson, then talk with Amber and her mother afterwards. They may not know the outcome of the arraignment."

I stand up, indicating I am ready to go, and the others stand more slowly, finishing their coffee and nodding at Ian in agreement. I almost race to the car.

Chapter 28

The hospital has a small café near the front entrance. If sunny, Mum and I would have sat outside, but today isn't that day. The weather is too cold and rainy. We are too anxious about Dad to endure anything uncomfortable. Last night, Dad insisted we go to a motel to rest. He was more worried for us than about himself. Mum decided it best not to worry him further, so we took a taxi to a nearby motel. It turned out the closest motels were in the centre of the town. Luckily, the one the taxi driver suggested had a double room with single beds available. It offered breakfast, which sounded good at the time. I don't think either of us slept. We rose, ate a hurried breakfast, not appreciating the quality of the food and returned to the hospital. We visited Dad immediately upon arrival, then went for coffee when the nurses arrived to check on him. They wanted privacy.

I walk smartly down the corridor and Mum seems happy to keep up. "Dad looks brighter today, but the bump is still nasty," I say to stop myself from thinking dire thoughts.

Mum looks at me, trying to be brave. "Yes, I think he will be his old self any day now." Her voice belies her thoughts.

I feel my forehead wrinkling up in a frown. "Mum, you heard what the doctor said this morning. The scan shows no haematoma or haemorrhage and no skull fracture. He has a concussion, which means he will be good to go shortly. They might have let him come home this afternoon if we lived closer. A car ride, a boat ride and then climbing up our hill is not such a good idea, especially with concussion."

Mum nods vacantly at me. "Amber, I understand that is what the doctor said, but your father is faking it. He is not himself."

I don't know how to respond. I know she knows him better than anyone, but she seems determined to make him sicker than he is. "Mum, he only regained consciousness last night after his turn the night before. It was this turn that has kept him here. We can't expect him to be perky. He didn't seem groggy this morning. I trust the doctor. He is a good man." I try to sound enthusiastic, but Mum knows I feel rather like her, a bit pessimistic no matter what effort I put into the speech.

I look around the café and note it filling up with staff. It must be a break time or a change of duty. My coffee is still sitting in front of me, untouched. I want it but don't have the energy to bring the cup to my lips. I notice Mum has only sipped her tea.

I am beginning to worry about her. "I hope the tea is good, Mum. My coffee is fine, but I am letting my imagination run away, thinking things are worse than they are. Perhaps we are both guilty of speculating."

Mum's eyes light up, awakening to my presence. For the first time since the altercation at our house, she is thinking beyond worrying about Dad. I forget all about her concern for me when coming here in what seemed ages ago. If I am honest, she has only thought about others. It is high time she begins to consider herself.

Then, she says something that upsets me. "Oh, darling. I am so sorry. I have been so worried about your father that I forgot the trauma you have endured. How are you?"

Somehow it strikes my funny bone, and I let out a small giggle. How ludicrous. I only suffered minor bruises, nothing like Dad. I don't want to think of the emotional turmoil. Despite not wishing my mind to contemplate what Malcolm did, my anger at him returns with a vengeance. "I hope that man is inside a jail cell, unable to leave until he is convicted. We should ring to find out what is happening to him."

Mum reaches across and touches my hand. "Amber darling. I don't think it will make any difference where he is. You must stay away from him."

I must reassure her although she does know me inside out. I am a bit of a bull at the gate. "Mum, the good thing is, I believe I have finally learned my lesson. For so long, I considered I was the one causing problems. It wasn't until I saw what he did to Dad that I understood he was truly evil. How could I have brought him into our house, our special place, and at *Matariki*, when all Daniel's family was home? I don't understand myself."

I put my face in my hands, my elbows rest on the table, and I rub my eyes. Mum comes around and sits beside me to cuddle me. "It is impossible to blame yourself, darling, for the horror that is Malcolm. Dad and I didn't like him, but we had no idea what a dreadful man he was. I wondered if my preference for Dan coloured my negative thoughts about Malcolm, but I think not. Malcolm hid his true self from us all."

While she says this, we see Dan, Ian, George, and their father through the glass wall at the front of the café. They enter the hospital, marching directly up to reception. Seeing them arouses something deep inside me. I am pleased they are here. It must show on my face because Mum says, "Speak of the devil. Here is Dan to see your father."

I correct her rather thoughtlessly. "Mum, it is Dan, his brothers and father, not only Daniel." But while I am protesting, my body says otherwise. I know I am pleased that Danny is here.

Mum and I stand up in unison and walk to the corridor to intercept them, greeting each one with a hug. Fortunately, Danny holds back and is the last person to hug me. I almost cry at his touch. It is so comforting. Oh, I don't know how to explain what I am feeling. It is like coming home after a long journey through a desert or a strange place. I don't want to release him, but I must.

"Lovely to see your family here, Danny," I smile shyly as if I am a wee girl again. I try to include his brothers and father, but it doesn't work. A smile deep in his eyes makes me wonder what he feels. Probably not the same as me, because why would he after all these years?

"It's good to see you too," he says, and, if I am not mistaken, his voice sounds more gravelly than usual. I grin up at him. He wants to put his arm around me, I feel sure. I wouldn't resist if he did, but he continues, "We are here to visit your father. How is he today?"

I feel a bit deflated, and it takes my mother to answer his question. "He is a bit better today, thank you. Come on down to see him."

Mother takes his hand and leads us down the corridor to the wing where my father is resting. I sense that Ian and George have something they want to tell us, but politeness prevents them from asking Mum to wait. I think it must be something about Malcolm, but I prefer not to ask. I would rather not know until I have to face reality.

When we reach Dad, he sits up in bed, calmly acting healthy when we know he is not. He favours his right side, so I suspect it is sore. His head is bandaged, which prevents Daniel's family from seeing the damage Malcolm caused. We chat, ignoring the reality, although Ian asks for details about the side wound and the head. He is happy with what Dad says, or maybe he is pleased with the way Dad says it. I'm not sure, but it is reassuring because I think I can still read Ian as I did when we were children. He is unable to hide his feelings the way George can. I suspect that is why George is a lawyer and Ian a doctor. My mind is roaming wildly around. It goes anywhere that isn't the present and preferably not the recent past. I am trying my best to put the incident with Malcolm out of my mind. I want to talk about anything that is of no importance.

"Where is Mike?" I ask rather lamely. Why should he use his work time to come to visit Dad?

"We left him with the wives and the children. We came from the police station, and seeing he wasn't in the house during the event, we thought it good for him to stay behind. The women are used to us not being there. Because he is single, we thought he was a good substitute for us, but it doesn't hurt for us to be there occasionally."

I understand Daniel's father is joking. Once again, I am impressed with the communication in this family. They joke, but they are always there for each other. It is implied in this statement that the two wives and their children are all together. They must feel the need for support because they also do not know what Malcolm will do next.

I respond trying to keep the topic light. "Of course, but the children must be at school today." I have a concern about how the children have taken all this and now I hope their day is as normal as it should be.

Their faces change as they see the effect the joke has on me. They all speak over each other, pointing out the logistics of tidying up the place after the long weekend and then getting the water taxi back to Picton. They could have used Dan's boat but decided to take the water taxi. They wanted to leave the vessel for Dan in case he needed it. Silly really, because Daniel was already in Picton.

Ian takes up the conversation to clarify the kerfuffle. "There are no worries at home. Mike drove off somewhere or other. The children are at school, our wives are working, and we must go to work too." He noted abruptly, then he turned to Dan. "Dan, perhaps you can stay here for a while. We will return this evening. Mr Jenson, I wish to talk with your doctor, if you don't mind. I want to ensure you are getting the best care." He smiles reassuringly. My father is surprised that Ian asks because he is the one who helped him at the house. He expects him to talk with the medical team.

Dan's family agree they must get on with their day, and I am secretly happy that Daniel will remain with us. My whole family is together, or that is how it seems.

Chapter 29

I am conscious of Danny's presence as we sit beside Dad. He has been constantly at my side since his father and brothers left. We whisper because Dad needs his rest. Mum wants to say something, but I am unsure if she wants to talk with me or Dad. It turns out Mum wants a private talk with Dad. On this pretext, she sends us off to have lunch together. Well, that is her excuse. I suspect it is a move to make Danny and me talk to each other. Her desire to speak has nothing to do with my father.

Danny's hand bumps into mine while we walk along the corridor. I want to take it but believe it is wrong when I haven't dealt with Malcolm. How can I show any interest in another person?

Danny stops me before I enter the café. "I think we should hop a taxi and go to the kebab shop in town; much better for us than pies. It has fresh salad vegetables and beautifully cooked meat. What do you say?"

My right eyebrow rises in surprise. "That might take too long. Mum needs a meal."

Danny has a solution. He is determined to have me to himself, or so it seems. "If she is hungry, she can pop into the café. Besides, with us gone, the hospital staff might bring her a meal when they bring your father's meal. I remember that happening when I was here with a football injury. Perhaps you can ring her to find out what she wants to do? We might be able to bring her something from town."

I must admit that café food is getting a little repetitive, and the thought of a kebab has my taste buds bursting. I take out my phone and ask if Mum would like a kebab.

I know my eyes are shining. I feel like I am going on a date. "Mum would love a chicken kebab. Dad wants one with all the fixings. That's settled. When did you develop a taste for Middle Eastern food?"

Danny's grin is as wide as his face, and his eyes light up. "I wasn't always a farmer. I travelled the world, had a wonderful time in Dubai and Istanbul, and loved the street markets. I also love Chinese food, but the real stuff is not here. They adapt the menu to suit our Western tastes. The kebabs at the Turkish restaurant here are splendid, more like the real thing. Perhaps we can travel there someday?"

He drops this last bit as if it is a new idea just formed, but it has the ring of distance. He must have been thinking about it for some time. A genuine smile cracks my face. It is the first time I have felt a smile reach my eyes since the incident with Malcolm. What am I going to do about him?

While I am not answering Danny's question, he is getting a taxi for us and indicating for me to hurry up. I return to reality with a thud and slip into the back seat alongside Danny. He tells the driver where to go, and we sit back and relax.

Unbidden, I hear myself saying, "I would love to travel with you, but there are a few things I need to sort out first. I must straighten out my life, but I am uncertain how."

Danny reaches across and takes my hand. An electric blue shock shoots up my arm. The tremor surprises me, and his eyebrows rise in a question, asking if it is okay to take my hand. I nod quietly and snuggle into the backseat, which feels comfortable, like a La-Z-Boy. A warm, happy feeling spreads slowly through my body, but unbidden, my mind takes over. I sit up straight and begin to frown. What am I thinking?

Danny looks shocked at my sudden move. "I am sorry, Amb. I don't mean to take advantage of you. I remember the good times we had together, and I hope we might be able to renew them. Malcolm is a problem, but that talk is for the restaurant. You don't have to fix things by yourself."

I am not sure how I feel about allowing Danny to help me. It is bad enough that I have caused this mess without involving Danny or anyone else. I scrunch up tightly, and Danny moves away.

I reach my hand out to him. I am horrified that he thinks it is his fault. "Oh no, Danny. You haven't done anything wrong. It is me. I should tidy up my own shit."

Danny's eyes narrow at my use of words. I don't often swear or even say shit, but it feels like it is the word of the moment.

Danny visibly calms down. "He is a dangerous man, Amber. He is a person who will take advantage of anyone, not only you. My brothers all feel the same. It is easier for me than them to take time off work to help you. George and Ian can't take time off easily, and Mike is under orders. The army governs his life, although he keeps a home in Blenheim. He wants your parents to use it until your father recovers. It has easy access to the hospital and physios. Mike will talk with your father tonight. I hope they take the option. I will organize a barge for our cars so we all have wheels, and yours needs to go to the garage for a check before anything else."

In my adult life, only my parents have been there for me. My mouth drops open while I gaze at Danny. What can I say? I know I have to get my car fixed. I have already rung work to ask for time off, which they readily granted. I have six weeks' leave owing to me, and they would prefer I take time off now rather than pay me out later. That sorts out the work part of my life. What a pity the other part is so difficult.

We arrive at the restaurant, and the taxi slips into a parking zone. Dan pays and requests a return trip in an hour. I slip out the left side of the car onto the pavement. Danny follows, putting his arm around me impulsively. I smile, feeling a spark, but I wonder what he thinks as he does this.

On entering the restaurant, we both order the same thing, a chicken kebab with garlic aioli and sweet chilli sauce. Danny orders a large size, while I want a regular one. We tell them about the kebabs for my parents but say to wait on making them until we are ready to go. We decide on apple tea and then pick up water and glasses at the water station before making for comfortable seats at a corner table.

Danny turns and looks cautiously at me. Something in his eyes tells me he has something vital to say. "Malcolm is out. He received bail and had a great lawyer if it is possible to call a lawyer great who twists facts. His charges are: attempted rape and physical assault. Other charges might follow, but that is enough for now. Malcolm must live in Christchurch and has a curfew. You understand now why we wish to help. You can only collect your things when he is at work, but he may have changed the locks and might be working from home. At the moment, we don't know what he is doing or where he is. He could be anywhere. On the plus side, he has no idea where you are either. I am sure he knows nothing of Mike's house, so you and your parents will be safe."

I am stunned by the news. I don't know what to say. I was sure the court would keep Malcolm for at least a couple of days. "When was he released?" I gasp.

Danny scratches his head and frowns. "The hearing was this morning, so I expect it was straight afterwards. Perhaps his lawyer arranged for him to reach Christchurch. The police didn't have those details when we were there. The arraignment happened during our interviews, so we were lucky to receive this information. It was George who received the news. He was the last interviewee because they wanted to grill him about what he did for you and your father. They were not interested in your talk with him. Of course, it is off-limits, client-lawyer privilege and all. They knew he would tell them very little. So, they could only ask what George saw and knew, but they were good to us, very fair. We worried about the Māori issue on the way there, but it wasn't a problem. I suppose our reputations in Picton and Blenheim are solid, so no problem."

I gulp. I have been tactless again. "I hadn't thought of that. I forget you are all Māori. You are just you, always have been. I can't understand why some people think otherwise." Then I put my hand to my mouth. "Malcolm! He wouldn't like that about you. Well, that is his problem." I say firmly, thinking about what I must collect from our apartment. Perhaps I should leave it all to him and fight for my half of the place only. Then I begin to think of my clothing, my photos and all my books. I don't see why I should leave it all to him. Most of it I owned before I lived with Malcolm. Then, there is the other problem. If Danny comes with me, Malcolm would be delighted to hurt him.

Danny takes my hand and squeezes it affectionately just as our food arrives.

Chapter 30

Dan settles Mum and Dad at Michael's house. Michael's place is a new three-bedroom home looking towards the Wairau Plains. The plains no longer have a myriad of orchards with fresh fruit ready for the Christmas rush. The fruit trees have nearly all gone to be replaced by vineyards. True, the wine produced receives accolades and awards worldwide, but I miss the orchards. Fortunately, there are still a few cherry orchards. I love buying a box of cherries at a roadside stand beside a farm at the beginning of the season. The fruit is crisp and juicy, a joy to crush in the mouth, but that won't be for a few months. We still have the depths of winter to traverse. Michael intends to return from Burnham Army Camp near Christchurch each weekend, but the house is big enough for us all. Michael's dad tells me in no uncertain terms that I must stay until my father recovers.

I protest. I am not some wilting flower who needs to be cared for all the time. "I must return to Christchurch to sort out my things if I want to keep anything. I really want my photos and some of my clothes. I don't think I should buy new clothes because I am too scared to pick up my own things."

We gather in the lounge. By 'we' I mean Danny, his father, my parents and me. Dad is lying on a leather couch, looking extremely comfortable. He looks at me. "Amber, I will worry if you go down there by yourself. I am not well enough to go, and I need your mother to help me. Your best option is to go with Dan. He is sensible and can stand up to the likes of Malcolm."

This revelation stuns me. I expect this from my mother but not Dad! Don't I have a say in my life? My thoughts are dark, but I think about how I have run my life to date. In review, it isn't too sparkling. I am the one who introduced Malcolm to the family. Who am I to say who or what I need? Obviously, my judgment is flawed.

I shrug as I try to show I am an independent adult who has lived quite a bit of her life alone. "If you think it is essential."

Deep down inside, besides my misgivings, I am pleased I have an excuse to be with Danny, even if it is at my father's orders. I guess to say 'orders' is a bit strong. Well, at his suggestion, sounds better.

Everyone breathes a sigh of relief at my comment. I mean, not just the people in the room; even the very walls seems relieved. I huff, thinking even inanimate objects are siding with everyone against me on every side. I wonder if anyone has considered what Danny wants, and then I remember it was his idea in the first place; well, his and his brothers. Danny has a Cheshire cat grin on his face. My frustration amuses him.

Danny's grin turns to seriousness as he presents what he thinks is a good idea. "I hope next Monday will be a good day to go to Christchurch. The main road will be clear of landslips from the storm, and I will have time to attend to the farm and ask the farmer next door if he will look in on the animals, especially the dogs. They hate it when I leave."

I think about the timing. I want to get there speedily, not because I think Malcolm will plan any nefarious thing, but because I want to clear my belongings out quickly before I change my mind. Yes, I still catch myself wishing to return to what I thought I had. The reality is taking time to trickle in. I must go to counselling, according to the hospital doctor. George also says it is a must because it will help my case no matter what I think. Once again, I find myself conforming. Isn't this attitude the one I am trying to change by leaving Malcolm? I know they are correct, not because of who they are, but because I need a direction. It would be terrible to use Daniel as a crutch to help me strengthen my outlook on life. If we are to become a team, I want it for the best reason. It must be for love and nothing less.

While I am away with the fairies, Danny is preparing to leave. I feel vulnerable as he walks out the door with a cheery wave. His eyes are taking us all in, not just me. This casual exit should not disappoint me, but it does. My mind is in such a muddle.

I find myself in the middle of the lounge, staring out the window on the other side of the room, not seeing anything. I don't expect Danny's exit to upset me, but it does.

Daniel's dad walks over and hugs me. "It will all work out for the best, Amber. The finest times of your life are to come."

He smiles and indicates I should sit in an armchair beside my father. My movements feel like a zombie's as I walk across the room. Mum perches on the edge of the couch beside Dad's legs, and then Daniel's dad sits down on another armchair once I sit down. I am following orders in a way I promised myself I would never do again.

Daniel's dad is welcoming and his eyes look kindly. "You have been through a great trauma, Amber, and you must not minimize it. The psychologist will be good, but the best thing is us. We are here for you any time, day or night. I mean, the boys and me. Your parents are right here, so no problem. Once you have picked up your belongings, think about a holiday. We have family in Rarotonga in the Cook Islands. That would be a great place to rest for a couple of weeks. They love visitors; give it a thought."

I look at Daniel's dad in amazement. "It is impossible for me to turn up uninvited, especially to people I haven't met."

He smiles, shaking his head as if he is a bit frustrated with me. "You know them, Amber. Remember Kahu and Louise? They came here the summer before you left for university. They love you and have already sent you an invite, not that you need one.

You are family like any of my boys. I hoped you would remember how much we love you."

He must have planned this for some time because he sat back with a deep sigh now that he had said it. I suppose he thought carefully about announcing this because he knows how touchy I am. I have nothing to say because I do not know how to respond. I am shocked that the news of my problems has reached Rarotonga. But I must admit, Raro is an island of my dreams, with clear blue water in the lagoon and white sandy beaches – well, mostly, and small enough to walk anywhere. It is almost unreal. I could swim all day or paddle a canoe around the lagoon, snorkel to view the inmates while listening to the sounds of the waves crashing on the outer reef. It seems like heaven.

My mother joins in the assault on my privacy. "It will be good for you, darling." She has a colluding smile on her face which shows me the idea is not new to her.

I regard her with a piercing look, trying to gauge when this idea emerged. "Let me think about it. I still have to get my things and deal with the apartment. Thank goodness for George. He has already sent a letter to Malcolm with my demands. They are not really demands because I am not asking for all he owes me, just the things of significance to me and half the apartment. But it is being misread because I am not talking directly to him.

My father rubs his forehead to remove a stubborn pain that refuses to go away. "Amber, you can't approach him. He is a violent man, intent on getting his way. Your lawyer should deal with it. Remember how quickly Malcolm acquired a top defence lawyer? I am sure he has already chosen a brilliant property person. You are playing with fire, and I do not want you to come out of it badly."

In my heart, I feel the truth of my father's plea for what it is, an appeal for me to be sensible. I hate that Malcolm's actions have hurt him. I must think of my family and me, but it is critical not to let them be hurt. I will harm them if I let things slide. I can feel my backbone returning to normal as I think about the implications. It straightens up automatically, and my face firms with a determined look.

I know I will not earn any peace unless I placate them all. "I look forward to going to Christchurch with Danny. Once that is over, I will think about a trip to Raro. I haven't been for years, and I love it. It will be better than a psychologist or a therapist any day."

I sit there looking defiant. I have killed two birds with one stone, not going to therapy and addressing the trip idea. Happiness, confusion and annoyance seem to flit over the faces of my audience. Somehow, I have managed to upset them all without even trying. I must do better.

I hold my hands primly in front of me, "In the least, I agreed to go to Christchurch with Danny," I say contritely, and then they all look at each other, beginning to giggle.

A buzz of agreement wafts through the room. "We have our old Amber back," my father says with a grin.

Chapter 31

Back on my farm, all is in order, except one of my neighbours, Bruce, is most upset I haven't cleared the road. I try to point out that I have had quite a lot to do and don't think it is the right time to clear any landslides yet. It is also not my job. I want to hurry out of here so that I can take Amber to Christchurch. Bruce can be annoying at the best of times, but this is not my best time. I don't want anything to delay my return to Blenheim and Amber.

"Look, Bruce," I say as I pull myself up to my full height, "See how water-soaked the land is. It would be futile to clear it now. I will only have to do it again tomorrow."

Bruce is a wee, pudgy guy who only comes occasionally to his bach. It is in disrepair, so much in need of maintenance. He seems to think I am the local roadworks person; no idea why. I guess I have just done anything like that because I own a tractor and didn't mind doing the work. I don't know what else to tell him, so I can get on with my work.

His face screws up until it looks something like a prune. "But I need to drive down to the dock. I can't manage to lug all my gear down there. I only came across for the long weekend. And the

Misses is annoyed at me enough. She seems to think I created this storm!"

He sounds whiney, and if there is anything that tries my patience, it is a whiney adult. A whiney child is irritating, but a young person still has much to learn. I feel like telling him to grow up.

My hands go to my hips without me thinking about them. "Bruce, I have rather a lot on my hands. Why don't you bring your boat round the point to my dock, then I will help you load it. My path is good to walk on, and the track to your place isn't bad. It will be much easier than trying to negotiate a landslide."

Bruce looks at me as though I am mad. "How can I reach my boat with the landslide there?"

I feel my temper rising. "You can walk and climb down there with not too much trouble. Just take care where you put your feet. Make sure you have on a good raincoat. Those clouds still look threatening."

I want to turn my back on him and begin my work. I promised Amber I would be back quickly, but I can see I will not get far if I don't help this man. I have no solution other than to help him and that means extra work for me. Not with the best grace, I say, "Give me your boat keys, and I will bring it around."

Bruce's face lights up. I must acknowledge that his smile made me feel better about the delay this will cause. He hands over the keys as if he hands over a favourite Easter Egg and stuffs his hands in his pockets.

His hands are shaking. "Thanks. I didn't think my old legs would get me down there, and a broken leg is all I need."

I smile rather weakly because I can't afford a broken leg right now, either. True, I am younger than Bruce, but not by that much. He is just not very fit.

I stomp off in the direction of his bay. It is a good half-an-hour walk across the hill. A half-an-hour I can ill afford to lose. I shrug my shoulders and get on with it.

Fortunately, the water is calmer than yesterday, and it will be a pleasant trip around the point to my dock. I start up the boat and head for the point near my place. I take a quick squizz around to check on the house sitting in all its glory as if it were meant to be on the beach. It seems safe enough where it is. There is nothing I can do about it, so I return to my dock, park the boat and rush up the hill to help Bruce and his wife with his things. The quicker I do this, the sooner I can get on with my agenda.

At last, I can get on with finding a barge for the cars, checking all the animals, talking with my farmer neighbour to see if he will keep an eye on the boys for me and anything else that needs caring for while I am away. I don't believe I will be away for more than a few days, so I am not that worried. We both share the responsibility for each other's properties when one of us has to be away. It is a good arrangement, and he is a trusted farmer, a person I have known for many years.

It takes the next two days to find a barge with time to pick up the cars and my truck from our beach. The barge company is busy helping stranded Marlborough Sounds residents and their guests, but I am lucky. As it turns out, they have space on one barge. It can fit the Jenson's and Amber's cars and my truck, to transport them to Picton without hassle. I say goodbye to my dogs, let my neighbour know I am leaving, and we are off to Picton. On the way across, I consider leaving Amber's and her parents' cars in the long-term car park near the Picton wharves, but then I ring Ian to help bring the Jenson's car to Blenheim. I know they need it to get around. I can take Amber's car to a local garage in Picton for a checkup. Once it is safely there, I intend to take the water taxi home to reassure the boys, then pick up my boat. It can wait in the marina for my return from Christchurch.

It would have been simpler to bring my boat across instead of staying with the cars on the barge, but my mind was a bit scrambled. I have a berth in the marina, so what is my problem? Julie and Jon need their car quickly. I feel bad about leaving my dogs by themselves, even with the careful ministrations of my neighbour. I know they will miss me, but they are in good hands.

Once the cars are at Michael's house, we can leave for Christchurch. That's Amber and me, I mean. I feel a little flutter as

I think of going away with Amber. I know I must play it cool, or all will be lost. But really, I am excited.

It has been five days since I last saw the Jensons. When I arrive at Mike's place, I note Jon has improved quite a bit. He still has a bump on his head, but the bandage is absent. His right arm moves more naturally, which I take as a sign his side is healing. Julie looks much less worried.

Jon stands to greet us when we enter the room, extending his right hand for a handshake. "We will return home in a couple of days. The quick healing has all been made possible because of your help. Mike's house is a godsend, a short trip to the hospital, physio, and shopping, and now you have brought our car. The taxi company will be annoyed. Think of all the business they will miss." His face crinkles into a smile.

I shake his hand and comment on how well he looks, "But this doesn't mean you have to leave the house," I say with emphasis.

Just then, Mike pokes his head around the door. "You can say that again. I came home to a spotless house and dinner ready in the oven. I don't want to lose their help too quickly. I have been trying to persuade them to stay for at least a month."

Jon's grin broadens. "He is very persuasive, but the last thing we want is to be a burden."

Mike is very quick on his feet when it comes to making a point. "You see what I have to put up with," Mike's eyes glow with glee. "It is me who should be thanking them."

We all laugh. Of course, Mike wouldn't need so much help if he found a girl to love, or so my mother thinks. Actually, he is a good cook, and cleaning is endemic to army life. I feel my insides flip while thoughts of Amber flit through my mind. I shake myself back to reality and return to the job at hand.

I turn to Jon and Julie, "I hope you don't mind us bringing our car here. There is plenty of space for yours. We will collect Amber's car when we return from Christchurch. We need you for more than cooking dinner for Mike when he comes home. You will also be guards for our cars once we collect Amber's."

I almost say for Amber and then stopped myself because a guard might be essential for her, and I know how she would react to the thought. The police say Malcolm is in Christchurch, but how do we know? Is she safe from him in Blenheim?

Amber's parents look stricken before understanding I wasn't thinking of Amber, only her car. I continue trying to cover up my *faux pas*, "Amber, is Monday still okay to go south, or perhaps we could leave tomorrow? Farm work is up-to-date; no worries."

It is more than a week since Malcolm hurt Amber and her father, but Amber is shaken by the idea of going to Christchurch. "I suppose we must do it. The earlier, the better, from my perspective. Maybe tomorrow is a good idea. That way, we can sleep on Sunday night and visit my apartment late in the morning when Malcolm should be at work. I will organise a motel."

I raise one eyebrow and grin down at her. "Don't worry about the motel. We have rellies there."

Amber puts her hand up in a stop sign. "No, I won't have that. I need independence. There is no telling what state I will be in once I have removed my things from the apartment. We must stop at a supermarket to pick up boxes because I need something for my clothes, photos, books and other odds and ends."

I want to lighten the moment. "Books!" I exclaim while my heart flutters at the thought of Amber and me in a motel together. "Are there many? Books are heavy. We may need help."

Amber laughs. "I saw plenty of books at your house. I only have a few I wish to take, archaeology texts and the like. I don't think Malcolm needs them. I have some papers, but they will fit into one medium-sized box. The clothes, well, goodness knows. I will take what I really love. I don't want things that remind me of Malcolm."

It looks to me that she has planned this and is quite comfortable with her list. "Whatever you say. Tomorrow it is, then. I am staying with Ian tonight and will be around nine sharpish. We don't know what the road conditions are like. I believe there is at least one stop light that takes its time to turn green."

I think of my dogs. Fortunately, I didn't tell them I would be back soon, not that they would understand. I shake my head slightly as I think of them. Then I brighten because I know they will be okay.

Chapter 32

Sunday dawns a beautiful clear day after all the rain and wind. It is calm and an excellent day to travel. Amber is ready and waiting for my arrival. Apart from the farewells, the only discussion revolves around my truck. Amber thinks we should take her car even though it is still at the mechanics. She does not relent until I point out the obvious; my truck has more room for her things. I smile, then break into a broad grin when I see her parents' faces. They are enjoying the domestic between Amber and me, and I realise we must look like an old married couple. I smile and hold the door open for Amber.

Amber's face opens up in delight. "Thank you. How thoughtful." Amber sounds as if she means it.

I hop in behind the wheel and try not to show my embarrassment. "Perhaps you can drive some of the way," I say playfully. I know she won't want to drive because my truck is not automatic. It has a gear lever. The gear lever is one of the reasons I like it. It is possible to set the gears for hills or plains to help the gearbox. We will see plenty of hills today.

We drive without incident to Kaikoura, stopping at Kekerengu just before the township for a cup of coffee. The restaurant is set on a beautiful spot on a hill overlooking the Pacific Ocean, popular with tourists. "When was the last time you stopped here?" I ask for no real reason.

Amber looks melancholy. Her face becomes drawn and worried. "On the way up. Perhaps we should drive to Kaikoura and stop at one of the cafés on the seafront. I won't have to think of Malcolm at one of the trendy places there."

I am halfway out of the truck while she speaks. I hop right back in and put it in gear. "Sorry, we don't need to remember Malcolm, well, not until we reach Christchurch," I say, feeling guilty because I forgot she only recently came up this road. It also reminds me how tender she is. She doesn't need any complications just at the moment. I must curb my desires until I can see she wants me. And yet, part of me is saying that she cannot rid herself of her negative feelings about Malcolm unless I show her how I feel.

The turn off for the centre of Kaikoura township comes up on our left, but Amber decides she isn't hungry. It is only a couple of hours ago from breakfast. We make a U-turn to stop for coffee at a café just prior to the turn off. It has seats outside to relax and watch the traffic.

After Kaikoura, the going isn't so pleasant. There are roadworks with plenty of men and trucks struggling to clear landslips. We have to wait for ages at one such location. It has a stoplight that doesn't seem to want to change, the one I heard travellers discussing, but the outlook is worth the wait. The seals are playing on the rocks, even at this time of year when they are free and easy. Their young are still to be born, not that they look after them so much once weaned.

Despite the delays, the scenery is spectacular. The Kaikoura mountains rise almost straight out of the sea. Well, there is enough room for some houses, the main road and even farms here and there. The peaks wear snow dresses almost down to the sea. With the mountains behind us, the blue of the Pacific enhances everything. The sea disappears at Oaru because from there, the journey winds through the Hunderlees until Highway One turns into the Parnassus Road. It is still the same road, just not so windy. The amount of work put in after the earthquakes is exceptional, and now so much has to be redone, but not at the same level as the earthquake repairs. It must be irritating for the road workers. It took one storm to knock out much of their hard work. We can sneak past all the construction on one-way stretches of road until we enter the mountainous road with its many twists and turns, that leads to Cheviot. The only stop we make before breaking for coffee is to explore a historic bridge. It was one-way in its day and is made from wood. Dad remembers travelling over it. The train travelled on top and cars below, so he used to joke about being run over by a train.

Amber surveys the scene and doesn't look impressed. "It looks so rickety. I suppose it was sturdier in the old days," Amber notes.

I feel a giggle rising from the pit of my stomach and I can't stop myself from embellishing the story. "I'm not sure about that," I retort. "My father said it was like being in a train, going clickety-clack when the car tyres hit each bump. And the river is so far below."

Amber nods, but she is entranced, and I mourn the old New Zealand, the days when most roads had one-way bridges and hardly any were tar-sealed. If we had left it alone, the damage might not have been so bad during the storm. Water seeps through the shingle and doesn't undermine the road.

We drive on in companionable silence until Amber suddenly pipes up.

Her voice is animated like the old Amber's voice. "Why don't we go via Hamner and stop to have a dip in the hot pools?"

I can't help from teasing her, but I am relieved to hear the lightness return to her voice. "Hot pools," I say as if I haven't heard of them. "I don't have my togs."

She is not to be deterred by any minor objection. "I do," Amber spouts. "And you can buy a pair of trunks in the shop there. It would be great, and it will take my mind off Malcolm. We never did anything so crazy."

Once again, Amber pulls me up. I keep forgetting this trip must remind her of travelling up. It wouldn't be that far out of our way, and I love the idea of getting her mind off Malcolm. Anything that does that is worthwhile.

Chapter 33

I feel strangely contented sitting beside Danny on this trip until we arrive at Kekerengu. It is great to see the wooden railway car bridge and to laugh at Danny's joke about his father, but memories of Malcolm flood back strongly. I feel I am in that bedroom again, not knowing what to do. I don't want to talk about it to Danny. He is being so kind, and I know he feels horrible for bringing up Kekerengu, but how is he to know that is where we stopped? Usually, I stop at Kaikoura. Tourists tend to stop at Kekerengu. Malcolm and I stopped there because I thought he would like it. It is modern and offers the types of food he likes. He believes anything in the provinces would be all pies and beer!

I am pleased Kaikoura is behind us, and we are on our way to Hamner Springs, where the hot pools live. I make myself look around. I haven't travelled to the hot springs this way. It is quite beautiful, with mountains, a small river, and valleys so green it would put the Emerald Isles to shame. I bet it isn't anything like this in the summer.

My mind is still whirling, but I am sure it is calming down with every kilometre we travel towards Hamner and the hot springs. "Do you think the dry seasons in Marlborough extend this far,

Danny? It is such a vibrant shade of green. I love it." I am really thinking of Danny, but I must make myself think of something else.

Danny has a wry grin on his face, as he turns to look at me, "I must say I like the view too." There is no mistaking which view he is talking about. I feel my cheeks redden as a warm feeling seeps throughout my body. I don't know what to say.

I feel my lips begin to pout. "Maybe the pools are closed," I want to change the subject. I suppose I deserved this comment because I started it. But Danny couldn't know what I was thinking. He isn't in my head like we were when we were children. Then, we always knew what the other was thinking, well almost. I remember being surprised that he had a fear of heights. He always seemed willing to climb wherever I wanted to go. I didn't give it a thought, expecting him to follow. I was thoughtless even then. No wonder I brought Malcolm home. I just expected he would love it because I do.

If I focus on our childhood, my mind stays off that ogre, Malcolm. However, the minute I stop, he is there like an ugly spectre on the edge of the light. I give a start as I realise I was thinking of Malcolm as ugly. That has been impossible for me to do because he is such an imposing presence. The development of this concept must be a step forward.

My revelation must be written on my face because Danny asks? "What's the matter, Amber? Did you have a shock?" Danny is looking at me, his big brown eyes looking concerned. He is driving casually with one arm on the steering wheel and the other resting on the edge of the door. What a picture. I want to curl up in his lap.

I shake my head in an attempt to keep my thoughts to myself. "Nothing. It was just an unpleasant memory, as if a ghost glided past. I survived the thought, no problems."

He didn't look mollified. "You know you can tell me anything, just like when we were kids. I don't seem to read you as well as I did. I suppose it is known as growing up."

A small snort escapes my mouth. "Funny you should say that. I was just thinking the same thing. Perhaps it will return. It was certainly reassuring to know someone understood even my wildest actions."

I scrunch back into the seat and look at the scene floating past my eyes. A few birds seem to think it is the right time of day to have a flight, soaring high up and diving down. I suppose they were shopping. It is definitely past our lunchtime. We didn't stop for a meal in Kaikoura, but we had a coffee. It was all I needed. A thought flits by. I wonder if Danny is agreeing with me to make me feel better. Maybe he needed a meal. I shake that thought out of my head; surely he would have said. A swim at Hamner Springs is much more inviting than a visit to Kaikoura. It is just what I need to clear my head.

I feel myself drifting off. I haven't slept much these last few nights. It feels good to let myself go. The warmth inside the truck, the sun shining outside, and the natural surroundings create a calming atmosphere. A sensation I haven't felt for what seems like ages.

Chapter 34

The drive seems to relax Amber because she nods off to sleep beside me. A good thing we left early because this little diversion will put around an hour and a half onto our trip. I am not tired, and the joy of driving through the Waiau Plains north of Cheviot makes me happy. It reminds me of home without the water views. I don't think I could ever live without the water, no matter the beauty of a place. It feeds the soul in a way impossible from any other natural phenomenon.

I remember talking to a desert Arab about the sea. We went to the Arabian Gulf together on a bus. He had never seen the sea before and couldn't understand what I saw in it. He loved the beauty of the dunes deep in the desert and found them cleansing. I understood what he meant but could not replace the sea for the sand. A great Arabian philosopher considered towns sinful and the desert peaceful, where it was impossible to be untrue to oneself. I suspect that doesn't hold for all, but it's the same for me with the sea. It is easier to meditate with water in front of me, but it is not for everyone. I acknowledge both the sands and the seas, had plenty of pirates. So, not all is peaceful there. It must be a state of mind where thoughts can roam free. I hope the hot pools will have that kind of effect on Amber. I can see she is still very hurt by what Malcolm did, and her constant blaming of herself isn't helping.

As we reach a fork in the road I take the left fork. The roads are narrow up here, so I tend to oversteer and must pull quickly on the steering wheel to line the truck up with the road. I glance across at Amber and notice she hasn't stirred, not one little bit. She needs sleep. I must be more careful, then perhaps the pools can work their magic.

Nearly an hour later we pull into the pool's parking lot. It isn't very crowded, which pleases me. I notice Amber rousing with a broad smile.

She stretches her arms and flashes her eyes at me. "You made quick work of that," she says, unaware of the actual distance.

I return her smile. "It was easy driving, not too many bumps to upset the slumbering passengers."

I feel acutely gratified that she seems happy. Her sleep must have been dreamless or happy dreams. It is possibly the first time since events on the hill. I sneak a glance to check her out as I get out of the truck and stretch. My neck gives a thankful crack in response. I have been sitting in the same position for far too long. Amber is as fresh as a daisy and is dancing around, asking me to hurry up and get my things. She already has her togs out.

At the entrance, I ask if I could buy some togs, but I am told I should go to the village. I look at Amber, "You go ahead. I will follow in a bit."

She nods and skips off to the changing sheds. I want to lie down on the cool grass and relax. I am happy not to swim. I think the heat will be enervating, and I still have quite a bit of driving to do before we settle for the night.

Once I see Amber in the pool, I buy a ticket, enter and find a spot where I can watch her. The day is warm now, and I feel my eyelids drooping.

The next thing I know Amber is stamping her feet beside me, asking why I am not in togs.

I look blearily up, "Too much concentration driving, Amb. It's time for me to have a rest."

She acknowledges my condition and settles beside me in away that I find arousing. I have to look away to control my thoughts.

Amber is determined to enhance my discomfort. The Amber I knew has returned in full force. "Not as chipper as you once were?" she asked cheekily.

I flick her arm gently and say, "Perhaps it's your turn to drive from here."

She looks horrified. "I take your point. You know I am not very good at stick shifts. That is why I wanted to take my car, but, as you pointed out, in no uncertain terms, it is too small for my things. I would need more trips. The thought of that doesn't thrill me at all."

I hope to bring her brightness back to the surface, if I can. "It's okay," I say softly. "It won't take long once we are on the road. It is a good road from here on. I believe contractors have removed the poorly cambered corners, and is tar-sealed all the way. Not a problem that a rest and a coffee won't cure."

Amber nods and leaps up to have another float. She is in her happy place. I drop off into a restful sleep and wake with a start. I do not know what startles me. I should have known, because Amber is smiling beside me.

She has a mischievous grin and an urgency showing she will not brook opposition. "I had to wake you up. I don't want us driving in the dark. We have about an hour before the sun disappears below the hills up here. It's time to go."

I shake myself, stand up and stretch, all thoughts of a quiet coffee gone. The week's events are taking their toll. Goodness knows how Amber must feel.

"We must get some food to go, perhaps a pie?" Amber has a query on her face. She likes pies, and so do I. I don't have them often because they are about as good for you as a hamburger.

"I asked the lady over there where we can get the best pies and coffee-to-go." I point to the ticket office in the middle distance.

I perk up. I have been hanging out for a coffee, and a pie sounds just the ticket, a matched set. Without thinking, I grab her around the waist and swing her around. Amber laughs, a deep belly laugh. I know she loves the feeling. I put her down carefully and gather myself together. I force myself to think of the present to control my feelings.

It isn't easy to speak casually when my heart wants to hold her tight. "Let's go, madam. You seem to be organising the tour," I joke. And we leave. Amber takes off at a run, waking up my body quicker than I intended, but it feels good.

Loaded with pies, coffee and a candy bar, we climb up on the truck and set out for Christchurch. What a day!

Once on the home stretch, driving across the Canterbury Plains, we start thinking about the seriousness of tomorrow. "How do you want to tackle entering your apartment?" I want to know. I hadn't told Amber, but a friend offered to pick the lock if the lock is changed.

Amber shrugs her shoulders. "I haven't thought that far ahead. We still have to find some boxes, but that is about it. I am hoping it will be easy. The motel unit has two bedrooms and a kitchen, and all I am considering is a pizza for tea and to retire early. However, my mother put together enough food for an army, well, for breakfast food at least. I think there are a few apples thrown in. We should have had them when we went to the hot pools. All I could think about was a pie, I'm sorry. Mum expects us to go out for lunch and dinner. Do you like pizza?"

The last is an afterthought. Amber has made her decision. I smile and say, "I will enjoy sharing a pizza and watching television with you."

Amber grins, "My thoughts exactly." She has been so self-absorbed during the travel that she does not notice she has taken command. I don't mind at the moment, but I hope it doesn't last. I have my limits because I am all for give-and-take.

Once at the motel, we order pizza and Coca-Cola, just enough for us. We settle in for the evening with the food between us. Much as I want to cuddle up to Amber, I don't want to put her under any pressure. I know my father said I should show my intentions, but it has to be right for us both. It isn't easy sitting across from her and seeing her eyes light up as she enjoys something special on TV, but I manage it without making a pass. I let out a loud yawn. I need to leave the room, or I will take an action I will regret later.

I fake a yawn and say, "I'm off to bed, madam. It was a great day. I hope we continue to have such good weather," I say, deflecting from the elephants in the room, Amber tonight and action tomorrow.

Amber turns towards me, her eyes shining. "Have a good sleep. I can't remember when I enjoyed myself so much. Thank you for making me feel safe."

Her smile lights up her whole body. That look almost makes me break my promise to myself. I want to rush over and hold her tight, to protect her so that no more harm can happen to her.

Amber's words have a profound effect on me. "Thank you, too. Let's sleep restfully and worry about things in the morning."

I walk out of the room quickly before I can change my mind.

Chapter 35

It miffs me that Danny didn't make a play for me last night, but in the cool light of the morning, I know he is right. I would have succumbed, and then what? It would have felt wrong. He is worth much more than a quick session in the sack. If we are to have anything, it must be when the time is right and when there is no Malcolm.

We have a quick breakfast, compliments of Mum, and then head to the nearest supermarket.

To my frustration, Danny takes command. "I'll go to get the boxes. You stay here and watch the car."

A quizzical look flashes across my face as I think of the implications. "The car doesn't need watching. What are you talking about?"

Danny smiles. I am sure he knows he is infuriating me. "You look so sweet when you are angry. I should annoy you more often." He chortles to himself, and leaves while I quietly fume about being treated like a child.

Cooling down, I think Danny is worried about me.
He doesn't want me seen with him in case someone reports back to Malcolm. Christchurch is big, much bigger than Picton anyway, so

the chances of anyone recognizing us are slim, but then, with my luck, it would happen. I don't know why I am so bristly. Perhaps I need to go to that psychologist after all. There will be time enough for that when I return to Marlborough. Six weeks holiday is a luxury not to be squandered, but the odd session with a compatible psychologist might help. Mum and Dad and even Danny's parents think so. I focus on the world around me while Danny emerges from the supermarket, laden with two piles of boxes stacked inside each other. He looks like Father Christmas gone wrong. No presents.

He approaches, and I grin from ear to ear. "You could have used me, in the least, for another arm." I reach up to take one pile from him while he reaches the truck to put the other pile under the tarp on the tray. Then I hand him the other bundle for him to secure. I look at the number of boxes. "I hope I don't have that much rubbish, but I suppose I might."

Danny looks at me with a grin, "You are a woman. I assume you will have more, but these boxes are sufficient for now. I am concerned Malcolm may come home at lunchtime."

I frown and think. "Malcolm has never done that before, but who knows!" I throw my hands in the air in frustration. I do not know this man, Malcolm, anymore. Probably, I never did.

"Hop in. We can't stand around here all day. No point in analysing him," Danny says this last bit to hurry me along. He knows me so well. I am dragging my feet. I don't want to do this, not today, not anytime. I climb reluctantly into the passenger's seat, musing that the step has grown. Maybe I am shrinking, like Alice in Wonderland. The closer I am to our apartment, the smaller I feel.

Danny drives sedately along the streets until we reach our apartment tower. It is set in a leafy green suburb, very special even for Christchurch. Christchurch is called the Garden City, and it is that, for sure, but this area is more so. The Avon River flows nearby, and Hagley Park stretches out in long green swathes towards the central city. It only takes about a twenty-minute walk to reach downtown. This distance is handy when contemplating having a glass of wine at dinner. The scenes from the apartment windows are spectacular. There are the river and park, with the Port Hills in the background, and further to the west, there is a glimpse of the Southern Alps. At this time of year, they are white dressed with snow, but they have many faces, from dry yellow to green, then onto winter white and all shades in between.

I look for my key, hoping I can't find it and will have to return to the motel to search my bag, but no, it is here, shiny and new-looking. I remember how I felt the first time I saw it. It seemed like my life had taken a leap towards a bright new future. So much for that.

Danny picks up one pile of boxes. "I think we should leave the rest here, just in case this will be sufficient."

Something in his eye tells me he is thinking something else. "Don't worry, Malcolm must be well at work by this time," I say with an assurance I don't feel.

We take the lift, using the fob on my key ring to access our floor, and I sigh. The lift door sweeps open, revealing the pale green of the carpet at this level. I walk tentatively up to my door. I find I am holding my breath. I shake myself to make my legs stand firmly, then put the key in the lock.

I begin to turn the key, and two things happen. Danny drops the boxes because the door opens before I complete the turn. Malcolm must be inside, and I steel myself. I don't have time to consider what I will say because a hand flies out and grabs my right arm, pulling me inside and shutting the door before Danny can react.

I am inside, alone with Malcolm.

If I didn't know better, Malcolm is his most persuasive self although his arrogance shows through. Doesn't he remember what he did to me? How can he believe I will listen to him?

His face changes dramatically. "You thought you could sneak back home without seeing me. You should know me better than that. I have been waiting for days for you to turn up. I knew you would."

I stand and gape at him. I have nothing to say. Slowly, my voice hits my vocal cords. "I have come for my things. My lawyer is dealing with the apartment."

Malcolm's laugh is almost manic. "You think you can leave me that easily. I don't think so. I need you."

I try to compose what I am going to say, carefully. I don't want it to have unintended consequences. "What do you need me for, Malcolm?" I begin to gain confidence.

He needs no time to compose his thoughts. "I'll show you." He grabs me around the throat and forces me against the wall. I wish I hadn't asked. I should have known. He pushes harder, and my mind tells me to act, but what can I do? I am wearing sneakers. They won't hurt much. I wish I had put on heels because they are good weapons.

Malcolm holds me firmly while he drags me towards the bedroom. I notice a gun on the side table in the lounge. I try not to go near there, but he puts my head in a headlock.

He is watching the direction of my eyes. "Hah, you have noticed the gun. It is there to protect me against invaders." His laugh is almost satanic. The hairs on the back of my head rise. "I want to have you one last time, then the balcony is conveniently placed, not to play Romeo and Juliet, but for you to jump to freedom."

I feel sick. "You want to risk your life for me?" I say sweetly. "I didn't know you were that romantic." I hope that if I show no fear, it will disarm him because it did last time. However, this time it doesn't have the same effect. If anything, it inflames him further. His free arm begins to wave around the room in frustration at my stupidity.

His voice is ominous. "You can't fool me, Amber. You are trying to distract me." But his words side-track him, and his hold slips. I take my opportunity and dash towards the door. I might win the four-minute mile if I keep this up.

He catches me again, but I act. I have had enough. Forgetting my sneakers, I stamp my foot on his bare toes while I throw my elbow hard into the soft area of his stomach. He makes a soft offing sound and releases his hold. It is all I need to get away, but I still need to reach the door. I race for it, open it and find no Danny there. Without thinking, I move through the gap and shut the door, but Malcolm's left arm catches between the doorjamb and the door. I pull hard, not knowing what else to do. He is much stronger than me.

My strength begins to wane when I hear voices, one a sweet sound I know well. Danny is coming with help. I pull harder on the door. It must stay in place.

Danny is yelling but sounds pleased. "Thank goodness. You escaped. You can leave the door for now because we will take over. The police are coming."

I let my hand relax, and Malcolm emerges, firearm in his other hand. He is right-handed, so the gun is in the hand he needs the most. I shrink back, but Danny is too quick for Malcolm this time. He leaps at him and grabs the gun while using his left hand to hit

Malcolm in the face. His move isn't well timed because, just then, the police enter the scene.

A loud shout rings out. "Here, here. You stop that." A young uniform is on Danny quickly, cuffing him before I can say anything. I understand how it looks.

Malcolm's voice sounds reasonable although somewhat upset. "Yes, Officer. This man came into my home and assaulted me. Here, see my arm. It will be black and blue by morning. Come on, Amber. Come home. The officers can deal with this lout."

I gape at him. He is so quick to turn the situation inside-out.

I want to intervene in a situation spiralling out of control. "Officer. This man," I point at Malcolm, "Assaulted me. Danny is trying to protect me."

The older officer is calm and collected. "Madam, what I see is a domestic. We will take statements and then take this man to the station for booking. I saw the punch he threw."

The older officer looks at the scene more carefully. "We will do as you have said, Officer, but I want to take this man's statement here." He means Malcolm. "Are you going to return home, young lady?"

I am distressed. I don't know what to say to make them understand. "This is all wrong. I am going to the station with Danny. Look, Malcolm has a gun. He was going to use it."

Malcolm stands tall and acts his best charming self. "Only on home invaders, Amber." He smiles serenely.

The senior officer is quite firm. He is not about to be pushed around, especially by a man who has been wielding a gun. "We can't have that here, Sir. You don't sound like you come from New Zealand. Wherever you come from, you will learn that we don't take kindly to people waving guns." It is the older of the two speaking. I sense he is beginning to understand things differ from his first thoughts. "We will take you, Amber, is it? And this one down to the station for questioning. Then we will return for your statement, Sir."

Malcolm smiles broadly. He thinks he has got us. "I will be ready and waiting." He almost salutes as we retreat down the corridor to wait for the lift.

Chapter 36

Amber and I watch while Malcolm closes the door on us, and we turn towards the approaching officers. The senior officer, Officer Thompson, shouts at the younger man, "Don't touch. We must photograph the position of everything on the floor. What are those boxes doing there?"

I feel myself losing control of my temper. I must cool down. "That is what I am telling you, Officer. Amber and I are here to collect her things. The boxes are for that purpose." I sound frustrated despite trying to sound calm.

Thompson finally puts it together. "Sorry, we had it wrong. When we arrived, it looked like you were the aggressor, but you were trying to save this woman."

I nod enthusiastically. The cuffs hurt my wrists because they want to move to emphasise what I am thinking. I must stop the impulse. "Yes. If you ring in, you will find that Malcolm has prior charges against him for hurting Amber. She is leaving him, and her lawyer has already written to him. Malcolm doesn't want to lose financially, and so is trying to make her stay."

The young officer says, "A strange way to try. Violence never works. He looks old enough to know better. You say he is a lawyer?" The young man harumphs in disgust.

I agree whole heartedly. At last, the real situation is beginning to sink in to the young officer's thoughts. "Oddball. I can't figure him out. All I know is that he isn't a man I want to know."

Thompson looks thoughtful. "Okay. I must call this in. CIB will want to be here to go over the place. Let me find out what they have to say. In the meantime, you can uncuff this man, Officer. I don't think he is a danger to us." He looks sharply at the other officer.

The younger man does as he is told, begrudgingly. He must have wanted the credit for catching me. I am happy not to oblige him. Still, I am not out of the woods yet. I am well aware of the optics, and Malcolm is a quick thinker. There is no knowing what he will come up with given time. He might do a runner and start again somewhere far away, but then he would have to get himself relicensed as a lawyer. He will need money to live. No, it's not a possibility. He will try to come up with a scenario that suits the scene.

Meanwhile, Thompson is talking on the phone, and it sounds like he is getting a bollocking. Whoever it is on the other end doesn't like how he has handled the crime scene. In fairness, there are only two of them, and they have seen Malcolm, although not at his rabid best. He was all sweetness and light for them. How are they to tell? The phone person has the benefit of his arrest files.

Finally, Thompson closes his phone and turns to the young officer. "Okay. You are to stay here and protect the gun and the boxes. Move nothing. You will photograph them for us, but CIB will come and take their own evidence. They want the carpet near the door clear of disturbance for forensic testing. If the man in the apartment comes out, you are to ask him to return inside. He is to wait there for CIB. They will interview him and inspect the apartment. There may be other guns."

Amber looks shocked. Her hand flies to her mouth, her eyes big and round. "Malcolm will not have any more guns. I am surprised he has this one. I don't think he knows how to use a gun." Even now, she can't help defending the man. I feel annoyed but what do I know? She was in love with him.

Officer Thompson is the epitome of professionalism. "We can't speculate. We must have evidence. That man's record shows he is dangerous," the senior officer states with some relish. "We will return to the squad car, where you will both wait in the back until we have this sorted out."

Amber begins to speak. "I was just thinking, if Malcolm goes to the station for questioning, perhaps I can collect my belongings during his absence. It will be safe because we will know where he is, and then I never have to return here again," she adds looking hopeful.

The senior officer looks at Amber, and his eyes soften. "Such action will be CIB's call, not mine, but I will suggest it. It depends on how seriously they take this incident."

Amber jumps in quickly. Her eyes look very dark. "I do not want to prefer charges," Amber says with a steely look in her eye. "It was bad enough in Marlborough."

The officer points out the obvious. "I don't think it will be your call, Madam. He has a weapon and one that is difficult to have licensed here. He will be charged for attempting to use it and possibly for its origin. We will not know that until we examine the evidence."

Amber cringes. I put my arm around her without thinking. I hate her being so lost. She smiles up at me but with no warmth in her eyes. She looks scared. My heart sinks. What can I do? Both officers look on. Their faces are hard to read. I put my arm down. I don't want to add to the story. While I do this, I can't help my eyes drifting towards the gun. Even at this distance, it looks odd. I go to step towards it. At the same time, the young officer walks up and puts his hand on my shoulder. He has finally something he can do that he understands. "Stop, stop right there, sir! I don't want you approaching the gun."

I stop immediately. I don't say anything, but I can see the safety catch is still on.

The officer takes a closer look at the gun to grasp what I am seeing. "Sir, the safety catch hasn't been released."

Thompson looks across at where we are looking. "My eyesight isn't that good, but perhaps you are right. It will not change his possession of the gun or its origin, but the lethal nature may change somewhat. Weapons are not my area. CIB will make the decisions."

The young officer's shoulders drop. He looks disappointed. I suppose he couldn't hold me for anything, and now he knows the gun is different from what he thought. I feel relieved that I didn't pick up the gun. It would have added to my situation, but I did knock it out of Malcolm's hand. I hope my fingerprints aren't on it. Besides that, I need to be out of here because my feelings for Amber may lead me into trouble.

I am pleased the senior officer takes Amber and me down in the lift to the foyer, and we emerge outside into the bright sunlight of a clear blue sky. We enter the squad car. I don't mind sitting in the back seat with Amber, although her hand is like ice when I brush against it. I glance at her and raise an eyebrow.

Amber looks like she has shrunk to half her size as she sinks back into the seat. "It's okay, Danny. It is okay. I feel it will be all right," she says with a milky smile.

She reads my thoughts correctly, but I don't believe the answer. "It will be, but not right now. We still have a bit to go."

She looks uncomfortable. "I'm so sorry for bringing you and your family into this."

I look at her in disbelief. "Amber," I say, not a little annoyed. "It is not your fault. You are not responsible for Malcolm's actions. He is a spoilt child who hasn't grown up. He thinks everything should go his way." I tap her on the knee to emphasize that I am not angry at her, just the concept. I hope she gets my message.

The senior officer, Thompson, is now seated in the front passenger seat. "I have seen it many times, a nice lady fooled by a shyster." He gives her a penetrating look, then returns to face the front with a satisfied look, almost as if he has solved the problem.

Amber and I watch while a team from CIB police arrive at the building. It includes some armed defenders. "Don't look shocked, Ms Jenson. It is a precautionary measure in case other guns are on the premises. Better to be prepared."

By now, Thompson has our details and regards us with some affection but Amber is not so much shocked as embarrassed. "What will all the neighbours think? They are all very polite and kind. Now, I am involving them in this!" She emphasises the 'this' as if she has run out of words.

The officer takes command. "My partner will join us shortly, then we can go to the station to take your statements. If CIB agrees, you can return to pack your things, that is, if your old boyfriend is on remand with us for a while."

Amber looks both relieved and annoyed at the same time. I suspect the reference to Malcolm being her 'old boyfriend' upsets her. I can't help but smile. I tap her on the knee again, "It might make clearing out your belongings much easier."

Chapter 37

I am relieved to know that the police waste no time in picking Malcolm up to interview him and to consider more charges. There are no extra guns in the apartment other than the one he used against me. The new charges must relate to that gun and the other threatening things he tried. However, he has no good reason for possessing any guns. Watching from Danny's car, it gave me great pleasure to see the police take Malcolm into custody, once again. The initial two officers look pleased. Before leaving, they arrange for me to pick up my belongings. They believe they have caught their man.

Packing my belongings takes less time than I think it will. I refuse to take anything that will remind me of Malcolm. I need my pre-Malcolm photos, one or two ornaments, my beauty products and the like and about half of my clothing. It is an opportunity to buy new stuff.

I smile while we pack the last boxes onto the back of Danny's truck.

Danny begins to worry about the clothes Amber is leaving behind. "Do you think you should take the remainder of your clothes to St Vinny's or another Op shop? It is a shame to leave it all here."

I like Danny's suggestion, but the idea of returning to the apartment leaves me cold. "Perhaps we can ask the police if they want to give it away," I said, knowing they are too busy to worry about such things.

For once, I am delighted for Danny to take the lead. I am exhausted. He says, "I will talk with them. Perhaps we can send in someone to take the clothing away. It is good stuff, too good to be thrown in the rubbish."

I nod in approval at Danny's idea, so he walks across to the police to discuss the collection of the rest of my clothes. He arrives back to me looking very pleased with himself.

Danny looks chuffed. "They say that Malcolm will be out tomorrow. It is impossible to keep him until his trial. Luckily, St. Vinny's can come if I ring. The police will let them in. They know it is only the female clothing. It will all be gone by the time Malcolm arrives back."

I sigh with relief because the thought of Malcolm having my stuff makes me feel sick. My favourite dress was in shreds in the wardrobe, so what would he do to the remainder? Probably throw it in the trash.

All I want to do is to curl up and sleep, until I can't remember anything that has happened. "Time for us to return north," I say more happily than I feel.

I know I need two things to happen until I feel truly safe. I need the financial settlement for the apartment and for Malcolm to be convicted. I have a strange feeling he will love prison because he will set himself up to be the lawyer for all the inmates who need representation. He might even make money out of it. That thought is not so comforting.

Then I say, "Before we leave Christchurch, there is something I must do."

Danny raises an eyebrow.

A sudden thought makes me worry about my workmates. They have been supportive of my recent work and incurred extra tasks on my behalf without complaining. "I would like to take my workmates out to lunch or dinner to thank them for their support and to let them know that I prefer to stay home until the trial."

Daniel sounds relieved. "Great idea, Amb. Ring them to set it up."

It works out nicely. Most are free for lunch. It will be a late lunch but a good one. We choose a favourite restaurant, recently saved from earthquake damage. The old English atmosphere is comforting. The lunch was satisfying, but most of all I enjoyed talking with my friends and reassuring them I was okay.

And so, my stay in Christchurch ends on a friendly note, a note that makes me want to return if only to visit friends. It was a thought impossible to imagine earlier in the day.

Danny and I decide to stay one more night to leave early in the morning. Besides, we both had wine at lunch. Approaching the motel a warm feeling inside me seems to grow, but those feelings cause me to worry.

I don't know how to approach Danny with my worries. He has been so gentle and caring this whole trip. "Danny," I say.

"Hmm," he responds.

"I am vulnerable tonight. I hope you will protect me as a friend." I smile shyly at him. We both know it will be easy to slip into bed together, but if that is to happen, I want to be in control of myself.

Danny smiles, "Amber, you should know I would never take advantage of you. I can wait. Perhaps we should plan to go to Raro once all this is over."

I nod and slip my hand in his. I know it will be okay.

Chapter 38

Six months have gone by in a flash. A short holiday, then working from home and therapy sessions ensured the time moved fast. The worst event was Malcolm's trial. I was on the stand for what seemed like hours to me. His lawyer was horrible, intent on proving that I asked to be raped. I ask you, what planet does this man come from? Fortunately, my mother's photos were allowed into evidence, which, coupled with the later police photos, showed I had resisted.

His second violent attempt at our apartment had some bearing on the result. He had a gun, even if the safety catch was on, and he threatened to push me off the balcony. His perspective was that I was threatening to jump from the balcony. If there was no gun to threaten me, I am not sure what the outcome would have been. After all, only he and I were there, but the police had collected good evidence, and that stood.

They grilled my poor father. He had fully recovered from the slice from the carving knife but not yet from the concussion. His doctor said it might be another few months until he was better, yet he had to take the stand.

The weight of the evidence turned out to be against Malcolm, and his sentence ensured he would spend a long time in prison. His shout at the end of the trial made my blood curdle. "I know where you live. I will be back," he yelled with a wild look in his eye. Even the judge accepted this man was crazy. Luckily, he chose not to go for an insanity defence. He might have won and lived in luxury in some centre until a psychiatrist declared him sane.

I believe he will never be normal. There is something broken in his psyche. They say I will be informed when he is due out of prison.

I refused to attend the sentencing. I felt physically ill just thinking about Malcolm. That's why I went to therapy regularly. Fortunately, my work colleagues were very helpful, but I knew my absence meant extra work fell on their shoulders. I could only do so much from home, yet they agreed with the boss that I should work at home until I decide my future. I could live anywhere in New Zealand because of the financial settlement, which came through rather quickly. Perhaps Christchurch wasn't my place any more. Then there was Danny.

Danny's work fully occupied him. He became busy in the time leading up to the trial. I suspected he wanted to give me space, and our families seemed to understand. When the trial was over, his work slowed.

Tonight, he has accepted a dinner invitation from Mum, which has put my head in a spin. I feel like a teenager about to introduce my date to my parents. It is madness.

Mum clatters around the kitchen, not letting me in. "No, darling. This night is yours. Dad and I are here to help out, that's all."

Help out! Help out when I am not allowed to raise a finger. Mum has spring-cleaned the house, and Dad has gardened until a weed would be ashamed to show its face. One would think the King of England was coming to tea. For my part, I find it impossible to decide whether to dress for the occasion or to act casually, and dress in jeans and a tee shirt.

Mum raises her head so she can look straight at me. "No, darling. You must wear a dress. The green one you bought on your last trip to Wellington will do nicely. Sandals are better than sneakers. If this goes well, we will invite Danny's parents on Saturday."

The penny drops. They have been collaborating to entice us into a relationship. The funny thing is, if they had left it alone, we probably would have got together soon anyway. Of late, I have noticed Danny sitting on the seat at the point, our favourite place. He has also been walking the dogs on the beach below us, in full view of our house. I am sure he knows I am looking, and, in truth, I was planning to go for a walk there tonight. Not anymore. No point. Danny will be right here. My heart flutters at the thought.

Everything seems to slow down, as I wait for six o'clock, the appointed time. I dress and change my dress several times before the given hour. I find Mum is right. The green dress is perfect, not too dressy and yet not too casual.

Danny arrives right on time, carrying a box of chocolates. "I thought flowers were overkill. Your father has such a beautiful garden full of them at this time of year," he says, grinning from ear to ear.

I am embarrassed; thus, my eyes drop to the floor. I say, "Thank you," very quietly. My tongue feels twisted as I search for a better response. Should I shake Danny's hand, hug or kiss him? I settle for moving my feet nervously on the door mat, with my hands holding the chocolates.

Danny laughs and pulls me towards him in a big hug, crushing the chocolates between us. "I have been waiting a long time to hug you. I hope I am not offending you."

I still feel embarrassed but try to sound confident. "Oh, no, Danny. I was just contemplating doing the same thing. Let's go inside. My parents are excited about your visit.
Mum hasn't stopped cooking all day."

Danny's face opens into a smile that reaches his eyes. They gleam while he says, "I am hungry and sick of my cooking. I am looking forward to this."

The conversation is inane. We all skirt around the subject uppermost in our minds, Malcolm.

In the end, it is my father who breaks the ice. "Malcolm got what he deserved, but I hope he receives help. If only to stop him from bothering us again."

Danny looks sad. "He is a broken man, and I hear he hasn't taken to prison life very well. He has a long way to go, and with his behaviour, he will not get out early."

I breathe a sigh of relief. I thought Malcolm would have been smart enough to act perfectly; then, he would be out in no time. But it sounds like this thought is only a bad dream. "Thank goodness for that. He is not the person I want to see any time soon."

With that, the conversation warms up, and we discuss the future and the possibilities.

Danny looks at me with both eyebrows raised, ready to ask a question. "I hope we can take that trip to Rarotonga soon, maybe in February, after the school holidays when the tourist traffic dies down but the weather is still hot."

Glancing at Mum and Dad, I am pleased at the approving lights in their eyes. "I have been looking forward to such a trip since your family mentioned it. Perhaps we can visit Niue Island too. I have heard it is very romantic, not so many tourists."

Mum, Dad and Danny all look surprised. I suspect they thought I would take some persuading, but I have already decided Danny is the one for me. It has been just a matter of timing.

Mum looks across with moist eyes, "Do you remember, Amber, that your grandfather proposed to Grandma on Niue? It is a special place."

Danny wants to put in his two cents worth. "It is a special place to our family too. Our bloodline goes back through Niue. So, this is a good idea." Danny has a cheeky grin even though he knows I want events to move slowly, but I don't want to upset the mood either by saying something to upset anything, but I do anyway.

My frustration level is on the rise. "Mum, Dad, Danny has just accepted an invitation to a meal, and you are both acting like marriage brokers. We will make up our minds ourselves, thank you, the Niue factor aside."

My parents look suitably chastened, but I catch Danny grinning at them. He is part of their conspiracy. I try not to feel annoyed because I know I need a push. Otherwise, I will use Malcolm to excuse my inaction for the rest of my life.

I speak as directly as possible, hoping to have an impact. "Maybe we will go to Niue or not, but have no expectations of me returning from the islands with a ring on my finger. I might never want to get married."

I feel a cool draft flowing from around the room. It emanates from Mum, Dad and Danny. I have hit my mark rather too forcefully. I have managed to upset everyone.

Chapter 39

Being a lawyer, I know our worries won't stop at Malcolm's sentencing. I say nothing about my concern to my brother Dan or Amber because it is not the time to ruin their happiness. Amber needs time to put Malcolm behind her now that the trial is over. My concern arises from the thought of the conclusion of Malcolm's incarceration since he is violent and will return to wreak havoc. This aspect of Malcolm is a worry, but another darker scenario is evolving. The Christchurch police sent his DNA to London to discover if the Malcolm there is, indeed our Malcolm. If this proves to be correct, it opens a can of worms.

While I think of all these issues, my parents walk in.

Dad is as affable as ever. "*Kia ora, kia ora,*[19] *tama*[20]. You look like you have seen a ghost." My father greets me like a young boy. I have no idea why it bothers me so much. My childhood seems far in the past, but it shouldn't worry me. I had a happy childhood, and now I am happily married. I have nothing to prove.

---

[19] Kia ora – A casual greeting.
[20] Tama – boy.

Mum recognises my irritation. "Ignore him, George. He is just jealous because you still have your youth." My mother grins impishly at my father.

Dad is not the least bit upset. "Woman, why should I want my youth again with all its problems? Besides, we would not have all these lovely *mokopuna*, my grandchildren."

They laugh together while Mum says, "They are mine too. Remember, I did the hard work producing their fathers."

To hear them tease each other warms my heart. They have acted this way all their lives together. I hope my marriage will last as long.

Both of them can read me like a book, despite my years learning how to hide my feelings in a courtroom. However, only my father comments. "Why are you so down, son? You look like you are trying to solve all the world's problems."

My father hits the matter on the head.

I explain the issue, otherwise I will have no peace. "I am troubled about the Malcolm problem. If he is the Malcolm the London police are trying to find, they might extradite him."

My explanation only confuses the situation further. "Well, surely this is a good thing. It takes him far away from here," my dad says with raised eyebrows.

I try not to look worried. "The problem is it might cut Malcolm's sentence here short, and then when he reaches England, the police there may not have enough to put him in prison for anything. The suspicion is that he killed his wife, but it has all the features of an accident. They need much more than DNA to convince any court of murder. The dead wife's family are pushing hard for the reopening of the case. They have some notion that something was wrong with the car. Because, at the time, nothing refuted the concept of an accident, they only checked the car for obvious issues. I believe the bolts and nuts on the steering linkage were loose. The assumption was that the damage occurred during the accident, but steering linkage nuts and bolts are locking nuts and cannot loosen themselves. The driver's seat had some issues too, and there were probably other unseen problems, but I am sure the car has been destroyed. Therefore, it is impossible to check. Hopefully, there are photos and reports, but it is still a risk. I wish they had sent the DNA to London before the trial. At that time, I could have argued for no extradition until he completed his sentence."

George's father rocks on his feet and puts his hands on his hips, thinking out loud. "This is why you are worried. If extradited, after completing his sentence, he might not bother returning here, but now……"

Dad needs no further explanation. "Yes, that is the issue. Malcolm will come straight back. Of course, we can request he serve his sentence before extradition, but we are not in a strong position. But there is another issue. If the evidence in the UK is not strong, he may not be convicted there, so will be free to return here." I frown and peer at the ground in front of me.

Mother gives me a nudge. "What are you planning? I see a plan running all over your face."

I wonder about my countenance. "Is it that obvious? I thought the years in courtrooms have taught me much about hiding facial expressions."

Mum laughs. "George, I am your mother. You hide anything from me at your peril."

I nod and feel a slight grin slip through. "I am thinking of returning to Christchurch to chat with the police and try to head them off at the pass. Better to be prepared than to let it eat away at me."

Both my parents look pleased and resigned at the same time. "When will you go?" they say almost in unison.

I have made my decision, no point in belabouring the issue. "I intend to leave when I have discussed it with my wife and cleared my desk here."

My father puts his arm around my shoulder. "Better to get it done. We can hold down anything that turns up here."

I laugh thinking, except for the work overload that will happen.

Chapter 40

Since the magical night I experienced at Amber's home, Amber and I have been almost inseparable. I feel like I have returned to the peace of my childhood. The difference is that now we are more of a team. Amber is thoughtful and willing to make joint decisions, although thankfully, the old impetuous Amber is still there. The difference is she is more mature in her responses to situations. Of course, this naturally happens as we grow older, I suspect.

She has a busy work schedule. Her boss in Christchurch seems intent on ensuring she knows she is welcome to return when ready, and he sends a slew of work for her to research online. The Internet connection out here in the outer Sounds is spotty at best, and Amber has taken to speeding across to Picton in my boat to visit the library. It only takes about twenty minutes with the boat ride and walk to the library. Their WIFI service is much better, so it is worth the effort. Of course, this trip is dependent on the weather. We are investigating Starlink, Elon Musk's system that is all the rage in Australia. The trouble is, neither of us like political connotations related to this system, but, once set up, the operating cost is hardly different from any other system available. It would mean Amber could stay at home. Maybe there is another Starlink system that will work.

No, Amber isn't staying permanently at my farm, but she is here so much she might as well live here. Her parents' house is only a short walk down the path to the beach and about fifty steps to a gently sloping hill. Their house is snug against a slight rise, sheltered behind from the winds by a belt of Pohutukawa trees. They and my parents are happy about us getting together, but Amber is still determined to take things slowly, and I respect this. It warms my heart to see how happy she looks.

Today, we are taking a day off to dive on the *Mikhael Lermontov*. This magnificent liner sank near a rocky coastline where it should never have been. When the ship was way out at Port Jackson, the Harbour Master decided it would be interesting to see if this beautiful cruise liner could fit through the shallow channel. There has never been any acceptable explanation for this choice, and both the Harbour Master and the Russian captain received bad press, but the Russians blamed the Harbour Master. He accepted this because his job was to keep the ship safe in the Marlborough Sounds. What a waste of an excellent vessel. Anyway, it makes a great diving site for adventurous divers.

Both Amber and I are qualified divers. Amber doesn't have as much experience as I do because my mussel farm means diving is essential. We decide we will dive only to twelve metres today. From there, we can play with the blue cod and all the other friendly fish that love to inhabit the wreck. To go any further, we would have to consider Nitrox, and I think Amber is still too tender for a technical dive. The currents can be sufficiently challenging without entering the shipwreck.

Fortunately, the weather plays ball. It is a beautiful, calm day. My brother Mike is in town, and I give him a ring to see if he will come. We need someone on the boat while Amber and I dive.

Mike sounds happy to be asked. "Sure thing, bro. No problem. I will be there within the hour." I smile because I know he will come as fast as possible.

Amber is smiling as well. "How wonderful to share this beautiful day with you and Mike. I hope he doesn't mind being topside while we have all the fun."

It pleases me that Amber thinks of Mike. I know he won't be worried. He'll dive if he feels like it. "He can dive after us. You might like two dives. We will see what he wants to do."

We are sitting outside having coffee on our favourite log. I can see Amber's mum putting out the wash. It is a good day for housework, but it seems a waste.

In no time, Mike arrives, full of bluster and carrying ham and cheese croissants from Seabreeze Café for us to have after the dive. Amber has already packed a lunch, but I must admit, the croissants look great.

His face is covered in a smile as he glances at the water. "Let's hope the Strait will be as calm as this."

Amber points to the unusually calm waters of the sound which surrounds my boat as we make our way to the sea. We all know weather in the Cook Strait is unpredictable, and anything can happen without a moment's notice.

I say, more to reassure Amber than for any other reason, "I checked the weather out, and all looks good."

The three of us laugh because we understand the limits of our weather reports, especially in this region.

We reach the dive spot in good time and hastily put on our gear while Mike watches. "I am happy to sit here in the sun today. It has been a busy couple of weeks at work. I need the rest. I might potter around this area. It is hopeless to drop an anchor because of the sandy bottom."

Amber and I nod as we sit on the rail, ready to backflip into the water. Once in the water, I check that Amber is okay. She failed to hold her mask tightly as she dropped into the water. I can see she has no problem clearing it. I didn't have to worry. She signals all is okay as she turns to fin down towards the shadowy sight beneath us.

I can almost feel Amber laughing as a cheeky blue cod comes up to investigate her. She reaches out to touch it, but it darts away. The cod is followed by a school of mackerel chasing or being chased by something. Then, an assortment of bright coloured fish dance around, some coming out of the gloom. All too soon, I signal Amber it is time to go up. She nods and fins effortlessly slowly up. She arrives, giggling as Mike helps her aboard, taking her fins and mask.

Amber is bubbling up with enthusiasm. "What a sight. I love those cheeky cod. Those smart fish have no fear. I am glad we didn't enter the ship. I have no desire to see dead dolls lost in one cabin and all that other stuff people want to gawk at. That's not for me. I love the sea life." She claps her hands with the joy of it. Both Mike and I look on, enjoying her delight.

Amber goes straight to the chilly bin to set out our food for lunch while I pick up a water bottle and take a long drink. She smiles, "I will have some of that too."

I hand it to her, saying, "There are more bottles in the bin over there, but no problems. Have all you need."

Mike's eyes are checking us out. He looks pleased. "You know, we can find a calmer spot. Just back around the point is a lovely bay where we can anchor and really enjoy the food at our leisure."

Amber looks chagrined. "I am just so hungry after diving and being out in the fresh air. I didn't give a thought to a better location. I can wait."

She sits down as Mike puts the boat in gear and races off around the point into the safer waters of Queen Charlotte Sound.

In all, it has been a perfect day. Much later, we arrive home happy and ready for the rest of our lives.

Chapter 41

The soft tropical warmth wafts quietly around us while Danny and I walk from the airport to our rental car. Hanan International Airport on Niue Island is like a step back in time, but with a friendly atmosphere. The sights and sounds are welcoming, and the air is not too hot. In Fiji some years ago, I remember walking under trees, thanking them for their moisture and shade. Such actions are unnecessary today, but the frangipani trees smell just as sweet, and the palms sway gently.

My body regenerates by simply being here. Marlborough Sounds are beautiful, but there is something special in the tropical balminess of Niue. All the locals smile whenever I catch their eyes, and even tourists seem to take a break to grin at us. Our car turns out to be an air-conditioned compact. Danny thinks there is no point in a large vehicle on an island so small. True, it is much bigger than Rarotonga, but it is still only sixty-four kilometres to travel around the whole island.

Now I must explain. We booked to go to Raro for a few days, and then a cyclone threatened to arrive, so we decided to wait until the season presented itself more reasonably. Then, we discovered it was impossible to fly from Raro to Niue. Well, we could, but it would mean returning to Auckland and starting again. We decided to make this holiday a Niue Island one only. So here we are. There is much to do here; two weeks will hardly do it justice.

Danny wants to hurry me up. He can see I am overawed by the beauty of the place. "Hop in Amb. Mooning around looking at nothing will not get us to the Matavai Resort. You never know; we could get lost between here and there."

I laugh at Danny's impatience. For once, we have time, no need to rush. "I am still getting used to the idea that it is yesterday. The idea of an extra Monday irks me, but my hunger pushes that odd idea to the back of my mind. Danny, I need to go to the restaurant for lunch."

Danny is on his best behaviour. "Me too. So, hop in." Danny laughs as he holds the door open for me. "Don't expect first-class treatment every time." His mischievous side is showing, and I love it.

The resort is just a short drive from the airport, but long enough for me to stare at the beautiful green vistas, the colourful locals, and to wonder about the local market.

Without much thought, I spout out, "We must go to a market, maybe this afternoon." I look hopefully at Danny.

Danny looks circumspect. "I thought we might want to lie by the pool while we plan where we want to go for dinner. We should go to the market in the morning. The goods will be fresh, so it might be the best time to visit, but perhaps we should ask at the resort."

I hadn't considered the best time to visit the market, only going there. I suppose Danny is right. My thoughts slip back to Malcolm. Am I letting Danny control what I want to do, or is it the sensible thing to do?

I am still desperate not to be controlled. One would think I should have put that away by now, but no, Malcolm's behaviour still buts into my thoughts. "I agree we should ask at the reception. If the morning is best, we should swim and enjoy the sun while adjusting to the idea of two Mondays."

This comment makes Danny laugh, but a flash of worry passes across his face. "I will never control you, Amber. You must not worry. I know you are an independent being, and that is one of the things I love about you," he says.

I can feel a lump rising in my throat. "Thank you," I speak softly because emotion catches the sound in my throat. "It is not you I'm worried about. It is me. I don't want to give up myself again. Can you help me maintain my equilibrium?"

Dan looks at me almost as if I am a recalcitrant child. I know I am being hard on him. I must listen to what he has to say before I judge him. "I don't want to do that because it could lead to control. When you were a child, you were always free with your opinions. You have regained most of your old self during the past few months. Don't change that by using me. I want you to be you, that is the thoughtful, caring person who usually thinks of everyone else before herself. I will aim to make you remember to think about yourself. I can do that all right."

We arrive at the resort as Danny says this. I nod but cannot add anything. We are here to enjoy ourselves and not to rehash past events.

The receptionist is helpful and points out the many brochures about places of interest.

She smiles politely at us. "There are brochures in your room. You can read those at your leisure. I can recommend swimming with dolphins, or if you are more adventurous, you can swim with humpbacked whales. Most tourists enjoy either trip."

Danny surprises both of us by saying, "Oh, we are not exactly tourists," Danny interjects. "My ancestors came from here a long time ago."

The receptionist looks at Danny carefully. "Then you might enjoy a trip to the museum. You will learn about your past and, you never know, you may have relatives living here still."

Danny responds, "We must plan our days to do all we hope to do. There is so much to discover and many activities that interest us, but we will put the museum at the top of our agenda."

Danny fits comfortably into this environment. It is almost like he is returning home.

We hustle to our room, a studio with a magnificent ocean vista, and unpack our luggage.

I can feel my stomach rumbling. "Let's go and have lunch before it's too late," I say, while my side of the room is still in a mess.

"Oh, you know how to put things away, I see." Danny laughs at me.

I am surprised. "I didn't have to go to the military to learn to be tidy. I can do it nicely, but it is such a waste of this beautiful day."

While I say this, I hang up some of my things and shove some in a drawer. "That will do," I say with emphasis.

I must address this challenge. "It's a good thing I am not a neatnik. Come on, let's eat."

Danny is amused at my attitude while we leave the room.

"I didn't even go out on the balcony," I say, a bit miffed at being moved on so soon, yet it was my idea to go to lunch. I am learning to deal with my emotions, but I still have a ways to go. I sigh and trudge behind Danny, marching like he knows the way. Despite my negative thoughts, it feels good to share this experience with someone who is so self-assured and yet thoughtful. I believe my confidence increases with each step.

Chapter 42

"Have a good trip, George."

Mum's words ring in my ear as I arrive in Christchurch armed with an appointment with the detective in charge of Malcolm's case. I know some detectives here, but this one is new to me. He is a Sullivan, which makes me wonder if he comes from down south, Temuka, or some such place, not that I know any Sullivans from there. I feel naked, not knowing anything about the man I need on my side.

The drive down is a dream. It takes just over four hours, even though I stop for coffee at a café in Seddon. I give them my business because they are still recovering from the 2016 earthquake. It hit the small towns hard. A couple of towns have almost disappeared. For me, the good thing is no road works to hold me up. Some parts of the road are still under repair, but I arrive while a woman in a Hi-Viz safety jacket waves the car line through.

I drive straight to the central police station and find it with only minor difficulty. Christchurch has changed since its earthquakes. There are one-way streets and other roads that should go through but don't. One road, Worcester Street, has at least three sections

- impossible to drive down it in one go. The original design of Christchurch placed the Anglican Cathedral in the centre of a square and then eight roads radiating out, forming the Union Jack with four avenues edging the flag. Extremely patriotic if you are English, but not so much for me. But I miss the simplicity of the city with the Port Hills popping up to help give direction to an otherwise flat city with only two rivers meandering through to upset ease of direction; so much for the garden city.

On arrival, without ceremony I walk to the reception and say, "Good afternoon, I have an appointment tomorrow for Detective Sullivan. Perhaps it is possible to visit him today."

The uniformed woman behind the counter looks something up on her computer. "George, is it? The lawyer from Blenheim?"

I am careful to be polite. It would suit me to see this man today. "That's me. I have just driven down and arrived earlier than I expected."

She responds positively to my attitude. "Let me see what I can do. Take a seat over there while I check."

I behave myself and take a book out of my rucksack, expecting to wait some time, but almost immediately she calls me back. I stand as I struggle to get the book back in my bag.

Her smile gives me the idea I won't have a long wait, even if I misjudged the immediacy of her request. "He will see you in five minutes and will come to get you."

I nod and return to my seat to begin reading.

Shortly, a burly man with a smiley face and deep blue eyes emerges from a secure area. He is in plain clothes but could have been in uniform, his stance and shoes, shout police. He extends his arm, ready to shake my hand when I rise to greet him.

He seems anxious to leave the office. "There is a café nearby. It makes sense to go there. I believe you have just made the trek from Blenheim to here. Food must be in order. It certainly is for me. I need a break. How was the road?"

I shake his hand, and his grip makes me want to curl my arm. I am glad I had to shear sheep recently for Dan. Otherwise, I might have shown my discomfort. I agree that a café is good.

We walk briskly along the road, talking about nothing of consequence until we are seated at a bright new café with lattés and mochaccinos. We have these in Blenheim, but not with such fancy food. Perhaps it is the display, shiny with aluminium and glass.

I shake myself to tune into Detective Sullivan. He wants to know why I am worried about the extradition. I explain my point of view.

Sullivan frowns. "I see," he says with a grunt. "He is a lawyer and knows how to manipulate. He was depressed at first but now!" He throws up his arms and shakes his hands in frustration. "Do you know Malcolm has already set up an office in the prison to advise prisoners of their rights? This concept is good, but how he does it makes the prisoners agitated. They become difficult to control and demand their rights loudly. The guards want him out quickly to prevent further harm, and this extradition plays into their hands."

I frown and say, "Tell them from me that if it happens, he will be back here before we can flick our fingers. If all the police have is DNA on a car that he must have driven many times and some issues with brakes and steering linkage, he will have that conviction quashed in no time. I don't want him back here hurting Amber Jenson. Given a second chance, he might do more permanent damage, if you get my meaning. Extradition at the end of his sentence would be ideal."

Sullivan squints and looks at me with a penetrating eye. "There might be a part of the evidence you haven't heard. It is being kept quiet. This evidence places him in the car scene before the accident. We have it on the best authority Malcolm will be convicted. Straightening up I take a deep breath. "Nothing short of fingerprints on the engine near faulty parts would do, but even then, Malcolm could have explored the engine to input oil or water. He can beat that, especially if Malcolm declares he knows nothing about cars and how they work. I believe he has already stated his incompetency regarding engines."

Sullivan relaxes and smiles. "It is better than that. The London police have a witness."

This news surprises me. "A witness to his wife's fatal accident? I already know a man saw it when he was out walking. That observation does not implicate Malcolm, but you haven't told me the most critical point. Does Malcolm's DNA match the London suspect's DNA?"

Sullivan smiles broadly now. "It is Malcolm's DNA. No doubt about it, and the witness is not the man who was out for a walk. You must keep the following information to yourself because we want him extradited. We especially do not want Malcolm to know this new information to give him time to plan his defence. We understand how tricky he is."

I assure Sullivan I will keep any information to myself, but only if it is in my client's best interest.

Sullivan doesn't seem deterred by my comment. I think he is keen to make his point. "I think you will find that it is. The witness is his mechanic. He showed Malcolm how to input brake fluid into his wife's car and even discussed the requirement to always use the manufacturer's brake fluid because of the danger of sediment, which, over time, can lead to the malfunctioning of brakes. He even discussed the steering linkage. He thought nothing of it at the time. Malcolm wanted to know about engines, especially the steering linkage, thus deflecting his interest in the brakes. The mechanic even told Malcolm about the locking nuts on the car wheels. He assumed Malcolm was interested in safety. One of the findings after the accident was that the brakes froze because of sludge and sediment in the fluid. He must have put in a variety of fluids from time to time, and this caused the fluid to solidify at the bottom of the sump. The brakes failed, and the accident became fatal when the car hit a tree. Thus, Malcolm had the opportunity, knowledge, and a motive. He made a great deal from his wife's death. He insured her life when they were first married. The sooner he is gone, the better from our perspective."

A shiver runs down my spine. Fancy planning to kill your wife right from the day of marriage? Amber is lucky. But insurance is something we must check. Malcolm may have an insurance policy on Amber, and I must have her car checked out for brake fluid issues. Why didn't I consider insurance, or the car's safety, for that matter?

Doubtful I have made any headway in having him retained here, I leave the police station. It is clear to me the system wants to get rid of Malcolm. He causes too many problems. Extradition is an easy out. Indeed, I am not sure I want him around any longer than he must be, but I am unconvinced for a conviction of the English crime. He will probably pull an insanity defence, then get out quickly because he will convince the psychiatrists his insanity is temporary. I must find out if my wife wants a trip to England. Maybe I can be a witness for the trial in London. This idea is not something I relish, but the plus side is we have been discussing a trip, but just not right now.

Chapter 43

The Gods, Huanaki and Fao, must be looking out for us because we see just about everything there is on this island. In case you don't know, Huanaki and Fao found Niue some one thousand years ago, and they are responsible for locating all the things we need to do, even some long-lost relatives for Danny.

We plan our visit carefully, but first, we circle the sixty-odd kilometres around the island, snorkel the Matapa Chasm and swim at the clear blue of the Limu Pools, and this is only our second day. We think it is enough for one day and establish that four in the afternoon is sacrosanct for a visit to the hotel pool with its bar set right in the pool. Then the evenings are ours to discover ourselves and relax in each other's company. The electricity I felt when Danny first touched me in the Sounds has increased, and yes, he feels it as well. We luxuriate in the big bed with its amazing view of palm trees and the sea. Our lovemaking is beyond my imagination; nothing I have ever experienced before.

The following days pass in a blur. We hike through stunning caves, swim with Spinning Dolphins and even consider swimming with the whales, but when I discover their size, I chicken out. Danny doesn't want to go if I don't, so I spoil it for him. He says not, but I know he wants to go. We dine at the hotel or local restaurants, and I try sushi for the first time. Danny has eaten it many times and even makes it at home. To my surprise, I love it.

Because of the whale thing, I say I will go Uga hunting. I am not keen because I remember seeing a beach covered in these huge coconut crabs in Vanuatu. Their pinchers are frightening and can break a man's leg. Danny won't go. I am uncertain if it is because of me or because he doesn't want to meet a coconut crab. It doesn't stop us from eating one at dinner.

Eventually, we arrive at a market at the best time of day. It is colourful, noisy and exciting. We eat pawpaw and bananas, drink coconut milk and slurp the freshness. The taste is so different from home. There is nothing like fresh tropical fruit picked on the same day.

On day three, we decide to add massages to our schedule for four o'clock. Then dinner and to bed! What a lovely way to end the day. What a life! I don't want it to stop.

It is not until towards the end of our stay that we visit the museum. We should have gone earlier, but we saved it up because we felt it might be the best experience of our tour. And, it is.

The director rings the people he says are Danny's relatives, and they immediately say we must visit them the next day. It is our last full day, but we think it will be the pinnacle of our visit. We agree and want to know what we should bring. They are horrified at the idea of our bringing anything.

A warm, friendly voice resonates down the mobile. "Bring yourselves. That is good enough for us. You have travelled far across the sea just to be here," the village headman says.

I hug Danny tightly because I feel an unimaginable emotion running through Danny's body and into mine.

My body is reacting to the fire in his. "I am so happy for you, Danny. This connection means a great deal to your family and you. How special to have relatives on this magic island."

All Danny can manage is a smile. It takes some time for it to sink in.

Finally, he says, "They will have a ceremony for us. We must find out what is appropriate to bring and wear. The small *taonga*, the sacred object Dad insisted we bring, may be a good gift."

The museum director smiles. "A *taonga* from Aotearoa would be the perfect thing. You don't have to worry about special clothes. What you have on now is perfect."

That settles the matter. A family member will pick us up and take us to the village at our sacred hour, four o'clock.

I am struck by the coincidence. "Strange, they managed to pick the right time. Perhaps they have worked out that four o'clock is important to us," I say as I tap Danny on the arm.

It is true; four o'clock has become a ritual to us, a relaxing time followed by a meal and then a getting to know each other session. Our room not only overlooks the sea, and the sunset is spectacular from there as well. Sometimes, we prefer to sit on the beach and watch the sun go down. I love the way it sinks in the tropics; boom, and it is gone. Afterwards, it is our private time. The only thing wrong with the timing tomorrow is we have set aside tomorrow night for a stargazing session. We did not decide on a tour. We wish to sit on the beach or find a dark location where the stars shine more brightly than at our hotel. Perhaps we will have to forgo this one thing.

The day dawns bright and sunny. We are going to do some shopping in Alofi, the capital. We don't want to arrive home empty-handed for our families. This trip is too perfect to mar it with such thoughtlessness. After a light breakfast of tropical fruits, which includes pawpaw with a squeeze of lime, we head out; what a day! It is hot for Niue, but even my skin enjoys it. Danny is as brown as a berry, and I have coloured somewhat. Shopping and lunch finished, we returned for a siesta. We have been too busy for such decadence, but Danny and I must rest. We have no idea when we will return.

Our ride arrives right on time, and we are off. I'm glad neither of us drives because the road we eventually take is unpaved. It is narrow, with deep ditches on either side. I suppose the ditches stop the road from flooding during a tropical downpour.

We approach the village and spot fairy lights while singing drifts out to welcome us. Danny takes my hand and looks deeply into my eyes. "This is what I love about being Polynesian. We welcome all comers even if they are only distant relatives."

On arrival, formal introductions conclude, but I have difficulty remembering which name fits with which person; not so, Danny. He calls everyone by their names when he has only heard them once. It is a skill I didn't know he had. His eyes shine. I think it is because he belongs here.

After lots of singing, dancing and talking, the *umu*[21] - a traditional oven, is opened to display the food for the night. The family spreads a long cloth on the ground, and the food is placed on taro leaves for all to admire. We are in the place of honour. There are fish, chicken, coconut crabs, taro, breadfruit and many more items. It is a real feast. Danny's closest relative whispers that we must begin eating because no one else will eat until we do. I begin immediately. Danny follows. Then, all sit down crossed-legged around the cloth. There are speeches to us about the history of the family. Impromptu chants occur throughout. When Danny finishes his *kai* - his food, he stands and speaks in Māori. He talks to his ancestors, to all the chiefs present, to everyone (including me), and then he presents the *taonga*. Spontaneous clapping and joy spread around the gathering. We all help clear the food away, and a show begins.

Young boys were giggling in the background just to the side of our vision before the speeches began. They were waiting for something. Then, they receive the signal to light their torches and perform a wonderful fire dance to honour the Fire Gods from

------

[21]Umu – an earth oven similar to a hāngī.

Fonuagalo, the hidden lands. The boys stamp and sing to commemorate the great event of the growth of greenery on the island and the abundance that follows. All goes quiet at the conclusion until Danny stands and speaks briefly about their skill and the honour it is for us to watch them perform. Then, he turns to me and says, "*Hei waiata*[22]."

In shocked surprise, I look at him. I only know one ancient *waiata* - or chant, and I don't remember telling Danny. But somehow, he knows. I stand, and he begins a beautiful ancient *waiata* that belongs to the Tuhoe people of Lake Waikaremoana, in the centre of the North Island. It is a *waiata* fit for any time because it is about when all the trees are gone, all the vegetation, all the birds of the bush, the whales in the sea, then the land, the land it will remain. It shows the connectedness of all time. It was written by an old lady around a thousand years ago, waiting for her loved one to return. It is soul-wrenchingly beautiful and fitting for this memorable night. Danny and his family have a tribal connection to Lake Waikaremoana. It goes back centuries.

We depart with tears in our eyes but warmth in our hearts, promising to return in the not-too-distant future, then invite them to visit us. I hope they do.

Contentment swirls through my body. "What a night," I sigh, entering the hotel, thinking sleep would be perfect.

---

[22] Hei waiata – a song, or let's sing.

Danny grabs my arm before I get too far ahead of him. "Not so fast, young lady. There is still one more thing we must do before we call it a night."

The surprise move brings out an odd feeling. "And what is that, kind sir," I say, feeling coquettish.

Danny looks serious, but I can see a twinkle in his eye. "Come with me."

I nod in agreement. Danny takes my hand and leads me from the hotel to a path we have trodden several times. It goes to a quiet spot in the bush. This location reminds me of our favourite seat on the hill in the Sounds. We walk until we stand beside a seat then sit down to gaze at the stars glistening brightly above us.

After a short contemplation, Danny takes my hand as he moves off the seat and kneels on one knee before me. He has something in his hand.

He hesitates as if he has something to say he has prepared, but is not quite sure for some reason. "Not quite what I thought I would give you, but it will do until I can find a better one."

Gazing at him in wonderment, and before he says a word, I say, "Yes, and I don't care what it is. It will be fantastic."

He hands me a ring with a natural pearl in the centre, flanked by chips of red coral.

I can't take my eyes of this exquisite jewel. "It is beautiful, Danny. But when did you buy this?" I stutter, overcome and delighted at his choice. It is so him. He must have bought it when we went to the market.

Dan is not as hesitant now. It must have been the ring that was the problem. "I love you, Amber. I always have and always will. There is no other woman who can match you in my eyes. Please accept it."

I laugh and cry at the same time. "In case you haven't noticed, I have already said yes."

I leap up and haul him off his knee to kiss him properly, and here, under the shimmering stars, the stars of Polynesia, we make love.

Chapter 44

The airport is ten minutes from the hotel, but we seem to arrive there instantaneously. We are reluctant to leave Niue. It has been such an enchanting time, and I rub my ring in excitement. I can't wait to show my parents.

Everything at the airport goes by in a blur. Then, time stops with a thud when we board the plane. The plane crawls across the sky for the three-hour flight to Auckland. Auckland airport is in a muddle. Frequent flyers tell us this shambles is a new normal since Covid. We must be patient and wait in the queues until we are through Customs, then there is the long walk to the Domestic Terminal. We can take a bus, but we both need to stretch our legs after sitting for so long.

We come out from the International Terminal into the bright blue sky, which isn't as blue as in Niue. I might be a bit prejudiced. The smell of cars, buses, and hot asphalt spoils the atmosphere. But joy comes from Danny. He holds my hand on the plane to Auckland, and now, during our brisk walk to the Domestic Terminal, he reaches down to take my hand once more. It makes me want to snuggle into him. I am ecstatic and sad together, unhappy to be leaving our island paradise but euphoric at the thought of the brand-new life which stretches out in front of us.

The plane to Blenheim is small and waits at the furthest gate from where we entered the domestic terminal, but we manage to get there to board on time. The jet resembles a toy after the international one, but it lands us safe and sound at Blenheim's little airport. Here, the terminal is efficient but without a fancy airbridge. Such a new-fangled thing is unnecessary, given the size of the planes visiting and the number of passengers. Before entering the terminal, I can't stop myself turning to Danny to hug him. He smiles down at me and lifts me up with exhilaration. I lean into the hug and feel my feet leave the ground. Danny makes me feel so safe.

Even before he puts me back down, he is speaking urgently. "We are home, Amb. It is time for us to plan a wedding and consider where we want to live."

This flabbergasts me. What is he thinking? "I thought we would live on your farm," I say, shattered.

A grins spreads over his face and his eyes light up. He looks relieved. "Do you mean that? I thought you would hate being out in the Sounds all the time. What about your work?"

I can't imagine what he has been going through worrying about his work and mine without reason. I will love to live on his farm. Taking his arm, I say. "We can cross that bridge when we come to it. I love your farm and the whole area. It is my home. I will work something out for work."

Laughing and arm-in-arm, we march into the terminal to stop stock still. Inside the building are my parents, Danny's whole family with their young ones holding a notice saying, "Welcome Home, Wanderers." They must have seen us hugging through the glass walls adjacent to the tarmac.

My heart stops. I can feel my face redden with excitement, and I hold my hand up so all can see the glistening new ring. Cheers go up all around the airport, not just from our families. Before we know it, it becomes a party atmosphere with singing and shouting to each other while the airport staff laugh while trying to move us along.

If this is what life will be like with Danny, it is the opposite of my previous existence. A warm, soft cloud envelops us. I know we will have a bright future.

My parents are thrilled and hug us warmly. Danny's parents are ecstatic, and his father dabs his eyes. I know it is something he wanted for many years. He joins in the hug with my parents, saying, "Now, we are one family as it should be."

It is impossible to tell which of us, Danny or me, begins crying first, but I know my face is wet from tears, tears of joy, not sadness. It is because so much happiness is almost too much to bear, yet I know it is genuine. I have never felt so joyful or supported in my life. I have finally turned a corner to find the people I always knew were there but didn't appreciate until now. Danny has always been the one for me.

Chapter 45

Danny and my wedding date rushes towards us. Despite the previous months' preparations, I start to think it will never happen. Perhaps happiness is a limited commodity in the world like 'good' is to some groups in Mexico. They see it is a finite item.

I had a charmed childhood and exceptional parents. We were not wealthy, but we were not poor either. I could have almost anything I wanted. In truth, that wasn't much because we spent so much time in the Sounds, and nature provided most of the entertainment I needed. I should say nature and Danny. We were inseparable then, and yet I pinch myself that now I am so lucky to have him, just for me. It is a dream that lost its way during my student days. I was overwhelmed by city life and all the excitement it brought.

The sun rises over the mountains and paints the sea with gold. The birds have been up for ages, and so has Danny. He is out with the animals, enjoying the calm of the early morning. It is an exceptional time of day.

It is time to make porridge for breakfast when I hear a boat coming fast. Nothing is urgent here, so it catches my attention. Then I hear Danny's running footsteps. He must have heard it. He is in a rush, but stops for a second to let me know that George is coming for breakfast.

I change directions. Porridge will not be enough for either of them. I must prepare bacon and eggs, toast, and maybe some porridge. I begin to fry the bacon and consider what else I should prepare. I feel excited. When I was with Malcolm, no one ever came unexpectedly to dinner, let alone breakfast. I sigh. There is the difference.

Both men chat while they walk up the path from the beach, and I wonder what has brought George out in such a hurry.
I didn't have much time to wait. He hugs me, walks into the house, and sits at the table, ready for food. Luckily, I prepared coffee earlier, so I can give them both a cup, not that they can't make their own. I liked this ritual in the mornings. Danny frequently makes dinner and sometimes lunch, though lunch not so often. His work on the farm usually takes precedence.

George looks glum. "Glad you look so cheerful," George says, making me wonder if I should be sad.

Now, it is my turn to look concerned. "Why, what has happened?" I ask now that he has made me anxious.

George is all efficaciousness now. I begin to worry. "I wanted to beat this morning's news. I didn't want you sitting in this house by yourself hearing it."

George has my full attention. "What news?" I say almost testily.

His next words shock me. I don't know what to say. All I can do is listen. "It's about Malcolm, of course. You know he escaped in the middle of his trial in London? No, he took advantage of lax policing and flitted out the door before they noticed. I rang the Crown lawyer in London to clarify the situation because I didn't want this to upset wedding prep. They had already caught him. Our news is behind the times because our news still says he is home-free, in the wind. He must have planned the move because a car was waiting for him. The driver was one of the jurors he charmed from the defendant's box. Gullible. She thought he loved her. You know the story."

Danny looks annoyed, with his face crunched up and no gleam in his eye. "They must know how tricky Malcolm is. He led them a merry dance when they returned him to England. The men in charge of transferring him thought Malcolm would sit quietly beside them while on the plane, so they removed his handcuffs. It caused quite a scene when he went to the toilet while they were emplaning the other passengers. He managed to exit through the First-Class entrance. The guards outside caught him, but how often must he prove he needs close watching?"

My feelings mirror Danny's. It was difficult enough when they extradited him. It was so early into his sentence, and now, if he keeps this up, he will be out of the country and on his way here. Maybe he will forget about New Zealand and decide some other country might welcome him.

George reaches over and pats my hand. "Don't worry. I think they have learned their lesson. They didn't think they needed me as a witness, but they are finding out he is the man I told them about. This move will not go down well with the jury. They have had to take the woman off jury duty. That leaves them with eleven jurors, but there is no need to worry about the jury numbers. Eleven is sufficient for a criminal trial in England. Malcolm's actions are not ideal but will colour their thoughts. It is not a problem."

I manage a weak smile, as I get up to deal with the breakfast. It is almost ready for us to eat. Both men refuse porridge, so bacon and eggs it is with lots of toast and homemade butter. Yes, I am getting into making it, just for ourselves. The routine helps me calm myself when I think of Malcolm and what he did. Danny is so patient because some nights, much as I want to, I cannot make love. It has zero to do with Danny, just me. The shadow of Malcolm and his actions are losing strength day-by-day, and my love for Danny strengthens because he does not push me even when he wants to be with me.

Now, I look across at Danny. There is concern in his eyes. I smile back. "Don't worry, Danny. I suspect this will guarantee he goes just where he should be. For the first time, I feel positive about his trial. I am sure he will be convicted and stay behind bars for years."

George nods vigorously. "This is how the Crown lawyer sees it. It won't be long before he is convicted, and we have a wonderful celebration coming up. What will you do for your honeymoon, go to Niue?"

I feign shock. "George! You know that is a secret between Danny and me. I am glad we waited for the wedding because it means your entire family can be here, and many of my friends have been away. It will be perfect."

Danny's right eyebrow rises. "I hope the *hāngī* will be laid in time."

The three of us laugh. We know the men in charge of the *hāngī* are old hands. It will be perfect.

Chapter 46

A week before the wedding the landline demands attention. Danny and I race to be the first to answer it. I raise the receiver, triumphantly smiling mischievously.

"Danny's Bar and Grill," I say, much to my surprise. I didn't plan to say this. It just popped out. I feel my expression change as I listen to the voice on the other end.

I hand the phone over to Danny. "It is your brother, George." Danny looks at me, and I squeeze my hands together, feeling like a little girl when Father Christmas brings her the best present ever.

Danny hardly speaks while he replaces the old-fashioned phone receiver on the counter. "It shouldn't be a surprise, but it is," is all he says.

I can't keep the nervousness out of my voice. "Did you hear what I heard?" I ask, in case I am mistaken because he doesn't seem elated.

He nods, barely able to contain his pleasure as it begins to bubble up. "Yes. Yes." He grabs me around the waist and pulls me towards him; my legs swing merrily off the ground. "Yes, we have no further worries."

Nodding in agreement, I say, "Yes, Malcolm got what he deserves, convicted and sent to the toughest prison in England. "

The thought is music to my ears. I feel a huge weight lift off my shoulders, and I realise I have been carrying this tension around since Malcolm's attack. I know everything will be okay. He is completely gone from my life. He tried to change his plea at the last moment, and the judge said:

You may not think like most of us because you only think about what is good for you, but you know right from wrong. You hide your true feelings well. You even managed to embroil an innocent juror in plans for your future. I will not change this court's proceedings. We will continue the trial as planned.

The judge's words, which George conveys, tell me something else. I do not need to carry the guilt around anymore. It is clear to all that Malcolm is crazy, but in a hidden way - hidden even from those closest to him. It has taken me all this time to put Malcolm in the box where he belongs. He is going to stay there for the rest of my life. He will not be able to manipulate or hurt me ever again.

I sigh and reach out to hold Danny's hand. "Thank God for you. You are my life. I love you Danny, and I want the whole world to know."

I become aware that George is shouting from the phone, "I guess I had better be getting along. I have a long day ahead of me."

I don't know how to show George that I am elated that he rang us with this news. What pops out is, "You should come over for breakfast again, George," I say, smiling broadly.

George laughs, "Oh, I can't come now. I have clients to deal with and wedding plans to complete." He laughs and shouts down the phone. "Welcome to our family, Amber. It is about bloody time."

The phone clicks and he is gone. Danny takes the phone off me and puts it back where it belongs. He looks very serious. I suspect, the news has raised other issues for him.

Danny looks at me carefully. "Unfortunately, I have work to do out there. I'll be in quickly. It won't take long."

I beam, knowing he must leave but will be back. I am not worried. I know he has work to do. A farmer can't just drop things. I reassure him I understand. I have much to do myself. I want to prepare the best meal, for one thing.

In the night, we make love like we have never before. It is sensual and loving, and I do not hold back. All my fears fly away because Malcolm is no longer in my life. I did not know what it would take to get rid of Malcolm, but apparently this news made the difference. No counsellor could have predicted this or even created such a scenario. It is life and life must take its course. I know Danny and I are meant for each other. When I think this, I remember his parents and mine. They have known this for a long time. I am the slow learner, but a happy one. I have never smiled so much in my life.

Saturday dawns bright and clear, a perfect day for a wedding. I stay overnight at my parent's house to make an entrance at the appointed time. My friends from Christchurch arrive on time. Six are already here, staying with us. I decided on three bridesmaids, but I wanted the others to help. Danny's three brothers will partner the bridesmaids. The little children are flower girls and boys. They will entertain us for sure. I watched George and Ian schooling the little one in spreading flowers. The girls cottoned onto the idea first, but then the boys saw it is also a good opportunity to throw them at the girls. What a site. I hope they don't decide to do this today. They look on their best behaviour.

Up the hill, there is bunting surrounding the lawn. We all helped to put up a large marquee complete with floorboards. It wasn't easy because it was an extra-large marquee. Once up, I see it is an excellent space with trestle tables for the food and others for the guests to sit to have their meal. We must clear a space later for dancing and the band.

We place a walkway of boards to the point above the bay for the marriage ceremony. No point in having high heels poking into the grass. The spot is close to our favourite star-gazing seat. After the ceremony, we will retreat to the marquee. I can hear launches arriving frequently. We have no idea of numbers because we haven't limited them. All are welcome. The overflow can eat in the house or even sit on the porch. No one will stand on ceremony. We want all to enjoy the day. I hope Danny's brothers have the *hāngī* well in hand. I have decided not to worry about a thing. Besides they are experienced in such things. I am the green person in this outfit and if there are bumps on the way, they will become wedding memories.

My dress is gorgeous. I have never owned anything quite like it. It is pure white silk, lined with taffeta, a body-hugging affair with long sleeves and a scooped neckline, lower at the back than the front. My mother spent many hours embroidering a sprig of roses to flow from the right hip up to the left breast. The roses are the palest of pink, and the leaves pale green. The train is separated and attached by hooks and eyes in the middle of the back. It has roses adorning the end of it. I wear a simple veil held on - you have guessed it - with a band of roses. My friends make sure my makeup is perfect. I hardly ever wear makeup. Well, some lipstick and face lotion, but that is about the long and short of it. Today, they insist I wear eye makeup and a bit of rouge, just a smidgeon. I am opposed to this, but I must admit it looks good. My lightly tanned skin sets off the whole effect.

When the time comes, my mother hands me a bouquet of roses, and my father takes my hand and walks me up the path while I try not to stumble. The little ones are throwing rose petals out in front of me and manage to do so without too much hassle. One of

George's boys can't help but through a bunch of petals at one of Ian's girls, but that only adds to the ceremony. The brothers and my bridesmaid follow Dad and I with Mum and my friends behind in a long procession. Danny and his family and friends are waiting on the point for us. The minister is there ready; all is set. I hear our band start 'Here comes the bride,' and tears begin to well in my eyes. I didn't expect to feel this emotional. Danny's face is a picture as he turns and sees me for the first time. His mouth drops open, and his face cracks with a huge smile. His father and brothers do the same. I look for his mother. She is standing with the boys' wives and children, smiling in an 'I told you so' kind of way. It is all I can do to stop myself from laughing out loud.

The ceremony continues stunningly, and the sun continues to smile at us. The day is enchanting. The trees and birds seem to think so. I am sure I hear the trees moan while we speak our vows and the birds sing at all the right moments. I know I have made the best decision in my life.

Postscript

We didn't do as expected at our wedding. That is, we stayed and enjoyed the party. The sun peeks over the horizon when we finally take our boat to the Bay of Many Coves. It is a luxury resort close to our farm, but they expected us in the evening, not sunrise. However, they treat us as if we arrived on time and show us our accommodation. We both drop down on the well-appointed bed with exhaustion. There is no time for lovemaking to make the marriage official. We sleep right through until lunchtime. We would have slept through lunch if it hadn't been for noisy birds deciding it was high time we surfaced.

We only booked two nights because we decided to go to Rarotonga - the Cook Islands - for our honeymoon. We chose Raro simply because we missed going last time and thought somewhere new was good for us, but we decided to delay the honeymoon until winter. Our parents thought we were crazy to postpone our honeymoon because it broke with tradition, but it made sense. We would have time in winter. Then, a temporary manager could look after the farm, and we would not be worried about what was happening at home. I know they wanted to ensure that Danny's and my wedding got off on the best possible footing, but this arrangement suits us best.

I have never felt so content in my life. I know we will have a wonderful marriage, and although the lovemaking is excellent, that isn't all that makes a marriage. We respect each other, and daily my love for Danny increases. And yes, the electricity is still there. It makes me wonder why I didn't return home to Danny years ago. I hope I discovered much during those years, but I learn from Danny daily. He is so thoughtful, but of course, he has some annoying traits, but nothing I can't stand. I look forward to the years ahead with excitement and a hopeful heart. Amazingly, I believe Danny feels the same.

Acknowledgements

Although this began as a romance novel, I discovered while writing, I liked exploring the psychology of romance in its good and bad forms. I used work and life experiences, as well as my research background, of chameleon-type characters and contrasted psychological dysfunction with a well-rounded intelligent young woman. The resulting interrelationship proved difficult for the woman as it does in real life. At work I was frequently told that a specific woman should leave her significant other. I hope this novel shows it is more difficult than simply walking out the gate.

I must thank the Picton police and former Detective Inspector, Dave Hazlett, for their help in creating the police scenes. I asked the barge and water taxi people about their experiences during the dreadful storm in 2022 which destroyed many of the roads around the Sounds. Thank you for your help. Friends from our Wine on Wednesday group helped with the cause of Malcolm's wife's accident. A farming friend helped with the situation for animals on the farm during stormy weather. And, of course, I cannot leave out Joan Rosier-Jones and the writers, at the writers retreat in the Marlborough Sounds for their encouragement and writing advice.

Thanks to Barbara Speedy for her generous help in crafting advertising material and other descriptive passages.

A special mention to Jess Marks, Chantelle Woodley and all the team at Seabreeze Café for your support, particularly for enabling the book launch. Jess, it couldn't have happened without you.

Thank you to my book launch members – Jess Marks, Pip MacFarlane, and supportive friends especially Joy Fletcher, Claire and John Welch, for your help in organising the event, and to Julie Robinson for setting up the Zoom meeting and video managing the event. You all took a great weight off my shoulders.

My editor, Gene Merica, had a bit to do with it, too. He edited and re-edited the material I sent him with helpful and insightful advice each review session. And the pre-readers particularly Lois Broadbent and Seren Williams, thank you for your perceptive comments.

Despite all this advice and the many rewrites, if there are still anomalies or mistakes, they are mine alone.

I hope that you, the reader, enjoys this quick romp through our beautiful sounds and find the material entertaining. Thank you for taking the time to read the story.

www.ingramcontent.com/pod-product-compliance
Lightning Source LLC
Chambersburg PA
CBHW071240300726
48975CB00002B/492